FLOOD RISK

By

SANDY NORK

For Bill

Part I

PROLOGUE

THE MYTH, THE MAN, THE MANDOLIN

Smithfield Bluegrass Festival
Smithfield, VA
Saturday, August 23, 1980
4:30 P.M.

CHARLEY HOPKINS STEPPED OUT onto the rough-hewn wooden boards of the stage, boots clicking, and positioned himself in front of the microphone. At first, he heard just a few people clapping at the front of the stage but after a few moments, applause swelled as more people recognized him.

In a quiet drawl he said, "Hello, y'all," drawing out the syllables as though he had all the time in the world. The crowd exploded with more applause and shouts as he positioned his hands on the strings of the mandolin and started his set with one of his favorite songs, "Ashes of Love."

He was nervous, more than he wanted to be. He'd been forgetting things again lately. He was only 40, but already he felt his age creeping up on him. Forgetfulness was just one sign. Thank goodness he hadn't messed up on stage during this tour. He wanted to feel good in front of his band, The Bantams, to feel at home, to feel like it was okay that he was on the road again. The band had been good to him when he battled memory lapses last year, covering for him. A few of them thought he should quit playing, just give up the travel and the long weeks away from home, but there was no way he would ever do that.

I'm a musician, dammit! How else am I gonna make a living?

Charley knew there was nothing else he was good at. Music was his only trade, his education learned from his daddy, his PhD earned on the road. Who would teach him to do something else now?

As he moved into a groove, the headache that had plagued him since midmorning faded a bit.

It's going to be okay.

Somewhere in the middle of the set, he got a little lost and improvised an extra phrase that he hoped didn't throw off his band too much. It sounded like they rolled with him, but he hadn't made such a noticeable error in so long that it startled him, causing him to breathe faster. He felt his blood hammer in his veins, a dull thudding that vibrated, something he'd never noticed before.

Or is it one more thing I don't remember?

He cussed inside his head. It was the instrument fouling him up, he was almost sure. That's what he got for borrowing this mandolin.

He rarely borrowed anyone else's instrument. But at the last moment before tonight's show, he couldn't find his Lloyd Loar F5, the one with a fancy scroll, the scribbled-on front, and the scratched-up back. Ugly, some called it, but it was his. And it meant a lot to him.

It was the one his daddy played sometimes when Charley was a kid.

It was the one Charley expressed an interest in playing.

Daddy was more of a guitar man anyway. It was no skin off his nose if the boy wanted the mandolin.

Charley loved the mandolin from the first note he picked on it. And over the years, he and the mandolin traveled the Middle Atlantic and part of the South, making music with his dad and later, any band who would have him. People liked Charley, so he played a lot.

The mandolin showed wear from all the days his dad played it, but now it was helped along by Charley's fellow musicians, who took to marking it after they played with him or shared the bill. Johnny Cash was the first to carve his initials into the wood, followed by Jimmy Martin, Earl Scruggs, and Jesse McReynolds, among others. Charley thought it was their way of blessing him.

When he got to the festival grounds that day, Charley had the mandolin's case in his hand, the one he'd stuck a "Nashville" sticker on and wrote, with broad strokes, his last name, "Hopkins," on the side, up near the headstock. Easy to see whose property it was. He left it in the van with the other equipment The Bantams brought with them. They didn't want to drag their instruments along while they walked around, eyeing the women and checking out the crowd.

Later when he looked in the van for the case, he couldn't find it. He borrowed another mandolin, an extra from the fiddle player in the band, who gave him a funny look and shook his head when he handed it over. It was an A-model with a rounder body than the F5, but the body shape wasn't the problem. Charley could play pretty much anything with strings on it, especially mandolins. The problem was that it wasn't his Lloyd Loar. He liked his own mandolin. He liked the way it felt, the way it sounded. Without it, he felt unmoored. Unblessed.

The next song featured the band. All he had to do was sing. But that strange nervousness he'd noticed earlier dried up his voice and he motioned to the guitarist to step in. He hoped the audience didn't see him swallow a few times to get his saliva back. He turned his body slightly away from the crowd and nodded to the band. He was okay, he was telling them in his way, I can handle the next song.

On the next song he played his lead, sang a couple verses, and played into the bridge. He closed his eyes as he played, and thought of his wife Maude, waiting at home with the girls: Hayley, ten, a little blonde comet with energy to spare, and twelve-year-old Paige, a somber redhead who followed Hayley around, keeping her in line. So different from each other. Picturing the two of them with their mother made him smile.

He especially missed Hayley tonight. What a voice she had! High and clear, powerful beyond her years. He taught her how to play the mandolin, too, and admired the ease with which she picked it up. He wished she was along to sing with him. Maude put her foot down. "Not this year," she'd said, so he promised Hayley she could go to the festivals with him next year, for sure.

Paige wasn't a singer or a player, but she was determined. She'd tried to sing along, to learn harmonies, but it was a struggle. She had a stiffness that lingered. Next year, when he took the girls with him, he'd figure out how to use her cute triangle face swept with freckles to wow the crowds.

The next song was an old Bill Monroe instrumental called "Roanoke." He pulled his energy together and focused on the song. He played hard and fast, then moved on. Back in step with the band now, he sang deep and strong, and worked through the rest of their set. By the time they finished, his fingers a blur on the frets during almost every song, the applause was deafening. He was drenched in sweat, but he felt he had done his best.

He thanked the crowd and stalked off, his boots clacking on the stage.

The band sauntered after him. Behind them the crowd continued to roar.

Backstage, he asked if anyone saw his mandolin and was met with blank faces. He returned the instrument he'd been using to the fiddle player. One of the stagehands said, "Hey, are you lookin' fer this?" and handed Charley the mandolin case. Charley stared at it, then grabbed it and clicked open the latches.

"Where have you been?" Charley muttered to the mandolin.

———— •●• ————

When they found him, Charley Hopkins was flat on his back in some high grass by the side of the road on the way to the parking lot. His eyes were rolled back in his head. He was holding the F5 case so tight to his chest that they had to pry his fingers loose.

The doctor said it was a heart attack. The band didn't agree. They thought it was because he had to play the A-model instead of the Lloyd Loar F5.

Maude understood their logic. That man hated to play anything but his own Lloyd Loar.

The band told Maude that Charley should be buried with the mandolin in his hands, just the way they found him. The story went 'round that when Maude buried Charley the following week, that Lloyd Loar F5 mandolin lay inside his coffin.

But that was just a story. What really happened was that Maude handed the mandolin to Hayley instead. "Do what your daddy told you," Maude said to Hayley. "Play it like he did."

Then Maude turned to Paige. "You take care of your sister," she said. "Make sure she does what she's been told. And bring all the money home to me."

BEFORE THE FLOOD

CHAPTER 1

Patton's Vintage Guitars
Phoenixville, PA
Wednesday, April 7, 2010
10:00 A.M.

"MARK? MARK PATTON?"

Mark almost dropped his phone. He knew the voice. Memories flooded back. Carefully he said, "Hayley Hopkins, is that you?"

Her laugh gave him chills but not in the way she undoubtedly intended.

"Of course, it's me, silly. Surely you didn't forget me. I know it's been a while."

Ten years? Fifteen?

"I haven't forgotten you." He hoped his voice didn't sound as sullen to her as it did to him.

"How are you?" she asked.

"I'm good. You still in Nashville?"

"Yeah," she said. "That's where the business is, right?" That laugh, again. It always sounded forced, to him. Even back then.

"I heard your song on the radio. A different version. They said you re-released it."

It wasn't the only song she ever recorded, but it was the one that everyone thought of, the one everyone thought was about her dad. Never Be As Good As You.

"Did you like it?"

"Sure. It's different."

Heavy drums and electric bass now. Electric guitar, too. He wanted to call it Rock and Roll but didn't. She might not like that. She might not have been shooting for that. Maybe New Country, the hot slot every country artist seemed to be shooting for these days. Still, what he said was true. The revised recording was definitely something different for Hayley Hopkins, something fresh, a departure from her bluegrass roots.

"I guess you'll be touring soon."

"You guessed right."

"And you are calling me because..."

"I'm putting a band together and I'd like you in it."

Mark fought the impulse to click off the connection. Instead, he said, "Really?" He knew there wasn't an ounce of enthusiasm in his voice.

"You were always a big part of the band, bigger than anyone else. Bigger even than me. You always made us sound good."

"Come on, Hayley, everybody wants to see the chick singer, you know that."

She laughed again and he shivered.

"Besides, you've had other guys in your band. Some of them have been pretty good."

"See? That's what I mean," she said. "Pretty good isn't good enough. Not this time."

"What's different? Except for the electric guitars, I didn't hear much that changed in your approach. So, what are you looking for? Am I going to handle the technical end? Do you really need me to ride along for that? I'm sure there are guys in Nashville who can handle this for you."

"I guess, but I know you. I trust you. And if we want to add some extra flair to what we're doing, I know you can step in and play."

"So mostly technical, but occasional filling in? I still don't know why you think I'm that important."

"I want you there. Daddy is getting inducted into the Country Music Hall of Fame this year."

He took a moment. This was big. Bigger than he ever expected.

"Their museum is going to showcase his mandolin. For nine months. They asked me to play it at the induction announcement concert."

"So, you won't be playing it on the tour?"

"Right." She sighed. "Time to rely on my own mandolins."

It crossed Mark's mind to ask her why anyone would come to see her play if she didn't play her father's mandolin as part of the show, but he didn't want to be mean. On the other hand, he was lured by the idea of being part of the band for the induction concert, but his history with Hayley was complicated. He wasn't sure he wanted to go another round with her.

"You know I have my own business now."

"I heard," she said. "I thought you could take a little time off."

"Did you? How little were you thinking?"

He couldn't believe he was even considering this proposition, let alone asking about it aloud.

"A few weeks to prep, two months of gigs. The kickoff is the big announcement concert. That's on May second."

"Two and a half months! And what about my business here?"

"I heard you have a business partner."

Mark thought about leaving Bic Travers with the responsibility for the shop for all those weeks. It wasn't completely unreasonable. Bic could do most things, but repairs would have to be farmed out. Still, the idea was overwhelming.

"I know this is a lot to throw at you after all this time. Why don't you take a day or so and think about it," she said. "But the truth is, the sooner you can get here, the better."

"Just one more question."

"What's that?"

"Does Paige know you called me?"

He knew the answer when she paused.

"Not yet, but I'll tell her. Come on, Mark. I need you."

"I'll think about it."

"That's all I ask."

There was another pause. They didn't seem to have more to say to each other.

"I've got to get back to work," Mark said. "Say hi to Paige for me."

"I will. It's been good to talk to you, Mark."

CHAPTER 2

Chestnut Hill
Philadelphia, PA
Wednesday, April 7, 2010
7:45 P.M.

"SHOULD I KNOW WHO HAYLEY HOPKINS IS?" Valerie asked as she bit into her burger.

Valerie and Mark were having burgers at Cantoni's, a bar that they frequented near her home in Chestnut Hill, the home she shared with her dad, Liam. Mark liked to come here with her. The burgers were good, and the beer was cold. It was the perfect place to tell her about his trip to Nashville. He could see that she wasn't angry about him deciding to go, so he was primed to talk about Hayley.

"She's a pretty famous mandolin player," Mark explained. "Not someone you might immediately recognize, but she used to be pretty big in the country music world. She's more of a mid-level player now. People in Nashville know her. Have you ever heard the song, 'Never Be As Good As You?'"

Valerie pretended to think about this, but she knew the answer immediately. Country music was not her interest, classical was. "No, can't say that I know it."

"It's the song that made her a star, back in the day. She always leaned on her daddy's history when she played and made sure to play his mandolin at every concert. Bluegrass fans loved it. They loved her dad, and after hearing this song that they guessed was about him, they loved her, too."

"Well, that's pretty cool."

"Not exactly. She was in her twenties when the song hit big, and all the attention was a tough adjustment for her. She didn't handle it well."

"That's too bad," Valerie said, not quite sure what "didn't handle it well" might mean.

"It feels like ancient history now," Mark said. "Last year she re-released the song. It sounds different. The arrangement is less blue-grass and more country rock. A lot of people like it, even people outside bluegrass and country music. It's become what they call a 'crossover hit.'"

"That's good, isn't it?"

"Very good, especially if you want to restart your career."

"And how will you be helping her? Technical stuff?" Even at this point in their relationship, Valerie wasn't quite sure how to refer to what Mark did. He had a shop where he bought and sold guitars and did repairs. But she knew he no longer played gigs as a guitarist, so she guessed he was being called in for his technical expertise.

"That's what she said. I may be called upon to do a little playing, but I don't think it will be much."

Valerie relaxed a little. She wasn't angry or upset that Mark was going. In fact, she was relieved. She was worried, too, but Hayley Hopkins was not the reason.

No, she was worried because she had been on the verge of telling her dad that she was thinking of moving in with Mark. She and Mark had started talking about it a couple months ago.

She wanted to refuse at first out of concern for her dad. That seemed crazy even to her, but after her mother died when Valerie was fifteen, she watched her dad descend into depression and struggle with drinking for a time. He rallied, but it took years. She still sometimes caught herself tensing up whenever he was drinking. She knew it was ridiculous to look at her father as though he was an alcoholic. He was not. She was just being over-protective, she told herself. But maybe it was time to make a change.

So, Valerie told Mark that she'd move in with him.

Mark was thrilled when Valerie agreed. He was less thrilled when he realized his tiny bachelor pad above his guitar shop was too small for two people. They had just started looking for a larger place. Then Hayley called.

"Do you think you'll be doing any recording while you're there?" Valerie asked, setting her thoughts aside.

"Not that I know of. Hayley didn't mention recording, just prepping for the concert and doing a tour," Mark said. "The concert's in honor of her father, Charley, among other people. He's going to be inducted into the Country Music Hall of Fame later this year, so they asked her to participate in the inductees' announcement concert. There are four other people who are nominated, so other players are involved, but it's a big deal for her. She's going to play her father's mandolin at the concert and then the Museum is going to put it in an exhibit for the rest of the year after the induction."

"Wow," Valerie said, even though she had no idea how big a deal it might be. Despite not sharing his affection for country music, she was impressed with the idea that the mandolin was going into a museum.

"Yeah, who knows?" Mark suddenly had a far-away look on his face. "Maybe she'll decide to do some recording while I'm there and make a deal to release it in conjunction with everything else. I'd definitely be up for that." He leaned toward Valerie and touched her arm. "I'm glad you're not upset about this."

"It's what you do," Valerie said. "I understand that."

She wondered why he thought she'd be upset. It was business, after all, his calling. Also, a friend needed his help. She understood.

What a great guy Mark was, to help an old friend when called. Yeah, we're probably not going to look for a place together until he gets back. But that'll give me more time to break the news to Dad.

"So, when would you leave for Nashville?" she asked.

"Hayley said she needs me there as soon as possible. I already talked to Bic, and he's cool with it, so I just have to get a flight. I'll probably go tomorrow."

Valerie almost choked on the last bite of her burger.

CHAPTER 3

Zimmer Investigations
Upper Darby, PA
Thursday, April 8, 2010
8:45 A.M.

HARRY ZIMMER WAS DEEP INTO PAPERWORK, buried under a mound of maps and photographs from his last case, when his phone rang. He was close to ignoring the phone, but he didn't. *Bad for business. Best to answer all calls.* He rooted under the paper pile until he found it.

"Zimmer Investigations."

"Harry Zimmer, how the hell are you?"

The voice on the other end carried a significant drawl. A Southern woman, no doubt, and it only took Harry a moment to place the voice.

"Olivia Farrell! How are you? It's been forever!"

"Not quite, but who's counting? And not my fault, surely. Why is it that you haven't been to Tennessee in all these years?"

Harry laughed. "Been a little busy. Opened my own place a couple years ago."

"Gave up the life of luxury, did you? TransReliable getting too stodgy? Requiring dinner jackets and ascots?"

Just thinking about his old employer, the gargantuan insurance monster that TransReliable was, gave Harry chills. He was happy to be working on his own with just a pair of employees. They weren't rolling in dough, sure, but that had never been his primary goal.

"Let's say they didn't care for my style. So now I'm enjoying a little more freedom, but not so much that I can travel like I used to. What about you? Still insuring those Nashville guitars?"

"Well, don't forget that we protect instruments for the Nashville Symphony, too, along with all the other instruments those Nashville cats use. Davis Insurance has been insuring those babies for at least sixty years now, thanks to my Uncle Beau. Remember Beau? The man who brought me into the business?"

"I do. I was sorry to hear that he passed."

"I miss him and his bourbon happy hour every day." Olivia sighed.

"But I'm sure you still celebrate."

"Someone has to carry on the tradition."

The two of them laughed. Harry could imagine Olivia, leaning back in her chair, holding a lit cigarette in her left hand, swirling bourbon in a glass in her right. Even if it was before ten in the morning.

"Beau would be proud," Harry said. "He loved those instruments. And the musicians."

"And their night life."

"So, if you're keeping up with Beau's traditions, you're still spending your nights in the honky-tonks? Or has some man forced you to give it all up for him?"

"Oh, one or two have tried, honey, but none succeeded. I only made that mistake once. Like you, I prize my independence."

"Is that what we have? Independence?"

"I think I do. You must, too, running your own shop."

"Sometimes I wonder."

The pause was longer than either of them liked.

"Well, regardless, I managed to hang around the insurance industry long enough to become President of the Council for the International Insurance Investigators."

"Whoa!" Harry whistled, thinking about her sharp wit and heavily mascaraed eyes. "Impressive. But no wonder, really. You have that natural combination of beauty and brains." From all his miles away, he could almost feel her blush.

"That's questionable, but let's move on. I'd like to ask you for a favor on behalf of this esteemed group."

Of course, she does, Harry thought.

Raquel Russo, better known as Rocky, pulled her little blue Ford Escort into the gravel driveway next to a beautiful suburban home in Chestnut Hill. She was picking up her partner, Valerie Sloan, at her home because she didn't drive but still needed to get to work at Zimmer Investigations.

Rocky couldn't imagine not being able to drive. Zooming around the countryside was one of the great pleasures of her life, along with blasting music at the highest decibel level she could tolerate. As if there weren't enough things she didn't understand about her work partner, Rocky also didn't understand Valerie's facial expression as she got into the car.

"Well, don't you look cheery this morning."

Valerie slid into the car and frowned at her driver. Rocky was one of the joys and sorrows of her job. It was nice to work with a partner, awful to have to depend on a driver. Particularly one with a penchant for loud eighties rock and the driving habits of a Formula 1 driver.

Rocky took a moment to turn down the eighties metal music blaring from her car's radio. It was Motörhead this morning. Lemmy was great for a workday morning. "Something the matter, Boss? I thought you had dinner with Loverboy last night."

Valerie rolled her eyes and fought the urge to tell her not to call her Boss. Or to call her boyfriend, guitar store owner Mark Patton, Loverboy.

"Yeah, we spent a little time together. Long enough for him to tell me that he's going to Nashville tomorrow."

"Wait, what? I thought you guys were talking about moving in together. And now he's moving to Nashville?"

"Not moving, going. It's just temporary. He's helping an old friend prepare for a concert. I guess we'll look for a place when he gets back."

"An old friend?"

Valerie bristled. Yeah, of course Rocky picked up on that. The expectation in her face said that apparently, she wasn't going to let it go, either.

"Yeah, a woman whose band he was in years ago," Valerie said. "Hayley Hopkins, some country singer. I gather she was popular once upon a time. You know a lot about music. Have you heard of her?"

"Sorry. Doesn't ring a bell. Country's really not my thing."

"Yeah, me, either."

"No kidding." Now it was Rocky's turn to roll her eyes. "If she wasn't born before 1900, you don't know who she is."

"That's not true. I know who James Taylor is. He wasn't born before 1900."

"I'm not impressed. So, get back to this Hopkins woman. If they were old friends, how old?"

"He hasn't seen her for years. I gather they weren't getting along well when they parted ways. He said he was surprised to hear from her."

"I'm surprised he agreed to do it, then."

"Not me. It's a gig, you know? He likes to do things like this when asked."

"Because he's flattered?"

"No. Because he can. Because he is apparently pretty good at what he does. I think. At least, that's what Bic tells me."

Bic Travers was Mark's business partner and one of Rocky's previous boyfriends. There had been a few boyfriends since Bic but remembering him still put a smile on Rocky's face. "Well, Bic should know. They've been partners in the guitar shop for years."

"I know."

"So, it's all good, right?"

"Yeah, just great," Valerie said, hoping that Rocky didn't hear the sarcasm. "He's going to be gone for weeks and I'm going to be here."

Valerie checked the tightness of her seatbelt, then checked it again, just to be sure she was safe. Rocky's aggressive driving made Valerie safety conscious. As they careened into the street, Valerie gripped the armrest and gritted her teeth. She reminded herself that she needed to look into driving lessons so she could depend less on Rocky. *We can still work cases together, even if we aren't in the same car. Right?*

Riding every car's bumper and yelling at drivers who couldn't hear her, Rocky drove their morning commute as though her little car was on a speedway. Valerie clutched the door, sometimes reached for the dashboard, and braced herself for curves and intersections.

By the time they pulled into a parking space in the tiny lot in front of the strip mall office of Zimmer Investigations, Valerie had almost forgotten about last night's discussion with Mark. Rocky's driving had made sure of that. Now all Valerie had to do was focus on work.

———— •❖• ————

"Remember all the conferences we attended over the years?" Olivia asked.

"Of course I do," Harry responded. "The Council always put on a good conference. The sessions, the food, the convivial companions. "Where was it we met the first time?" Harry asked, although he remembered vividly.

"Seattle."

"Right." Mentally, he could still see the skin-tight leopard dress she wore to that one.

"But I haven't seen you since the D.C. conference in 2004."

"Yeah, I know." He let his mind drift forward to the orange dress with the big bow at her cleavage that she wore there. With matching stilettos. "That was memorable."

"I haven't seen you on the guest list since then. You could have called me."

Harry could hear the pout in her voice. He came back to the present.

"I'm sorry. You noticed that?"

"I watched for you at the conferences for a few years. Then I got on the planning committee and saw the reservations come in. I didn't see you on the lists. I'm guessing that coincided with you going solo."

"Yeah, not a lot of time or cash to work the conference circuit when you just start out. You could have called me, you know."

"Not something a lady usually does, at least not in my town."

The accusation hurt. He liked her enough to care about hurting her. He simply didn't think she thought it was a big thing.

One more woman I don't understand. It's becoming a pattern.

"Things are getting better, though, easing up as we develop our client list," he told her.

"That sounds good. Maybe you can help me out of a jam."

"I can't imagine you have a jam you can't get yourself out of."

"It's not for me, it's for the Council."

"So, what can I do for the Council?" he asked.

"I'm working on putting together this year's conference. It'll be held the last week of April, here in Nashville. We've lined up a great selection of programs, but one of my presenters has had to cancel, so I'm left with a hole in the schedule."

"And?"

"I seem to remember reading a story about your agency being involved with the disappearance of a guitar. A Gibson Les Paul if memory serves. 1958. Kind of pricey."

"Two of my agents worked on that, yes." He didn't mention that they were his only two agents. "Valerie Sloan and Raquel Russo."

"It sounded interesting, especially to me. Davis Insurance works with the musicians' union and the Nashville police to thwart instrument theft. We are putting on a joint session at the conference. I thought you might have some insights to share with us. I thought you could do an introductory session, present the case, and answer questions about it."

"But I'm not the one who worked the case."

"Meaning, you won't do it?"

"It would be better to have Valerie and Rocky present the program."

Olivia was silent. Harry, thinking about the opportunity this could be, found himself nodding. "Yeah, they would probably do that."

"Well, I'm not sure..."

"Let me talk to them and see what they say," Harry said. "I'll encourage them to do it."

"Encourage them to do it? Wait a minute. Aren't you their boss?" Olivia asked, laughing.

"You don't know these two. There is no way I could order them to do anything."

"They're women, right? Women love you. I'm sure they'll do whatever you ask."

Harry felt heat rise from his neck. "I think I hear them coming in now. Let me talk to them and give you a call back."

"All right, Harry. I'll talk to you later."

Harry hung up the phone. He called out to Valerie and Rocky as they entered the office, "Hey, guys, I've got a surprise for you!"

CHAPTER 4

KH Precision Machine
Nashville, TN
Thursday, April 8, 2010
9:00 A.M.

SUZUME KOJIMA ADJUSTED HER POSITION in the office chair, blinking her eyes to clear them for a moment. The walls of her office felt close, like they would squeeze the breath out of her, despite the windows that looked out over the Cumberland River.

She was an Outdoor Girl, not of the Great Outdoors but of the Cities of the World. She preferred walking city sidewalks. She knew that other staff members would kill for this corner office, no matter how tiny. She hated it. She wanted to be downtown, in a café or a honky tonk, smoking cigarettes and drinking a cocktail, eyeing up the young men available to her.

These inventory figures will make me go blind. How did I end up in this little outpost of Hell?

She knew exactly why she was assigned to this level of purgatory but preferred to think it was not her fault. Just a little slip-up. Her brother be damned.

In the parking lot outside her windows, a silver Nissan Infiniti slid into a parking space between her father's Lincoln Town Car and her own little red Nissan 370Z. She watched as the Infiniti's door opened and Uncle Naoki got out.

She stood and flapped her hands at him, trying to get his attention, but he was concentrating on something else and didn't see her. She sat back down, deflated, and went back to the evil spreadsheets.

Voices in the hallway stole her attention. She opened her door a sliver so she could hear better. Her father Hoshi's large office was next to hers and though they shared an interior door, opening that one would have caught her father's eye. The door to the hall was much safer.

Uncle Naoki stepped into Hoshi's office. Visiting him was not unlikely since Hoshi and Naoki were partners in KH Precision Machine, whose inventory was bedeviling her. She eavesdropped on their greetings until her uncle spoke the word favor. She looked up, sharpened her hearing, and strained to decipher the words that followed.

"We are organizing a little party for the plant employees," Naoki said. "We want to reward them for a good quarter."

"Yes?" her father responded. After a long pause, he added, "Is this what you've come to tell me? Why would this involve me?"

The voices faded slightly.

They must have stepped into Daddy's office. Suzume inclined her head closer to her open door.

"I'm looking for someone to entertain at the function. I thought you might know of someone who would fit the bill. Someone we could get inexpensively."

Naoki emphasized the word *inexpensively* and Suzume immediately knew what that meant. He was looking for a band that would work for free, a band who owed her father a favor. That happened a lot in her father's line of work. Not the parts-machining arm for whom she currently worked, but the drug-supplying arm that operated within his import-export business, Oriental Exchange.

Suzume pursed her lips.

Oriental Exchange was monolithic. Ostensibly run by her father, there were locations in many cities of the United States: New York, Philadelphia, Baltimore, Savannah, Tampa Bay, Baton Rouge, New Orleans, Los Angeles, Seattle. Others. Technically they were run by a local staff but ultimately, they answered to her father, who answered to his bosses in Japan.

Yakuza bosses.

In the U.S., the Yakuza's influence mutated into local gangs of other names, like Green Mountain, Gold Tooth, Dragon. But the structure, methods, and ground rules were strikingly familiar, and her father somehow sat at the top of one of the three large gang pyramids in the country, Dragon. KH Precision was her dad's side gig, a company he opened with Naoki. Naoki wasn't really her uncle, but her dad treated him like the brother he never had. They were always up to something.

"When do you need them?" Her father's voice was faint, but she had years of practice deciphering his words when he dropped his voice.

"The first day of May."

"Celebrating Golden Week? Here?"

Uneasy laughter followed. The day would have been included in the Golden Week festivities in Japan, but not here in the United States.

"Workers' Day."

"Hmm."

"It will be a day of picnicking and celebrating. With entertainment. I ask you to recommend someone."

"I will consider."

Their voices got louder as they said their goodbyes and Suzume backed away from the door. She returned to her desk and the spreadsheets on her computer, but her brain whirred with questions.

Why is Naoki asking Daddy for this favor? Couldn't he just ask one of the other bosses? This is Nashville. You can't throw a stone without hitting a band here. What, exactly, is he looking for?

Suzume frowned. There was a time her father would have shared his secrets with her. Naoki's, too. There was a time he assigned her more important work, more interesting work.

Spreadsheets. Huh.

CHAPTER 5

Davis Insurance
Nashville, TN
Thursday, April 8, 2010
9:05 A.M.

OLIVIA FARRELL EDGED FORWARD on her desk chair as she put down her phone. Talking to Harry Zimmer brought up old memories, old feelings. While on the phone with him she heard herself let her accent broaden the way she liked to do when people were listening to her. She knew it made her sound as though she was from further south than Nashville and she noticed that men really liked that twang. That Harry really liked it.

She sipped from her coffee cup, thinking about her last gentleman caller, a dapper man who said that her coffee contained more cream and sugar than any human being should put into a beverage. He didn't understand that nothing pleased her more than a loaded cup of coffee. Except, perhaps, a fine bourbon. The gentleman certainly didn't please her half as much as either beverage. A man that fastidious was certain to try to change her and that was never going to happen.

That brought her thoughts back to Harry. *Harry was like a fine bourbon*, she thought, *so smooth, with a fiery finish.* She had no doubt he was the kind of boss who could get his employees to listen to his suggestions. She certainly remembered him as delectably persuasive when they met. Afterward, they stayed in touch, visited each other, drank a lot, told stories. Oddly, it never went further, but she liked that about Harry. She had respect for the man. An uncommon feeling for any man in her life, except Uncle Beau.

A lot of musicians knew either the name Beauregard Davis or, at the very least, Davis Insurance. Davis insured instruments, and in a town full of them, Uncle Beau had been a busy man. But a few years ago, when he passed and left the business to Olivia, more than a few people scoffed.

Most musicians knew Olivia, too, but that had less to do with insurance and more to do with the way she looked. They thought she was a vapid, entitled freeloader with a penchant for hanging at the bars and honky-tonks. They didn't know that the woman who looked like a shallow Southern belle was a tough businesswoman who had worked for Uncle Beau since finishing school. And after twenty years under his tutelage, she could hold her own. When her uncle died, she became a busy woman. But not too busy to help the Instrument Theft Reduction Task Force.

She poured herself a fresh cup of coffee, doctored it to her liking, then stepped out onto the porch overlooking the parking lot behind her building. Every day she used this porch to relax and think, and every day she found that she never regretted keeping this odd, antiquated building that she inherited from her uncle. She thought of it as a Victorian with a shot of Deco, a turret in the front and a widow's walk on top. It looked like a small, but grand, old lady in between the modern office buildings and apartment towers in the Gulch area of Nashville. The house was like a petulant dowager who refused to sell to big business.

Olivia never regretted choosing the second floor for her office rather than the first, either. The first floor was currently rented by an incredibly quiet accountant. She always thought of him as a buffer between her and the rest of the world. She liked that.

The third and fourth floors were apartments. The third floor was split into two apartments, one slightly smaller than the other. The smaller one was currently unoccupied. The last tenant moved a few months ago. She hadn't found a replacement yet. She was picky about choosing renters.

She kept the third-floor apartments as a cushion. Extra income for months that seemed a little thin, although after clients adjusted to dealing with her rather than Uncle Beau, those thin months were further and further apart.

She lived on the fourth floor, repairing drafts and leaks as needed. Sometimes she felt like this house was her job, not the insurance policies she wrote, the protection advice she gave, or the investigations she conducted. But the house was a labor of love and a reminder of her affection for Uncle Beau. And every day, when she sat out on the porch, she thought about how lucky she was to live there.

She turned her mind to her other current focus, the Task Force. Officially the ITRTF was part of an existing police jurisdiction. They worked with the local musicians' union and, because of her history with the union and her experience with instrument insurance, the Task Force called Olivia in as a consultant.

She was glad they contracted with her early in the process, while they were still developing resources to assist with their work. Together they developed a list of possible perpetrators by talking to studios, recording companies, and music shops. They uncovered leads from several bands who were tired of having their equipment stolen.

But everything for the Task Force was in the talking stages. Everyone wanted to press charges on known thieves, including her, but there was never enough hard evidence to make a charge stick.

She sipped again.

It will happen. It just takes time. The Task Force has the best interests of everyone at heart. Except for the thieves, of course.

She laughed at her own mordant humor and thought again about the women she had just invited to the conference. *Will they be able to tell us anything we don't already know? On the other hand, if I know anything about this business at all, I know you should talk to everybody. Help can come from anywhere.*

CHAPTER 6

Zimmer Investigations
Upper Darby, PA
Thursday, April 8, 2010
9:15 A.M.

"THE TWO OF YOU HAVE BEEN INVITED to present at the Council of International Insurance Investigators Conference on..." he consulted the notes he'd made while talking with Olivia, "April twenty-eighth. The President of the organization asked for the two of you to talk about the Cafferty case."

Harry wasn't prepared for the silence that followed his announcement. The women stared at him.

"You don't seem excited," Harry said, tapping a finger on his desk. "What's up?"

"We're never going to get away from that case, are we?" Valerie said with a sigh.

"Why would we want to talk about it? It's history," Rocky added, looking puzzled.

"You don't think retrieving a guitar worth $250,000 is important? Or interesting to other agents? The rock and roll dentist, the wacky thieves he hired. It was important enough to attract the attention of a couple newspapers and an insurance newsletter," Harry said, waving one hand toward a copy of the newsletter framed on his cluttered wall.

"This sounds like something you should do," Rocky said. "Representing the agency and all that."

"Me? I didn't work the case. You did. The two of you can represent the agency."

"What about the cases we have now?" Valerie asked.

"I'm working on the last of the paperwork on my current case before I take it to court. I should have some time after that. Bring me up to date on what you've got, and I'll see if I can't fill in."

"For both of us?" asked Rocky. "That sounds pretty ambitious."

Harry sighed. "Look, the president of the organization asked for you two, specifically. I think it's a good idea. I'm willing to set aside the time."

"Well, I suppose we could take a day off," Valerie said. "We'd be able to plan for it, work around it."

"About that. It's going to take more than a day. The conference is in Nashville."

"Tennessee?" Valerie's brows knit together. "We'd have to be away for a couple days."

"It's a three-day conference. If I'm sending you to do a presentation, you should go to the whole shebang. And you'll have to allow for travel time, of course, so I'm guessing five days in all." Harry scratched his head.

"Valerie, tell Harry what you told me this morning, about Mark working there," Rocky said.

Harry looked at Valerie, his eyebrows raised.

"Yeah," Valerie said. "He's helping an old friend prepare for a big concert."

"I'm sure he'd be happy to see you there, right?"

"I guess," Valerie said. "He might be pretty busy."

"Oh, for crying out loud," Rocky interrupted. "You're his girlfriend. Of course, he'll be glad to see you."

"Yeah, I'm sure he will. Okay."

"Jeesh! Don't sound so excited." Rocky rolled her eyes. "It's going to be fun!"

"Yeah, yeah, I know."

"Think of it this way," Harry said. "The conference is a good way for investigators to come together and exchange ideas and information. You learn new procedures and review the ones you think you already know. You get to know other investigators. You meet representatives of companies that make products we use. I imagine that you will hear new ideas for improvements to our own company."

"In other words, a paid vacation!" Rocky pumped her fist. "Yeah!"

"No, Rocky, it's not a paid vacation. I know Nashville has a reputation as a party town, but I expect that you will be working most of the time. You may get a little sightseeing in, and I imagine that Valerie will get to see Mark, but work comes first."

Rocky deflated. "That's no fun."

"Maybe not, but it is an opportunity to raise our profile a little," Harry told her. "Remember, our clients deserve investigators that know what they are doing. It doesn't matter if we are working with insurance brokers, agents, adjusters, or clients, we need to be the absolute best we can be. Enthusiastic. Efficient. Thorough. Knowledgeable. Going to the conference is educational. Doing this presentation improves our status in the investigative community."

"Whew," Rocky said. "How long have you been preparing that speech?"

"This is the first time since I opened the doors that we've had a little breathing space to participate in something like this." Harry glared at her. "We've been busy just trying to keep our clients happy. This is a chance for you to broaden your knowledge and to help others in the process."

"It does sound like something we should do," Valerie conceded.

"Good. I'm glad you agree," Harry said. "By the way, who is this friend Mark is working with?"

"Hayley Hopkins."

Harry scrunched up his face a bit. "Don't know the name. Do you know her, Rocky?"

Rocky shook her head. "Valerie said she plays country music. I don't know much about country music." Her expression brightened. "Bret Michaels made a country album. Does that count?"

"I don't think so," Valerie said. "Mark said Hayley had a hit some years back but left the business. She's trying to make a comeback now."

"So, is he in the band, or what?"

"Sort of. He's going to be her technical guy, making sure all the instruments are in good shape and keeping them tuned properly and all that. But he did say she might ask him to play a bit."

"Wait, what?" Rocky said, even more puzzled. "Isn't he just going to be the tech guy?"

"Yeah, but Hayley could decide she needs him to play guitar, so he might do that, too."

"Huh." Harry said. "Don't take this the wrong way, but that sounds odd."

"Odd?"

"Yeah. Aren't there, like, a thousand other guitarists in Nashville that could help her out?"

"Well, apparently she's burned some bridges in her earlier career."

"Ah."

Rocky wrinkled her nose. "She could have asked Bret Michaels to help her."

"No, Rocky, I don't think so. And all I'm saying is that Mark is probably going to be busy while we're there."

"Well, buck up! We're going to Nashville! Cowboy hats! Boot scootin'!" Rocky did a little scuffling dance into the outer office where she acted as receptionist. "Harry just said it's a partying town," she called over her shoulder. "You don't necessarily want to be tied to your boyfriend for that, do you?"

Valerie glared at her back.

"So, what do you think? Are you in?" asked Harry. "They want to make arrangements for you to stay on-site. I need to let them know that you're coming."

"You bet!" Rocky hooted from her desk.

"Of course, I'll do it," Valerie agreed. "For you. For us. It will be good experience."

"That's the spirit!" Harry said, sounding more certain than he was. As Valerie went to her office in the little cubicle next to his, he couldn't help but wonder how this was going to work out.

CHAPTER 7

Hayley Hopkins Residence
Franklin, TN
Thursday, April 8, 2010
10:30 A.M.

HAYLEY HOPKINS DOODLED TWO MORE NAMES into her notebook, then dropped it onto the couch beside her and flipped her long blonde curls out of her face and behind her shoulders. She gathered her hair and twisted it into a bun on top of her head and looked across the room at her sister Paige, who was bent over a worktable by the wide windows at the front of the house.

Paige's head was tilted down, her straight red hair creating a barrier that made it hard for Hayley to see the side of her face or what she was looking at. But she knew what Paige was doing. She was doing what she always did when they had some downtime: reviewing the spreadsheets.

"You don't have to do that, you know. We pay people to do that."

Paige put a tip of a finger to the sheet to hold her place and looked up at Hayley. "The record company pays people to do the basic figures, to tell them what they need to know. I go over them to make sure they are correct. And to make sure you get paid properly."

"You don't trust them?"

"No, I don't. I know too many people who trusted their accountants and lost a lot of money to them." She sighed. "Hayley, you know this. I'm just making sure it's not going to happen to you."

"You sound like Mom."

"You make it sound like that's a bad thing."

The sisters locked eyes.

"What's the matter, not enough to do?" Paige asked. "I thought you were looking for someone to replace the tech who cancelled on us."

"Hey, if you were going out on the road with Keith Urban, you'd cancel with me, too."

"I'm just saying, you'd better find someone good to handle Pop's mando."

Hayley puckered her lips as though she'd tasted a lemon. "I already called someone," she said.

"Who?"

"Mark Patton."

There was a long silence while Paige absorbed this information. "Are you sure you want to do that?"

"Mark was always good with our instruments. I read that he's considered one of the best luthiers on the East Coast these days, but he said he's willing to help."

"When was this?"

"Yesterday."

"You called him without consulting me?"

"I wanted to feel him out, to see if he would even consider it. He wasn't sure at first, but he called me last night and said yes."

The expression on Paige's face was the one Hayley expected, the hard set of her jaw and the downturned mouth.

"I've been over it and over it in my head, Paige. If he can get past the past, so can I."

And beggars can't be choosers, Paige thought. *It's gonna be hard enough to find musicians, let alone a tech that will still work with you, one that doesn't remember how you used to treat people. If Mark can forget, and Hayley can forget, then I can forget, too, I guess.*

Paige blew out a short breath. "Okay. Your call. What about the rest of the band? Who else do you have?"

"I locked in Todd Bruce on drums."

"Boomer?"

"Yeah. He's been reliable for me."

"Okay. Who else?"

"Des Oakley for guitar. He can play fiddle, too, if we ask nicely." She was going to ask him to play just the fiddle but knew he was one of the only guitarists in town still willing to play with her. Mark was her backup if Des didn't work out. Hayley lifted her notebook back into her lap. "Kenny Harbold on bass. Des says he likes working with him."

"That sounds good, so far."

"I still need to figure out some others. I haven't found a banjo player yet. And if I can find one available, maybe a pedal steel guy."

"Five guys? That's a lot, don't you think? It's going to get expensive."

"Yeah, well, if I want to play something more than bluegrass, that's what it's gonna take."

"And Justine to do your hair and makeup, of course," Paige added.

"Yes, she'll be there."

"I would imagine so," Paige said, turning back to the spreadsheets. "It's not a show without Justine."

CHAPTER 8

Patton's Vintage Guitars
Phoenixville, PA
Thursday, April 8, 2010
11:30 A.M.

"SO, LET ME GET THIS STRAIGHT," Bic Travers asked, his eyes squinting with the effort of trying to understand what Mark was telling him. "You didn't tell Valerie you'll be working with your ex?"

Mark leaned over the worktable, examining the bass guitar that he was setting up for a client. "She didn't seem all that interested."

"But you did mention that she was your ex-girlfriend, right?"

"Well, not exactly," Mark said. "Because Hayley wasn't, exactly. So, there was no reason to put it that way."

"Exactly?" When Mark looked up, the tip of Bic's tongue showed through his teeth, as though he had paused just before saying something he shouldn't.

"What?" Mark said.

"Dude, I think you might want to be clearer about this," Bic said. "You know, women don't like surprises unless it involves spending a lot of money on them."

"Valerie's not like that," Mark replied. "I told her the truth. I'm going to help an old friend play a concert. And a short tour."

"Yeah. Right. That's a lot more than one concert. And it sounds like more than just business to me."

"But that's all it is, Bic."

Bic's dark hair, pomaded off his forehead with a few slicked curls rolling down into his eyes, shook a little as he expressed his disapproval. "I don't remember you talking about it that way when you first told me about it. And didn't you say you weren't sure if you should take the job or not?"

"When I realized that Hayley was just offering me the job because it was just that, a job, I decided it was okay." Mark put the bass back into its case and wiped his hands on a ragged towel he pulled out of the waist of his jeans. He tossed the towel onto the table. "That's what I told Valerie and she's okay with it. I don't know why you think this should bother her."

"Okay, dude, I guess you know what you're doing." Bic frowned and turned away from Mark so he wouldn't see Bic's expression. Bic pulled a guitar from the wall and plugged it into one of the test amps. He played a fast, searing run, ear-splittingly high on the fretboard, until Mark yelled at him.

Bic felt a little better after that, but he had the feeling Mark was going to feel worse. Soon.

———— • ◆ • ————

Closed off in her tiny office at Zimmer Investigations, Valerie worked on a funeral fraud case that required her to do research for the Attorney General's office. It had to do with clients who had invested their cash for prepaid funeral services. The funeral director transferred the money to her personal accounts instead of holding it in escrow for her clients. To make matters worse, she ran a side business of supplying bodies and organs to research facilities, who trusted that the families had agreed to the arrangement. Unfortunately, not all of them had.

Valerie was absorbed by the phone calls and account checks the case required. It was mid-afternoon when she found time to break for a cup of coffee and a stale doughnut from a box Rocky had brought with her in the morning. Valerie realized then that she had already missed lunch because she was so wrapped up in her case. Now, too tired to walk somewhere for food and not quite finished with her research and calls, she found herself dunking the tired pastry into the hot liquid, at least making it a little easier to eat.

It was quiet in the office. Rocky was out running an errand for Harry. Harry was doing some surveillance in Frankford. Valerie leaned back in her chair and closed her eyes. She could feel how sore they were from staring at her computer screen.

And yet...

Her brain whirled away from her current case and dredged up the conversation she'd had with Mark. She wasn't upset, she told herself, but she hadn't been overjoyed, either, when she found out he was going to Nashville.

I'll miss him. But if I go to the conference, I still won't be able to spend time with him because he's working.

When she opened her eyes again, Hayley Hopkins' name popped into her head.

Who is this woman?

She had accepted Mark's description without question. Now she realized that she ought to find out more about her.

She opened a new screen and tapped Hayley's name into the search engine. A list of entries came up. The first article was a brief bio, including her recent background; her recording history with the mention of a re-release of an old hit, "Never Be As Good As You," in the last year; her awards and most popular songs; and in the "Early Life" section, a story about her father and his mandolin.

The mandolin Hayley inherited. The mandolin she was going to play in the concert Mark mentioned. The mandolin that was going into the Country Music Hall of Fame and Museum.

Pictures of the mandolin showed how beaten, worn, and down-right damaged the thing looked. Valerie's personal love of violins extended to all stringed instruments, and she felt almost offended by what had been done to this one. She was used to the gloss and glow of a well-polished violin. This mandolin appeared to be so defaced that she couldn't believe there was any value left in it.

Then she read the story: how Hayley's father, Charley, inherited the mandolin from his own father and how, when Charley began to play the touring circuit in the Southeast, other musicians marked his mandolin with their advice and well wishes.

It made a peculiar kind of sense.

When she went back to the documents list, the next articles verified everything Mark told her: how Charley Hopkins was being inducted into the Hall of Fame, how his daughter was scheduled to play a concert featuring the mandolin, and how the instrument would be moved to the Hall of Fame Museum.

Further down the list of documents, Valerie found Hayley's older personal history. This was quite different from the more current information.

Apparently, Hayley had a big country hit in the nineties, the song, "Never Be As Good As You," the song she just re-released. Hayley followed that success with a long period of losing herself in alcohol and drugs. Valerie double-checked Hayley's birthday with the personal bio: Hayley would have been in her late twenties then.

Valerie followed the link to a video of a young Hayley Hopkins onstage with a band. With no one else in the office to bother with the sound, Valerie played the video, turning the volume up. It was a fast bluegrass number with guitar, banjo, and vocal harmonies framing the sound of Hayley's voice and mandolin. It sounded upbeat, but when Valerie played the video a second time, she paid more attention to the lyrics. It was all about Hayley's quest to be as good as... who? Her father? That was Valerie's immediate guess and the guess of most of Charley Hopkins' fans. The anthem to her father reeked of jealousy and defeat.

Valerie looked at the video a second time, then a third. The third viewing gave her an unexpected shock. The guitar player to Hayley's right caught her eye, a guy with long dark hair and full beard, wearing faded jeans and a worn buckskin jacket. It was Mark.

The video ended and Valerie pushed herself back, away from the desk and away from the old image of Mark. If she had passed this version of Mark on the street, she would not have known him. She might have even tried to avoid him. He was rail-thin and pale. The coat hung on his shoulders like it had captured and drowned him, the sleeves too wide and long for his arms, bunched at the elbows while he played. His only discernible feature was his eyes. Valerie recognized them, but only after studying the video.

Valerie clicked back to Hayley's bio. After this song got popular, Hayley went on some sort of rampage that managed to alienate almost everyone who ever helped her. It took years for her to rebuild a positive image.

Valerie played the video again. This time she noticed that Hayley looked at Mark every few seconds while she played and sang. They seemed to have some sort of energy between them that made for compulsive viewing.

Valerie did a quick search of both their names and the explanation became painfully obvious.

Mark was Hayley's ex-boyfriend.

CHAPTER 9

KH Precision Machine
Nashville, TN
Thursday, April 8, 2010
2:30 P.M.

HOSHI KOJIMA SAT IN THE OVERSIZED LEATHER CHAIR at his desk, eyes down, focused on the magazine in front of him. The desk held the usual office items, stapler, note pads, a telephone. One corner held a framed photograph of his son, Ichiro, in happier times. He was dressed in his best black suit. The boy's round face beamed at Hoshi, a child on the brink of manhood, a boss in training.

Hoshi hovered over the pages of the magazine he'd been reading, *Bluegrass Unlimited*. He loved reading this magazine, loved spending time in the bluegrass world, at least in his head. Sometimes it allowed him to forget for a while the boy in the photograph.

Hoshi indulged his passion for country music whenever he could because this was the town for it. Occasionally, listening to the music was not enough. Even seeing the bands play in the downtown honky tonks weren't quite enough to fill his heart. In those moments, something elevated him to the heights of desire, to hold something physical in his hands, something that would shout his love for the music, and he was looking at one of those things right now.

He was looking at photos of Charley Hopkins' mandolin.

"Look at that mandolin, Ichi," Hoshi whispered to the photo of his son. "It's a mess, isn't it? A beautiful mess."

The mandolin, on its surface, looked like a wreck. The wood was hacked at the edges; scribbled on in pen, pencil, and marker; defaced in a manner that could only be called irresponsible. Except these markings made this instrument special.

As if it wasn't special enough being a Lloyd Loar-designed F5 mandolin, with its scrollwork head and slim belly. As if it wasn't special enough having been played by the great Charley Hopkins right up until his death in 1980.

What made it special was that these were the signatures of the people who loved to play with Hopkins, the marks, the touchstones of respect and awe that they left behind.

Respect. Awe. The same things that Hoshi wanted for himself.

"I want this mandolin, Ichi. It's meant to be mine."

Currently, the mandolin was in the hands of Hayley Hopkins, Charley's daughter. Hoshi had quietly been funneling financing to the band after contacting the other Hopkins daughter, Paige, and asking what they needed. Paige was delighted to accept his support "since you are such a fan."

She had no idea.

Hoshi was hoping to negotiate for ownership of the mandolin but knew that if he presented that idea first, she would turn him down. Instead, he offered her some financial stability. He'd pay off their debts and even offered to put them up in a downtown condo while they rehearsed for the Hall of Fame Induction Concert on May second in Centennial Park. As the band's sponsor, he had his All-Access Ticket already. He practically salivated, thinking that he might hold the instrument in his hands.

"If I could just get it away from her, Ichi, away from the stage, away from all the other people," he said. "I'd protect it. I'd hang it in my office at home. I know the perfect spot for it, in front of my work-table, next to your picture. I could look at it every day, touch it, run my hands over it." He breathed in deeply, then exhaled. "I might even play it. What do you think about that, Ichi?"

Ichi didn't care that his father was not a musician. Ichi was, after all, dead.

Hoshi sat forward on his chair and placed his hands flat on the magazine, as though he could touch the mandolin just by his fingers touching the photo. He thought about Naoki's request and knew exactly who he was going to "ask" to "help out." Maybe he could get earlier access to the mandolin. Maybe he could divert it from its path to the Country Music Hall of Fame Museum.

Voices outside his door interrupted Hoshi's thoughts. His face folded in on itself like used tinfoil when he heard his daughter's voice mingling with that of his assistant, Bana. Hoshi slapped the magazine closed and took another deep breath, this time to prepare himself for Suzume's arrival. He hoped for the best and prepared for the worst.

Hoshi heard his daughter long before he saw her. Suzume had one of those high-pitched, nasal voices that grated on his nerves. He knew she was in the hallway when she greeted Bana and heard her voice get louder as she got closer to his office. He heard Bana try to stave her off.

"Your father is busy."

"Not too busy for me."

The door flew open, and Bana stumbled backward, catching his bulk on the handle of the door. Suzume swept in. She was dressed in black jeans and a flowing black shirt that dwarfed her and made her look even shorter than she was.

A long time ago, someone told Suzume that dressing in all one color would make her look taller. It didn't. It made her look lost. But she is still a beautiful girl. Outside.

Suzume ignored Bana's awkward twist and flowed to the side of Hoshi's desk, shirt billowing behind her, her anger reverberating in the air.

A beautiful girl with no manners, but it is obvious she has something to say.

He stood and held out his arms to his daughter, foolishly expecting her to greet him cordially.

"Daughter, it is good to see you."

"Good to see me? I work in the room next door!"

"I know, but you are busy with the spreadsheets…"

"Yes, the spreadsheets. It's always the spreadsheets. That's what you tell me. But I think you're still punishing me."

Hoshi eyes opened wide. This was unexpected. He thought she'd settled into her new position.

"What would you have me do?" He held his hands out, palms up.

"Include me in your important work."

"I do. You are doing important work."

"I am not!" Suzume sputtered. "Why won't you let me work for Oriental Exchange? You used to let me acquire pieces for you to ship. Why did you stop?"

"You know very well why."

"That incident in Philadelphia? That was months ago! Surely, I have demonstrated my worth since then. Why can't I help?" When Hoshi didn't respond, she said, "You *are* still punishing me."

"You're punishing yourself," Hoshi sighed. "Until you see that you are part of the structure here, part of the staff, you will always be unhappy."

"But I am not like everyone else here," she said. "I'm your daughter. I deserve better than this. After all, I'm going to inherit the business someday."

"Inherit the business? You are too careless! You almost got yourself kidnapped!" Hoshi snapped. "There are people who would love to get their hands on you so they could control me. Think about what happened to your brother."

"Yeah, yeah, my dear dead brother, the one you always hold over me." Suzume picked up the photo of Ichiro from her father's desk. "The other two gangs, blah, blah, I've heard this before."

Hoshi grabbed the photo out of her hands. "You put yourself in danger, running around Philadelphia alone."

"It wasn't my fault! Itoh left me at the warehouse. He took all the men with him! How was I supposed to defend myself?"

"Itoh was doing what he was told! You were not!"

"But then that Sloan woman…"

"Stop it! Stop it right now!" Hoshi yelled, still holding the photo, pulling it tight to his chest, his face flushed. "You heard me before? Well, I heard you, too, and every time you complain it sounds like excuses for very bad judgement. Look at you! Until you can prove to me that your judgement and your self-control have improved, I cannot call you my daughter. You are not worthy."

Suzume stared daggers at her father. "You can't be serious!"

Hoshi took a deep breath and stared back at Suzume. She always brought out the worst in him. Always. But then he thought, *Am I being too harsh?*

"Maybe there is a way."

Suzume's chin jutted forward. "What can I do?"

"Find some new items for me to offer my buyers. I know you can do that. As you say, you've done it before."

He laid the framed photo flat on his desk, face down.

"What are they looking for?"

"Something special. Something that will take their breath away. Something that's one-of-a-kind."

"Artwork? Gold? Jade? Diamonds?" Suzume tilted her head and pursed her lips, thinking. "Seems like there might be something here. The architecture of some of these buildings is so... old-world. Maybe something from one of them. Do they have museums here?"

"That's not what I'm talking about," Hoshi interrupted. "We're in Nashville, Suzume. Buyers in Japan want instruments. The kind with country music connections. Something like this."

He pushed his magazine in front of her and she looked at the images on the pages. Some ugly stringed thing, a mandolin, but damaged. *Why on earth would anyone want this?* She started to reach out, to take the magazine from his hands, but he snapped it back to his chest.

"Even I would like something like this," Hoshi said.

Suzume saw the naked lust in his eyes for the mandolin. "I could work better in a larger office," she wheedled.

"No," Hoshi snorted. Suzume started to talk back to him, but he held up a palm and said, "If you need more space, I'll approve you using my office."

"Your shrine to Ichiro?" she said, scanning the multiple framed pictures of her brother hung on the wall across from her father's desk.

Where are the pictures of me? Not even one, not in that room or any other.
"No thanks! I'll stick with my own office."

"Fine." Hoshi puffed his cheeks. "But I'm going to assign someone to you. For protection."

"Who? Bana?"

"No, he is working on something for me. But I'll make sure you have someone to keep you safe."

"Ugh!" Suzume huffed loudly and left as quickly as she came. Bana stood back to watch her stomp to her little office and slam the door. He stepped into Hoshi's office and closed the door gently.

"Sir? I believe I know just the man."

CHAPTER 10

Zimmer Investigations
Upper Darby, PA
Thursday, April 8, 2010
3:30 P.M.

VALERIE FELT AS THOUGH SHE'D BEEN KICKED in the stomach. She realized now why Mark had been so nervous to tell her about going to Nashville. He was going to see his old girlfriend.

Mark picked up his phone on the third ring. "Hey, babe, what's up?"

"When were you going to tell me that Hayley Hopkins used to be your girlfriend?"

She could hear Mark swallow hard on the other end of the line.

"I tried to tell you last night," he said.

"No, you didn't," she said, incensed. "You could have told me any time. You could have told me on the phone before we went. You could have told me over the beer, over the burgers, while we waited for the check, while you drove me home. None of those happened. You barely told me anything, except about the concert and the tour." She hoped Mark could hear just how angry she was.

"That's because she is not my girlfriend. Not today and to be perfectly honest, not then, either."

"What do you mean, not then either?"

"I wasn't her boyfriend. I was a guitarist with her band." Mark heaved a heavy sigh. "She shredded every man she ever went out with, and she went out with plenty. When she got to me, I said no. She was furious and fired me."

"When was this?" Valerie asked, still suspicious.

"1994." Mark paused a moment before he added, "She was drinking pretty heavily. I heard later she went into rehab, but that was after I moved to Pennsylvania."

"Wait. I'm confused," Valerie said. "You moved to Pennsylvania in 1994, but you didn't open the store until 2002?"

"Like every other musician in Nashville, I thought I was going to make it big. It didn't happen. I thought they just didn't recognize my talent. Then I came to Pennsylvania and got a second taste of reality. My talents weren't in demand here, either. I was playing in a band some nights, sleeping all day. I crashed in a crummy apartment with six other guys who also had no money. Sometimes we got lucky, and a friend or family member gave us a little cash."

"Lovely."

"It wasn't lovely, it was awful. But that was life for me then."

"Obviously that changed. What happened?"

"I told you when I met you that it took me a long time to figure out what I wanted to do," Mark said. "I met Bic in 1999 while he was still working for WMMR radio, and I was still playing out weekends. He wandered into the bar where I was playing and talked to me during a break. We hit it off and started discussing music and instruments. We shared a jaundiced view of the music industry here. I've told you that part of the story before, too."

"I remember," she said. "You said that after you met him you realized you needed to pull some money together if you wanted to open a shop."

"Right. I got a day job that paid better than bar gigs. I moved out of the apartment and slept on Bic's couch and saved up. I still played out some, but at least I had a goal. Bic's encouragement really made the difference."

"And you didn't hear from Hayley until now? Seems odd."

"Not really. She only calls people when she wants something from them."

"So, what does she want from you?"

The pause was longer this time.

"I think that all she wants is for me to help her prep for this concert."

"You think?" Valerie ran her hand through her silky hair, grabbing a handful in frustration. "But you're not sure?"

"I didn't ask her directly," Mark confessed. "After she told me it was for the Country Music Hall of Fame, the only questions I asked were 'When?' and 'How much?'"

Valerie unclenched her hand.

"So why didn't you tell me all this?" she asked again.

"Because there was nothing to tell. Hayley was hell on wheels in the nineties. I was glad to get fired, glad to get away from her, even sort of glad to have an excuse to leave Nashville. I didn't want to agree to work with her without discussing it with you first."

"That was a pretty selective discussion."

"But all true."

"So, what should I think about the pictures?"

"What pictures?" Mark sounded genuinely puzzled.

"Online. Pictures of the two of you together."

"Oh. Those. Yeah." Mark paused. "Photographers." His tone was dismissive. "Honey, I don't know what else to say. There was nothing between Hayley and I then. There is nothing there now."

"Those pictures..."

"Forget the pictures."

"Then what about the articles?"

"Oh, right. The articles."

Valerie could almost see him slapping himself across the forehead. *How could he forget these details?*

"Hayley thought it would look good, the two of us being a couple in the band," Mark said, adding quickly, "It was a sham."

Valerie let the comment dangle in the air between them. Finally, she said, "I've got to go. I'll talk to you tonight."

Part III

WELCOME TO NASHVILLE

CHAPTER 11

BNA-Nashville International Airport
Nashville, TN
Friday, April 9, 2010
2:30 P.M.

TO MARK, THERE WAS SOMETHING RELAXING about being in an airplane. Maybe it was the low whooshing of the air as it recirculated through the main passage or the drone of the pilot's voice as he greeted fliers and gave them updates. Maybe it was the smiling attendants, or the calming music piped into his headphones. Even though the video screens in the plane were all tuned to the latest news about the Deepwater Horizon explosion, it had less impact without listening to the sound. Mark read the closed captions. Now that the rigging sank, reporters had turned their attention to the huge oil slick left behind.

He leaned his head back, not wanting to watch the coverage any further, even without sound, and closed his eyes. Visions of Valerie danced in his head. *What I told her was true but perhaps I should have told her everything.*

By the time he opened his eyes, the video screens were off, and the pilot was announcing the Nashville airport.

I'm here. All I have to do is catch a shuttle downtown and get to the condo that Paige arranged for Hayley and the band. But first, the ritual: Lower Broadway.

That's where the honky-tonks were. Grab a drink or two, check out the bands, then on to whatever brought him to town. He took a taxi from the airport, asking the driver to drop him near Robert's Western World. He shouldered his duffel and looked around, trying to decide which direction would lead him to the best music. Down the street he heard a banjo being played at high speed.

Banjo Bob. Good god! It's been sixteen years since I moved out of this town, but every time I come back, he's still here. Always reliable, always here, always playin' for tips. All these years.

Mark maneuvered himself out of the crowd on the sidewalk, listening to the music and watching the constant nodding of Bob's Stetson. After a couple songs, he rejoined the crowd to walk down the block to Lulu's.

Except Lulu's was now called DaisyMae's.

So, there were some changes in town.

Mark slipped into the cool dimness of the honky-tonk, inhaling the familiar scent of fried boloney and beer. The band on stage was playing a raucous country swing number and he grabbed a seat at the bar.

Well, the name of the bar may have changed, but the inside sure hasn't.

Mark ordered a lager and a shot and let the drinks soothe him. Nashville had its own vibe and liquor was a part of it. That was something else he hadn't mentioned to Valerie. She was so sensitive about her dad's drinking that it made Mark feel self-conscious at times. He was careful not to drink as much as he might like to when he was around her.

He let the lager slide down his throat and pushed the bottle toward the bartender. Mark wasn't quite ready to face Hayley. Or Paige.

He ordered another.

When Mark got to the sixth floor of the Athenian Towers condominium, he stepped out of the elevator and took a moment to orient himself. He was feeling warm and fuzzy until now. The beers and shots had done their work and made him mellow but when the elevator doors opened the mellow turned to nervous anticipation. He adjusted the heft of his duffel and steeled himself to enter Hayley's world. It felt like his reality was about to disappear, like he was stepping off a ledge into nothingness.

He pressed the buzzer next to the door and it opened immediately. The guy who looked at him from inside the door was about the same height as he was, but he was fully bearded, and his hair was a lot longer than Mark's. A lot. He had topped it with a baseball cap.

Shades of the nineties, Mark thought. *Didn't I used to look like that?*

"You the new dude?" the long-haired guy asked.

Mark held out his hand. "I guess I am. Mark Patton."

The guy looked at his hand like it was a foreign object. "Boomer. I'm the drummer. C'mon in," he said and stood aside to let Mark pass into a high-ceilinged, open space that, by its clutter, appeared to be the living, cooking, dining, and practice space shared by the entire band.

Several people were in the room. The bass and guitar players were sitting on a long couch working through a tune. They were playing unamplified, but Mark could hear that they were struggling somewhat with timing. Across from the couch a young Black keyboard player sat in front of an electric piano, trying to assist. It wasn't smooth, but they were getting it. All three glanced up as Mark came in, but didn't acknowledge him in any way, just kept on playing. A fourth man, older than the others and sitting off to himself, was fiddling with a pedal steel guitar, testing the pedals, and adjusting the strings. He did not look happy.

Mark didn't recognize any of them.

There was also a woman, her hair pulled up on top of her head in a bun, that he also didn't know. She was in the kitchen pouring herself a drink. The refrigerator door hung open while she did so. *Who the heck is she?* he wondered.

Instruments were everywhere.

Typical, thought Mark. *Like a tornado went through. The Hayley Effect.*

The guy who met him at the door hollered next to Mark's ear, "Hey, Paige! Your guy is here!"

Mark would have liked to punch the guy but held himself back. His attention was diverted by Paige popping up in the kitchen. She was probably looking into a low shelf of the refrigerator. She walked to the door to greet him, her feet bare and her red hair swinging from side to side as she walked. Mark remembered her with shoulder-length curls all those years ago. He remembered freckles, too. The freckles were covered with makeup, he could see as she got closer, and she'd let her hair grow into a smooth-as-a-waterfall long sheet, attractive on her triangular face. Paige's smile was a sight to behold but he could see that her eyes were icy. This was all business.

"Hi, Mark. Glad you're here."

She made no move to reach out to him, to shake hands, or to hug him. After the near lack of acknowledgement from the guy at the door and the musicians in the room, Mark was feeling distinctly unwanted. He stood awkwardly in front of Paige.

"Good to see you," he said and heard a slight questioning in his own voice.

Paige looked down at Mark's duffel, which he had dumped on the floor. "We've got a spot for you on the left, there, just past that table." She pointed and he picked up the pack and followed her to the hallway. Past the mentioned table, she knocked, then pushed open a door. Inside, he saw two queen beds, one of them with the blankets tossed back and the other with a large suitcase open and its contents laid out across the bed's surface. That's when he realized he'd be sharing the room.

"The guys are all sleeping here," Paige said by way of explanation. "Keeping us all in the same suite is the plan."

"So, no one runs off?" he asked without thinking. He was gratified to see a slight smile curve her lips, but it disappeared quickly.

"Let me get your roommate." She turned and yelled, "Clay! Get back here and move your stuff off the bed. Mark's here."

"Thanks," Mark said. "So, we're all staying here? Even you and Hayley?"

"And Justine."

"Justine?"

"Hayley's gofer." Paige said dismissively. "Go ahead and unpack. If you need to, just dump Clay's stuff on his bed. I'll let Hayley know you're here." As she left the room, she yelled again, "Clay! Get back here and clean up your stuff."

She closed the door behind her, and Mark looked around the room. There was no way he was going to touch his roommate's clothes. They were arranged in outfits, with the shoes placed near the outfit they complemented. He was sure anything he did would cause havoc. He would just have to wait for this Clay fellow to come in and move them.

Mark tried to figure out just how big the condo was. It was a little mind-boggling considering the honky-tonk he'd left not that long ago. *They could have put several bars in this condo*, he thought, and unzipped his bag.

He heard a light tapping at the door. When he opened it, expecting Clay, he was startled to see Hayley standing there, all five feet of her. She looked taller, but it was because she was wearing a pair of high-heeled cowgirl boots, flashily covered in glittery gems that were emphatically pink. "Nashville" was emblazoned on the front of her boots in black letters edged with gold, also glittery. Her t-shirt was snug and proclaimed, also in pink and black and gold, "Come for the music, stay for the party."

Yep. Hayley was back.

And now, so was he.

She laughed at his silence and the way he'd once-overed her with his eyes.

"Still can't hide it," she said. "I know you love me. Give me some sugar, Sugar."

She moved into the room, a tiny tornado that eliminated breathing. She hugged him fiercely.

"You can run but you can't hide," she said. "At least, not forever."

"Even if I wanted to."

"Right." She grinned. "When you're ready, come on out and I'll introduce you to the guys. We're gonna play a little right now, but after we'll chat about where you fit in."

"Won't take me long," Mark said. "I'll be right out."

She left the room, closing the door behind her. Mark found himself staring at the door after her. He'd gotten a better reception from Hayley than he'd expected. They had not parted on a happy note, so either she completely forgot or decided it didn't matter anymore. It was Paige who held the grudge. And Hayley obviously still worked with Paige.

CHAPTER 12

Athenian Towers
Nashville, TN
Friday, April 8, 2010
6:30 P.M.

CLAY WAKELAND, MARK'S "ROOMIE," turned out to be the young Black man playing keyboard when Mark arrived. Clay knocked on the door before he entered the bedroom and immediately apologized for leaving his clothes and shoes everywhere. Up close, he was exceedingly good-looking, with buzz-cut hair, smooth skin, deep brown eyes, and a warm smile.

"I don't travel light," he said, laughing as he picked up, folded, and stored his clothes in one of the small dressers. "I spent a few years as a model and tend to overthink my wardrobe. Do you have much for the closet? There's only one and, Lord knows, I've got a few things to hang up in there."

Mark was taken with Clay's smile and his easy self-deprecation. He didn't act the way Mark thought a model would act. But he didn't act like a musician, either.

"Go ahead," Mark said. "I'm a tosser and dumper, myself. Don't wear many different shirts, wash em when I get the chance. Nothing for the closet."

"Not even your jacket?" Clay paused and stared at him.

Mark was wearing his old Fender blue jean jacket, knowing that it would take a beating while he travelled.

"No, not even my jacket. I'll just put it over the chair." He pointed to the only chair in the room.

"Well, laundry facilities are down the hall. They're small, but functional." Clay finished hanging his clothes and moved on to his shoes, organizing them on the closet floor. "Paige told us you're the best luthier in the business, but that you no longer play. Is that right?"

"Right."

"You don't play at all?"

"Only for myself. And my girlfriend sometimes."

"Why'd you quit?"

Funny, Mark thought. *I don't get that question much.*

"Didn't care for the hours. Or, often, the bar managers. Sometimes the other musicians. It led me to some bad habits."

"Ah, yes. I thought that might have something to do with it. I heard you used to play in Hayley's band. Were you here for her meltdown?"

"Yeah, I was."

"You were her tech?"

"I played guitar for her back then."

"Hm. Well, Hayley seems to be conscious of the bad habit thing these days, considering who she hired. Boomer has a bit of a rep as a party boy, but from what I've seen, Hayley's put the fear of God in him. One slip and he's gone. The rest of us are all clean-living guys. I guess she learned from the past."

"I'm sure she did," Mark agreed, then asked, "How did you end up in a country band?"

"Are you asking because I'm Black? I know there's not a lot of us in this end of the business, and not a lot of people are willing to hire us even now, but we are here and interested. In my case, it was because of my grandmother that I'm here. She used to listen to the Grand Ole Opry every Saturday night when I was a kid. I loved the music."

"And you came straight here?"

"Direct from Alabama. Via New York City," Clay said, and just as Mark was about to ask how that happened, Clay seemed to tire of talking about himself. "That's enough about me. Do you know the rest of the band? I'm the new guy, I think. Paid to fill in for any other instruments Hayley couldn't hire. Brass, strings, I can make the keys sound like that. The rest of the guys played with Hayley before. They're her 'real' band."

"I only talked to the guy with the long hair and baseball cap. That's Boomer, right? I didn't know him."

"Yeah, Boomer, our drummer. Todd Bruce is his real name. People kid him about being Jack Bruce and Ginger Baker's love child. Let me just warn you, he's heard it before. He doesn't like it."

"I'll keep that in mind," Mark said, though it was something he'd never have thought to say. "What about the rest of the guys?"

Clay sat down on his bed, warming to the subject. "Des Oakley is playing guitar now. Do you remember him from your days with Hayley?"

"No."

"Hayley and Des have been working together since 2002, according to Des."

"That makes sense. I left in 1999 and she 'took a breather' for a couple years," Mark said, using air quotes.

"Right. Des is a nice guy, I guess. Sounds like an old fogey to me, constantly whining about this or that. I think Hayley gets tired of his attitude, but he's an okay guitarist."

"Just okay? She should have someone better than just okay. She actually said something like that when she asked me to come here."

"I'll let you remind her of that. I'm the new guy, remember?" Clay laughed his easy laugh. "Des is supposed to play fiddle, too, but Hayley's not happy with that. She says she needs a dedicated fiddle player. Unless and until she finds one, I'm doing some of that, too."

"It's a little late to bring in someone else now, isn't it?" Mark asked. "She's running out of rehearsal time."

"Yeah, but Hayley's got a mind of her own. I bet she'll find someone. If not for this concert, then by the time we tour."

"I hope you're right. Who else do I need to know about?" Mark asked.

"Kenny Harbold is our bassist. He barely says two words a day, but he and Boomer really set the stage. Kenny's a good bassist, from my perspective. Gives us solid structure. Just keeps to himself."

"And the actual old guy?" Mark asked.

"Luke Carson. Pedal steel. He's not old, just seasoned," Clay laughed again. "Boomer calls him 'Twinkletoes,' but I wouldn't say that to his face. Still, he's a fine pedal steel player. In this town, he's got lots of competition, but from what I've heard him do, Hayley got a good one, don't ask me how. That song she plays about her daddy, 'Never Be As Good As You?' He adds a depth to that song that just wasn't there before." Clay's eyes took on a misty look. Mark was sure he was listening to the song play in his head. "He's an asset, for sure."

"The original song didn't have pedal steel on it. It was straight bluegrass." Mark didn't object, it was simply his observation.

"Yeah, yeah, I know," Clay said, "But this new version is supposed to crossover into new country. At least, that's what Hayley says."

"And what Hayley says is what happens."

"Pretty much. Anyway, that's the band."

"Thanks for the overview," Mark said. "Hayley hired me but didn't give me many details. I figured I'd catch up when I got here."

"You're welcome. Let's go talk to the rest of the guys."

CHAPTER 13

Davis Insurance
Nashville, TN
Friday, April 23, 2010
3:00 P.M.

"IT'S BEEN A WHILE SINCE I TALKED TO YOU," Olivia said to Harry several weeks later. "Is everything going according to plan? Do you need anything for Valerie and Rocky to prepare for the conference?" The truth was, she simply wanted to talk to Harry, hear his voice, and remember. She cradled the cell phone in her hand and allowed her voice to sound like aural honey.

"Oh, yes, the ladies are excited," Harry confirmed. "They have the presentation ready to go. I've seen the bulk of it. I asked them to make a few changes. I think you'll be very happy with it."

"Good," Olivia said. "I'm sorry you won't be joining them, though. I'd love to see you again."

"I'd like that, too, but somebody has to keep up with the work here."

"I know." She couldn't quite remove the regret from her voice. She realized that she really did miss Harry. Even though he explained that it was not his case, she was truly sorry he wasn't coming to Nashville to do the presentation.

"Listen," he said. "Maybe you could visit when the conference is over."

"I'd love that, honey," she replied, her accent thickening, her regret palpable, "but I'm in the middle of this Task Force push. A visit will have to wait. But I'll certainly let you know when I can."

"Great," he said. "How is the rest of the conference coming?"

"Well, you solved the biggest issue I had. Now it's all the fine details and getting it underway."

"That sounds good. Anything else? Anything I need to tell Valerie and Rocky?"

"No, I think everything is set. If they pick up the shuttle at the airport, they'll get to the hotel without any difficulty. I hope they have a great time here. I look forward to meeting them."

"Thanks for inviting them," Harry said. "I'm sure they'll do a good job."

"I'm sure they will," said Olivia.

— • ◆ • —

Running KH Precision Machine could be a chore. It was a very small part of Hoshi's business empire but, although he made money with it, its hassles often caused distractions. Sometimes Hoshi felt he spent entire days on the telephone. This was going to be another one of those days. He supposed he could delegate some of his calls to an assistant, but he liked to stay on top of things himself. His daughter once called him a control freak. Once.

Today was going to have at least one highlight. He was going to call Hayley Hopkins' sister/manager to ask them to play for Naoki's little soiree for the employees on May first. He wanted to say that he intentionally waited this long to call them about it, but the truth was, it had just slipped his mind. Even after Naoki reminded him. Twice. And then he decided that the extra pressure of calling them this close to the date would be fun.

Let's see how high they jump, Hoshi thought.

Paige answered on the second buzz. She was obviously using her cell phone because she knew who he was when he called.

"Mr. Kojima, how are you?" she said, in that fake happy voice she used whenever she talked to him. He loved it. He knew she felt indebted to him.

"Well, I'm calling you because a friend of mine is in a bit of a bind. He's putting on a little party for his employees next week and is looking for some entertainment."

There was a slight hesitation before she said, "And how can I help you with that?"

"I thought your sister could play for them. And her band, of course."

"I don't know, Mr. Kojima," Paige said. "Her schedule is tight right now. As you know, she is rehearsing and doing some small shows to prepare for the Country Music Hall of Fame Induction Announcement Concert and after that, she's going on tour for a few months."

"All the more reason to do this show," Hoshi said. "More buildup, more people to show how much she's changed."

He knew the reminder that Hayley was not always loved by her audiences would strike Paige in a tender spot. He was right.

"Well, give me the details and I'll discuss it with her."

He did so, then added, "I need to know today so he can announce it to his employees."

The sigh Paige emitted was not meant for his ears, but he heard it. *Oh, such a challenge,* Hoshi thought sarcastically. *How hard is it to play a couple hours? I'm sure they've done this before.*

"All right. I'll call you later."

He clicked off his phone and sat back, smiling contentedly. If Hayley refused, he knew he could threaten to collect all the money he had fronted them to do this tour. He was thinking of doing that anyway, but maybe later in the tour, after they had made back some of the cash. He wasn't sure exactly when he would play that card, but it was within his hand. And he could still pry the mandolin away from Hayley before it transferred to the Museum.

Threats could be so useful.

CHAPTER 14

Pedestrian Bridge
Nashville, TN
Friday, April 23, 2010
3:30 P.M.

Paul Pratt walked toward downtown Nashville on the pedestrian bridge over the Cumberland River, checking out the visiting tourists. Paul liked using the bridge because it was a good connector between his room at the seedy Crystal Hotel and Lower Broadway. He only had to walk one and a half blocks from the hotel to get to the bridge, and at the end of the bridge, the Schermerhorn Symphony Center, home of the Nashville Symphony. From there it was just a few blocks to the honky tonks. If his efficiency apartment was on the parking lot side of the hotel, Paul would be able to see the Schermerhorn from his grimy third-floor window.

Paul had lived in Nashville for over ten years. He knew how the town operated. He knew how to get around. The Crystal's location was important to him.

Paul considered himself one of the better criminals in town. In any town, really.

If there was a Hall of Fame for Thieves, I'd be in it. In fact, I would be featured.

Paul was a chronic thief, generally a thief for hire, but if he saw something valuable and easy to resell, he'd be happy to lift it for himself. After all, just as he knew the town, he knew people that could liquidate his finds.

It beats having a regular job, he thought. I'm good at this. I can lift anything that a tourist doesn't keep an eye on. No tourist can outsmart me.

To prove the point to himself, Paul slipped between two walkers, a man and his wife. They each wore a light windbreaker. She had a fanny pack cradled in the small of her back, offering easy pickings for a thief like Paul. But Paul saw something even more straightforward and probably more lucrative: the man's wallet, outlined lightly inside his back pants pocket.

Paul zipped three steps ahead of the couple, then nimbly cut back behind them. They paid no attention. Paul lightly slid the wallet out of the guy's back pocket while his wife pointed out a park across the river. Paul walked by without them ever noticing him. He laughed to himself.

The guy won't even realize his wallet is missing until they go to dinner.

Paul got far enough away from them to peek inside the wallet. He counted over two hundred dollars in cash in it, which he pocketed, then he dropped the wallet on the walkway for them to find when they got to that spot.

If they even notice.

CHAPTER 15

Hilton Hotel Downtown
Nashville, TN
Monday, April 26, 2010
1:00 P.M.

WHEN VALERIE AND ROCKY ARRIVED at the hotel, it was all Valerie could do to keep herself from becoming a typical tourist, craning her head to see everything, eyes wide, drinking it all in. She stared upward at the floors above them that were open to the reception area below.

The Hilton Hotel Downtown was majestic and gorgeous, with white tile floors and an atrium with high white arches. A grand staircase faced the entrance and Valerie could imagine women in ballgowns and men in tuxedos doing a dance number there. Huge clay pots of fragrant white flowers, predominantly roses and magnolias with a bit of ivy tucked in for background, studded the room. People milled about the lobby and their voices echoed off every surface. The sound of rolling wheels and staccato footsteps surrounded Valerie and Rocky.

A coffee bar marked the center of the atrium, a large television tuned to weather and news hanging above it. The television appeared to be muted, but it was hard to tell over the rest of the sound in the room. Real-time closed captions were running at the bottom of the TV screen, sometimes overlapping the news chyron.

Valerie glanced up at the TV but didn't register the weather report running its alerts at the top of the screen. She was too overwhelmed by the sound of other travelers checking in, meeting friends, asking questions, and talking on their phones. Rocky charged across the lobby and Valerie called to her to keep her from getting too far away from her.

I need a leash for that girl, she thought.

To their left was an entrance to a restaurant. A line of fifteen or so people waited to enter. More white flowers trimmed a sign which pointed them to the reception area on the right. A few people were waiting there, also, but the lines moved smoothly.

Valets were quick to offer help. Valerie turned them down. She and Rocky simply didn't have that much luggage with them, just one bag each. They checked in and found their way to the elevators.

The elevator doors closed, and it felt like they were in a hermetically sealed box. It was the first noise-free space they'd been in since they left Valerie's house to go to the airport. The last vestiges of the prior guest's perfume lingered in the air.

On the ride to their floor, Valerie glanced at Rocky's single bag. "I know you're planning to do some shopping," she said, gesturing to Rocky's soft-sided suitcase. "How are you planning to take things home?"

"There's a little extra space in there. I have an expansion section that zips open."

"But you were talking about buying boots? Are you planning to wear them home?"

Rocky laughed. "You talk as though I'm only going to buy one pair," she said. "I'll ship the ones I don't wear right away."

Oh, boy, Valerie thought.

They rode to one of the higher floors in the building, an area that required them to use their keycard a second time to ascend. When they found the right room, they stood just inside the door and looked at each other.

Valerie was the first to break their shocked silence. "Wow! We got a suite, not just a room! I didn't know they booked us a suite!"

"Do you believe this? Look at this place! And the view!" Rocky moved over to the window and pushed back the sheers so they could look out.

"This is really great." Valerie sat down to test one of the queen-size beds. She stretched out and felt giddy, delighted to find it was long enough to fit someone of her extended height. "Ooh, it's so fluffy! Look at these pillows!" Thinking that she sounded like Rocky, she immediately tamped down her enthusiasm. "You know, it's actually a relief to get away from Philly for a few days."

"Because of Mark?"

Rocky looked so innocent when she said it, Valerie almost laughed, but she let the comment slide by. She couldn't help but babble, patting the bed. "This is amazing."

"I'm hungry. How about if I research the restaurant in the hotel? Or maybe ask the concierge for suggestions?" Rocky was already moving toward the door.

"Okay but try to stay out of trouble."

"Okay, Boss!" Rocky said and saluted her on her way out the door.

Valerie didn't even try to tell her not to call her "Boss" anymore. She knew Rocky did it just to annoy her, so she ignored her, at least outwardly, no matter how hard that was. It was hard to ignore any-thing Rocky did.

Valerie gave her about thirty seconds, then punched in the code for Mark on her phone.

"Hey, Mark, I'm in Nashville."

"You made it! How was the flight?"

"It was all right. How are you doing?"

"I'm okay. Been working, mostly. The concert is Sunday. And there's a private party that Hayley agreed to play Saturday night. We've been working like crazy to get the songs down. We're just about there. You'll be here until next Monday, right?"

"Right."

"I got tickets for you and Rocky for the concert. Is Rocky there? I don't hear her."

"She's already out exploring the hotel."

"I bet," he laughed, then added, "It's really good to hear your voice."

CHAPTER 16

Lower Broadway
Nashville, TN
Monday, April 26, 2010
4:45 P.M.

PAUL PRATT STROLLED DOWNTOWN to the honky-tonks. The pickings were usually good there, and easy. He passed a banjo player busking on the street, a guy he saw pretty much daily. The banjo player glared at him. Paul guessed he knew that Paul was the guy who stole the tip money out of his case a few weeks ago. He'd been giving Paul the stink-eye ever since and keeping his case cleaned out.

Paul wasn't worried about it. The guy was around town all the time. *He'll make the money back. He'll get over the theft and get sloppy again and I'll clean him out again. The cycle of life.*

Paul kept walking and chose a random honky-tonk to visit, Sweet's Lounge and Bar-b-que. He looked up at the chalk board with the list of bands playing that day. The one onstage was some group called The Happy Charlottes.

It doesn't matter which honky-tonk I hit, Paul thought, *because every-one is watching the band, not me.*

Inside, he was sure that something or someone would catch his eye. He knew he'd find a target in the crowd.

Aaron Gentry was a young guitarist, new to Nashville. Today he had a gig with a working band, The Happy Charlottes, that regularly played the honky-tonk circuit downtown. Pumped up, excited to be gainfully employed as a musician, he took his Fender Telecaster to the gig. To his delight, the gig went well. The front man even gave him a shout-out from the stage, asking the crowd to applaud his first appearance there.

After the gig, the band packed up and headed out. The next band was already loading in. Aaron said his goodbyes and then placed his guitar, snug in its gig bag, to one side of the raised stage so he could make a quick trip to the john before he left. He called out to the incoming musicians that he was just leaving the guitar there for a minute and to keep an eye on it for him.

Paul Pratt sat at the bar, watching Gentry. When Aaron disappeared to the back of the bar, Paul finished his beer, walked over to the side of the stage, and casually picked up the gig bag. The band, busy setting up, never noticed. The bartender and the bouncer, busy talking to each other, didn't notice, either. Paul walked out the door, bag in hand.

Paul knew how to act casual, as though picking up this instrument and walking out the door of the bar was what he did every day. He took measured strides, didn't make eye contact with anyone, breathed deeply, kept himself calm. Outside the sun was still bright and the crowds were busy, but no one noticed him.

Paul had just started to relax when he heard a shout behind him. Aaron came flying out of the honky-tonk, running in his direction. The bouncer was behind him, waving something in his hand and half-heartedly jostling along, as well. Paul lifted the bag above his head and started weaving in and out of the people on the sidewalk, a maneuver that he thought of as "swimming the crowd." He kept glancing over his shoulder to make sure the guitar player wasn't gaining on him.

He was not. Eventually the guitar's owner gave up and disappeared from Paul's view.

———•●•———

"I can't believe you talked me into this," Valerie muttered as she and Rocky crossed Lower Broadway. Honky-tonks surrounded them. Every open doorway exploded with music from another band. "I do not need boots. I am not shopping for cowboy boots. You shouldn't be shopping for more, either. How on earth are you going to get these things home?"

"I told you already. I'm shipping them."

Rocky had already bought two pairs of boots at a place called BootsBootsBoots that held what looked like thousands of pairs of boots and boot-styled shoes. It had taken Rocky over an hour to narrow down her choice.

Valerie was ready to go back to the hotel and take a nap before dinner.

"We still need to find you a pair," Rocky insisted.

"No, we don't."

"You should have looked closer at some of the other shops," Rocky insisted. "That last one had sizes that fit you, I'm sure. Look over there! There's Robert's Western World."

"That's a bar, not a boot shop."

"They have cowboy boots. I read about them. Besides, aren't you parched?"

"'Parched?' You've been watching too many old cowboy movies." Valerie gauged her thirst level and relented. "But yeah, I could go for a beer."

Inside, while Rocky ordered their beers, Valerie was startled to see an actual row of boots lined up along one side of the bar. "Are those boots really for sale?" She aimed her question at Rocky, but the bartender answered.

"Sure are, if you really want them, but we don't usually sell boots to wear anymore. People buy them more as a souvenir of the bar than to actually wear."

"Thanks," Rocky said and tipped him extra when he slid their bottles across the bar. "Told you so," she said to Valerie.

They took their beers to a table and watched as a band finished setting up to play. As soon as they started their set, Valerie realized she didn't want to stay long. The music was good and the band personable, but they were also loud. The sound bounced around the room, overwhelming her with the vibration. Louder than Valerie liked.

"We should go."

"Why? This is what honky tonks are all about."

"It's giving me a headache. Let's head back to the hotel."

Rocky rolled her eyes. "Okay, spoilsport. Come on."

Valerie made sure they tipped the band before they went outside. *Mark taught me to do that,* she thought with a sudden pang of longing.

"I still want you to get some boots," Rocky said when they got outside.

"Maybe another day," Valerie said and started walking in the direction of their hotel. Rocky followed her, sulking. Across the street a banjo player picked a country song and sang to a small gathering of about eight or ten people. Valerie didn't know much about banjos, but the guy wasn't making mistakes that she could hear, plus he was singing in tune. *Two points in his favor.*

They hadn't gone much further when Valerie saw a guy walking toward them carrying a guitar case. Valerie wouldn't have thought anything of it normally, but the guy was wearing a hoodie, not typical Nashville wear. Her eyes narrowed to watch him. At that moment another guy, this one wearing a cowboy shirt embroidered across the yoke, came running out of one of the honky-tonks, yelling.

The guy in the hoodie ran right between Valerie and Rocky. The yelling guy followed close behind. Then a second man ran out of the honky-tonk, a large, ungainly man waving one fist in the air. This man started to run, but his bulk suddenly stopped. He took a rigid stance and pointed his right hand in Valerie and Rocky's direction, steadying it with his left.

"He's got a gun!" Valerie yelled and grabbed Rocky, pulling her down to the ground. People around them screamed and collapsed to the ground with them.

Valerie lay flat on the sidewalk watching the gunman. He suddenly seemed to wake up. He looked at the crowd of people on the street and put his gun back in his pocket. Then he pulled out a cell phone and made a call.

Banjo Bob was always glad when the sun started to set. The blue sky settled into gold and orange hues, the humid air got a tiny bit cooler and incrementally fresher, and the tourists got drunker and more generous. He'd been playing since ten that morning in what he deemed a prime spot a few hundred feet away from Ernest Tubb's Record Store and only now was he seeing big bills, rather than loose change, in his banjo case.

Recharged by the sudden bounty, Bob picked a few of his personal favorite tunes: "Fireball Mail," "Roll in My Sweet Baby's Arms," and "Flint Hill Special." Audiences recognized them, liked them, and sometimes asked for them. As the sidewalk filled with listeners, he tilted his head down, letting the brim of his Stetson cover his face. He studied their shoes, figuring out which pair would leave the biggest tip. It was a game he played to pass the time, and often, he was right.

Bob was about to launch into "Foggy Mountain Breakdown" when he heard a loud shout. He looked up, still picking, and heard another.

"Stop that guy!"

Looking beyond the crowd to his right, Bob saw motion and heard more yelling. He paused his playing and watched as a skinny guy in dark clothes, a guy Bob had seen many times before, took off running down the street. He was holding a gig bag in his hands in front of him almost like a battering ram, but higher, above his head. His body twisted left and right, dodging the people around him. Bob could tell he was just trying to keep the instrument inside the case from hitting anyone and slowing him down.

Bob had seen motion like that once before when he cornered a weasel on his grandad's farm. After Bob cornered it, the weasel, still holding the egg he'd filched from his grandad's chickens in its mouth, ran toward Bob with the flock squawking around him, dodging poultry left and right. This guy was running just like that.

They used to call George Jones "The Possum," Bob thought. *This guy is definitely "The Weasel."*

People in the runner's way ducked and flattened to the street or against the buildings, making a racket much like those chickens. The Weasel leaped over several humps of humanity as he tore his way up Broadway across the street from Banjo Bob and headed in the direction of the lavender walls of Tootsie's Orchid Lounge. He turned left at Tootsie's and crossed the street against the light, causing cars to screech to a halt and blow their horns.

Bob immediately realized The Weasel had come out of one of the honky-tonks. After he heard the shout, Bob stopped playing long enough to watch a young man giving chase, followed by a burly bouncer type who was no match for The Weasel's speed. Burly Boy had a pistol in his hand. He must have thought he could shoot the thief, but he hadn't counted on the mass of innocent tourists filling the sidewalk, no matter that they crouched out of the line of fire.

Burly Boy holstered his gun and replaced it with a cell phone. Cops arrived a few minutes later.

By that time, Bob had continued picking his banjo. The incident would be tidied up shortly. No need to disappoint the tourists. The tune he chose was "Long Journey Home," in honor of the trip Bob suspected The Weasel was going to have.

But from his vantage point across the street, Banjo Bob had seen the entire thing. He recognized the thief. He was the man who stole his tips a couple weeks ago. Inside his head, Bob snarled.

CHAPTER 17

KH Precision Machine
Nashville, TN
Monday, April 26, 2010
4:00 P.M.

SUZUME LEANED OVER HER LAPTOP, checking her list of contacts, looking for the right fit for her father's request. Despite Nashville being full of instruments, it was hard for her to imagine very many that would be interesting to the clientele her father served. Maybe something used by a star. Maybe something custom-made. Maybe something unusually old or expensive.

She'd talked to a couple fences in the area that she knew well and had worked with often. Neither had anything to offer her. On the other hand, she knew that just rattling a few chains might bring her something later. It was always good to put out feelers.

Then she remembered Sailor Lang. She'd worked with him a few times. He occasionally contacted her with items she might be able to use. Like the puzzle box he acquired. That was the first time he worked with her.

Sailor had called her and asked to meet. She had heard of him, of course. His reputation as a safecracker and lockpick preceded him but she was suspicious, especially when he said he had an item she might be able to identify for him.

"Why me?" she had asked.

"Because I hear you know about Japanese antiques."

Yeah, she knew the antiques of her home country. She learned about them at the knee of her father's best dealer, Kiyoshi Itoh. The man she thought of as her grandfather, even thought he was no blood relative.

"You know about Hakone boxes. I want to know the value of one I found."

"Most of them are mass-produced these days," she'd told him.

"Not this one."

She agreed to meet him in a busy park. He carried a backpack, not unlike her own, but larger and made of burnt umber oiled canvas rather than the lush black lambskin that was hers. He pulled a Japanese puzzle box out of the backpack.

The box was beautiful. Mosaic woods, colors that swirled and danced in the light. Shined to a glow. She marveled at the way Sailor handled it, lightly and carefully, yet turning and twisting the edges deftly, opening layer upon layer of hidden inner chambers. When completely open, the box created a star shape of miniature boxes. She gasped with wonder.

The quality, beauty, and practicality of its design made the puzzle box a worthy acquisition. Negotiations ensued.

"I only wanted to know what it was worth," he said. "I'm not looking to sell it."

"I will pay you well."

Money was the key. She argued that he wouldn't have to find a buyer himself, she could do that. She thought he might have a fence already, or a collector in mind. But his head turned at the amount she offered.

"All right."

After he demonstrated the secret to opening the box, slowly so she could keep up, she paid him. And paid him well, as she had told him.

It was, she could see, a very old example of Hakone. A valuable one. She was able to take it to her father and impress him. And Daddy did not impress easily.

That was the first of their occasional interactions. None of his later offerings were quite as impressive, but the items he brought her were always high quality and unique.

In short, Sailor Lang might be of assistance. The problem was conjuring him up.

Mr. Invisible.

Sailor was sometimes hard to track down, a good thing in his line of business. He would appear when least expected and disappear before you could pin him down. Rumor had it that he knew every nook and cranny of this city and could put his hands on whatever you needed without leaving tracks.

Yes, Sailor Lang might just be the man for this job.

She heard a rap on the door and closed her laptop.

"Suzume?"

It was Bana, her dad's assistant. It was never good news when Daddy sent his second-in-command to see you.

"Yes?"

Bana stepped inside the door. This was not a social call.

Bana was a large man, built like a weightlifter, which Suzume guessed he was. As he moved into her office, she saw the man behind him, a much younger man sporting a high pompadour which he ran his fingers through expertly. He turned his face slightly, showing her the angle of his chin and the arch of his eyebrows. He wore a silk bomber jacket zipped low. The thin shirt he wore underneath looked skintight, to show off the smoothness of his chest beneath. She suspected that if he opened his jacket fully, she would see the outline of his nipples through the material.

"This is Ryu Tanaka. He will accompany you should you decide to travel in the city."

"I don't need a babysitter."

"Think of him as your bodyguard."

Suzume's eyes went back to the young man, whose face was still angled slightly away from her. His eyes watched her, his lips pressed together in a sharp-edged smile.

Not only does he know how good-looking he is, but he has also practiced this look in a mirror many times.

She knew better than to argue with Bana. An order from him was just an order from her father, filtered through Bana's voice.

"And what am I to do with him when I am in the building?"

"Maybe have him wait for you outside the door?"

As you do for my father, she thought. *But it might be fun to have a bodyguard. Let's see how useful he can be.*

She nodded, each nod pronounced and slow.

"Sit down, Ryu."

"Thank you." His voice had a nasal edge.

"I'm sure you two will enjoy each other's company," Bana said.

As Bana left, the door made a sucking noise that reminded her of being sealed in a bag. She and Ryu stared at each other for a long moment. He looked ready to argue with her at the first opportunity. She was the first to speak.

"I believe we are stuck with each other."

"What would you like me to do? Shall I sit outside your door?" He tilted his head back and screwed up his nose and lips when he said it, as though it was something beneath him. Yet she knew it was what Ryu expected her to demand, and, as he said, what Bana expected her to do.

"So, it seems I am your punishment." She almost laughed at the thought.

Ryu's face changed subtly. His eyes sharpened and he looked at her more directly.

"You didn't think I would guess," she said. "What did you do?"

Ryu's cheeks darkened. "Spoke out of turn."

That must have been some comment, to earn you time with me, she thought.

"Well, let's hope you have learned a lesson. I don't expect that you will repeat it. On the other hand, I do expect that you will talk to me. With respect."

Ryu nodded. She believed his respect was relative and that he would turn on her as soon as he had a chance.

"I have some business to arrange." When Ryu stood to leave, she stopped him. "No. Sit down. I just need to make a phone call."

He sank back into the chair. She picked up her cell phone and punched in a number. Holding the phone to her ear, a little thrill ran through her when a man's voice responded.

"Hello, Sailor."

CHAPTER 18

Crystal Hotel
Nashville, TN
Monday, April 26, 2010
6:30 P.M.

PAUL PRATT, GUITAR IN HAND and still running, was headed home. Home was the Crystal Hotel, situated on the eastern side of the Cumberland River, perched on a hill near the end of the pedestrian bridge. At one time the Crystal was a nice hotel where folks could stay for a decent price and basic amenities. Those days were long gone.

There was also a time when the Crystal was used exclusively by drug traffickers and their clients, but the diligence of the local police helped to curb that. Eventually, the Crystal closed for a couple years, then some investors tried to bring it back to life.

It almost worked. Almost. The building needed a lot of renovation, more than the investors realized. They sold the building to the first buyer they could find.

Now the words *Crystal Hotel* equaled *squalid* and *ramshackle*. No longer a haven for travelers, it became the refuge of the old, the indigent, and the almost forgotten people of the city. It was a bastion of cheap rentals and a wild diversity of downtrodden tenants. Including Paul Pratt.

I probably should've thought this part of the plan through better than I did.

Paul enjoyed taking more time to scope things out. But this was a sudden opportunity, the sort of chance that made Paul's life exciting. The guitar's owner leaving his guitar unattended in a bar on Lower Broadway with no one watching over it was fortuitous. The guitarist assumed wrongly that, because there were lots of people in the bar, and because the bartender and the bouncer were chatting with each other at the front corner of the bar near the stage, that he could safely leave the guitar there. Paul made a snap decision and almost immediately had to run away from the guitar's owner and the bar's bouncer.

What was it Sailor said about every theft?

"For every action there is an equal and opposite reaction."

He said he learned that in school. Sailor went to a very different school than I did.

But now Paul had to deal with the fallout.

He'd run in the entrance of The Crystal like a man on fire. He was out of breath and paused inside the doors to lean over and suck some of the hotel's stale air inside his lungs, hoping that no one noticed him.

Paul looked around him. Sometimes he forgot that this was The Crystal Hotel, where no one saw anything, and no one mentioned it if they did. And it looked like there was no one around to see anything anyway. But Paul knew that behind those closed doors, on every floor, the hotel was populated by old folks with their ears pressed to the door, hazy druggies collapsed on the floor, and losers feeling sorry for themselves and looking for ways to "get over" on the other tenants.

And thieves, of course.

Thieves like me.

He poked the button on the elevator panel to call it to the lobby. He was amazed to hear the elevator wheeze its way down. It was often "Out of Service," according to a sign regularly posted there. *Looks like I might get lucky,* he thought, *although it's probably faster to run up the stairs.*

Ethel, the manager, poked her head out of her room and into the lobby, skyrocketing Paul's heart rate again. He tried to look nonchalant, but suspected he just looked guilty.

"Oh, it's you," Ethel said around the cigarette in her mouth, her gritty voice like rough sandpaper in his ears. For a moment Paul thought she was going to question him about the guitar case. Instead, she said, "I thought you were Harriet. She left her umbrella down here again. I'm surprised no one has taken it yet." Ethel tsk-tsked, then added, "I've been watching for her, but she hasn't come back. If you see her, tell her it's over there in the corner." Ethel pointed a gnarled finger at the umbrella.

The umbrella's garish flowers in neon colors would be hard to miss. Some of the canvas webbing had separated from the rods and the spine of the thing bent horribly. Paul wondered why anyone would bother to steal it. He understood why Harriet didn't take it with her.

"I'll let her know if I see her," he muttered as calmly as he could. The elevator door opened. He got on, pressed the 3, and the elevator creaked its way to the third floor where he lived.

CHAPTER 19

Davis Insurance
Nashville, TN
Monday, April 26, 2010
6:30 P.M.

OLIVIA FARRELL HUNG UP THE PHONE and tapped one long fingernail on the top of her desk. It was the sort of thing she did to help herself think.

Especially when someone from the Task Force called.

The phone call was quick, all business, too short for Olivia to comment much. Unusual, for her.

"Do you know a guy named Aaron Gentry?"

She recognized the voice on the other end of the call as the new addition working on the Task Force, Detective Watson Dodd. She'd talked to him twice before and found him professional but dry.

No fun at all.

She thought a moment, then shook her head even though Dodd wouldn't see it through the phone. "Can't say I do. Should I know him?"

"He just had a guitar stolen. From Sweet's Lounge and Bar-b-que. A Fender Telecaster."

"Hardly worth reporting unless it was something special." She didn't mean it to sound dismissive, but it did.

"It wasn't, according to the owner." Olivia thought Dodd sounded miffed. "He's mostly angry and wants to catch the guy."

"And the Task Force is involved?"

"Of course, we are." Dodd sounded really annoyed, now. "We want to hear about any instrument being taken, not just the expensive ones. These small-time offenders can become big-time criminals in the blink of an eye."

Olivia knew that was true. "What happened?"

Dodd gave her the gist of the story.

"He was a newbie, eh? That hurts. Poor guy. Probably ready to get on the bus and go home," Olivia said.

"Yeah, probably, but that's not our concern. We need to get the guitar back to him. If we work fast, maybe we can track it down. Maybe we can even find the guy who did it."

"We?" She bit her tongue before she said something rude. Instead, she sweetly asked, "What do you need me to do, honey?" She would lay money that if she was in the same room with Dodd, she would see surprise on his face.

The hallway of the Crystal was quiet. Paul Pratt saw no one, heard no one. It was as though the building was holding its breath.

Or maybe that's just me, he thought as he unlocked the door to his apartment.

Inside, a quick scan of the room told him no one had been there since he left, not even Ethel, who sometimes let herself in, supposedly to "clean." He'd never seen much of an indication of any cleaning and suspected she might have been looking for drugs or stolen goods she could squeal to the cops about. Or maybe sell to the highest bidder.

Plenty of options in this building.

He flopped the guitar case on the bedspread and collapsed across the lumpy mattress next to it, exhaling heavily. For a while he watched the clicking fan on the bedside table oscillate, moving dank air around the room. The bedspread scratched his hands where the sleeves of his hoodie didn't cover them. He turned on his side and looked at the guitar case lying on the bedspread next to him.

The back of the gig bag was plastered with stickers from the owner's travels, some peeling away from the fabric. Only a few made sense to Paul. Most were stickers advertising bars where, he supposed, the guitar had been played. A few stickers were band names: Highway Dave and the Varmints, The Eskimo Brothers, Deranged Rover, and a bunch of other names that Paul didn't recognize. Paul's playing days were long past, and he no longer kept up with the real music world. Only the instruments. Only the buyers.

A light rap on the door startled him. Paul shoved the guitar case under the bed, ignoring the dirt and random crap embedded there. "Pratt!" a voice called softly through the door. "You in there, Pratt?"

"Yeah!" Paul called back. He recognized the voice, jumped up from the bed and pushed the guitar further back with one foot. He almost got to the door before Sailor burst in.

"You could have waited," Paul grumbled. He hated when Sailor did what he did so well, broke into the room by jimmying an admittedly pathetic lock.

"I think not," Sailor responded. "I like to keep in practice."

He was a small man, shorter than Paul. Paul guessed him to be about five and a half feet tall, a good three or four inches shorter than him and only slightly heavier. Sailor had blond hair cut short in a casual style that Paul thought might work in almost any corporate office, although Paul hadn't seen the inside of a corporate office except in movies. Sailor had hazy gray eyes, the color of mist on water. His smile tilted up on the left side, the only outward indication of something off. If he didn't smile, he looked absolutely forgettable.

It was a talent, being that invisible. One that worked well for his real job. Sailor was the best fence Paul had ever met. And in his line of work, Paul had met more than one. Doors and safes were just a hobby for Sailor. He enjoyed moving stolen goods far more. Add his invisibility and Sailor had all the makings of a formidable criminal. He was also a great teacher, and taught Paul some of his tricks.

I owe him, Paul thought. *Let's see what he thinks about this guitar.*

"Hey, I have something for you to look at," Paul said, then scrutinized Sailor, who was wearing a crisp suit and pressed shirt. Sidetracked, he asked, "What's this all about?" He waved a dismissive hand in Sailor's general direction. "Going to a funeral?"

"Very funny. Haven't you ever heard about dressing for the job you want, not the job you have?" Sailor said, dusting his fingers over the lapels of his jacket. "Spiffy, no?"

"What the hell are you talking about?" Paul fumed. There was no job on earth that he wanted to waste his time doing. He did well enough supplying clients with instruments that they wanted. Well enough to live at The Crystal, anyway. Although, to be fair, sometimes he asked for Sailor's help.

"I just talked with a friend," Sailor told him. "She's asked me to coordinate a job. And it's a job that's perfect for you. But you must apply for it. And you need a uniform."

CHAPTER 20

Station Inn
Nashville, TN
Tuesday, April 27, 2010
11:45 A.M.

THE TABLES WERE EMPTY, the chairs neatly arranged around them. The stage was bare except for two high stools. The house lights were up, and the lighting techs, all two of them, were adjusting lamp angles and strengths for the cameraman who was going to record Donna MacCloud's interview with Hayley Hopkins for Nashville local news on WHIM.

Donna was a darling of the local channel, and when Hayley got the chance to talk with her -- in no small part because Paige set it up -- she jumped at it. With any luck, the interview would be picked up by the news affiliates and bring in more people to see Hayley's show on Sunday.

To further enhance the interview, Hayley's band would play a song or two afterward, giving the audience a taste of what to expect at the show.

Hayley sat on one of the stools, eyes closed, attempting to

deep-breathe her jitters away. She didn't do many interviews anymore, and this one was important. Her assistant Justine fluttered around her, dusting her face with powder to take down the shine and touching up her glittering eyeshadow. She made sure the curls in Hayley's hair sprang in a controlled way, not too bouncy, but not too flat, either.

"There," Justine whispered to Hayley. "Just right."

Hayley opened her eyes and saw the wide smile on Justine's face, a sure sign that she was pleased with her work. "Thanks," Hayley said. "I couldn't do this without you."

Justine squeezed Hayley's shoulder and slipped the powder brush into the makeup case. She picked up her gear and said, with a wink, "Break a leg, honey," and disappeared backstage.

Donna MacCloud sat on the other stool and eyed Hayley. Donna's layered silver hair was sprayed into submission and she, too, had slathered on the eye makeup.

It might be for the cameras, Hayley thought, *but sometimes I think we wear makeup for protection. We don't want anyone to see who we really are.*

"Are you ready?" Donna asked.

It must be noon, Hayley thought. She nodded and Donna cued the camera operator. From somewhere Donna's theme music played on the house sound system and when it faded, Donna took over.

"We're here at the legendary Station Inn," Donna said, her voice brighter and louder than Hayley thought it needed to be. "Visiting with us today is the one and only Hayley Hopkins, bluegrass mandolin player without peer. She's the daughter of Charley Hopkins, the man who some say made the mandolin a critical element of bluegrass. Hayley, welcome to the show!"

"Thank you," Hayley said and realized from the motions the

cameraman was making that she needed to talk louder. "Thanks for inviting me."

"It's great to have you here. In January, you re-released your song "Never Be As Good As You." It's become a huge hit that's crossing over from bluegrass into the country world. You must be proud."

"It's a good feeling knowing that people like it."

"It's been a long time coming, though, hasn't it? Originally you released it in 1993, and your last big concert was in 1994, isn't that right?"

"Yes, that's right," Hayley replied, feeling her smile fade. She didn't think anyone would bring up her past, let alone make it the second question asked. She forced herself to shrug off her panic. "After all these years, my life is very different from what it was then. For one thing, I came to terms with my father's legacy and what he meant to me and to my music. That's why I re-released the song."

"Let's talk about your dad," Donna went on. "Do you think he is the driving force behind what bluegrass became in the seventies and eighties?"

"I let the philosophers and critics talk about that," Hayley said with a guarded smile. "I only know that he was a giant to me. And I let the music talk for me. What I learned from him, what I learned from all the people I've played with over the years, and how I can translate that into how I play, that's what matters to me now."

"But your new song is an admission that you can never play as well as him or move the bluegrass world the way he did."

Hayley nodded. "I've often felt that way, but the truth is, we all make our own way in the world and do the best we can. I think it's okay that I'll never be as good a player as he was or that I many never change the music world"

"What do you think your father would say?" Donna asked.

"I think if my father could tell me anything, he'd tell me he was proud of me and what I did to get here and what I do now. I think he'd be happy that I followed his path. But I also think he would tell me that it didn't mean this was a competition."

"So, do you think you are as good today as he was then?" Donna leaned forward, her eyes piercing Hayley's.

Hayley sighed. This was the question she expected.

"I think I am my own self, my own player. I simply want to honor him with the concert coming up on Sunday and offer his mandolin to the Country Music Hall of Fame."

Hayley was delighted that she was able to work in the plug. She honestly thought that's what this interview was going to be about, not whether she was as good as her father.

Donna didn't seem thrilled with her answers. She continued to stare at Hayley and pushed the question further. "Will you be performing with his mandolin on Sunday? Or will you use your own?"

"I plan to do both," Hayley responded, "but I'll probably play his a little more. It will be the mandolin's last public use before it goes to the Hall of Fame Museum."

"And will you be performing your own songs or his?"

"Well, Daddy didn't write a lot of songs, he was known more for his playing. I'll be doing some classics that I know he played, but I'll also be doing a few of my own songs."

"Including the new version of 'Never Be As Good As You?'"

"Of course."

Donna leaned back again, her interview nearly concluded. "I believe you and your band are performing a brief sample for us here today. Why don't you introduce the band?"

Hailey nodded and waved to the guys to come out on stage. As they prepared to play, she introduced them, heaping each one with praise. Then she looked around the stage like she'd lost something. She waved at Mark backstage, and he came out ducking his head reluctantly.

"I have a great band, but I couldn't do the show this weekend if it hadn't been for my old friend Mark Patton," she said, wrapping one arm around his waist. "He came down here all the way from Pennsylvania to help me get the instruments set up and the show sounding right."

"Well, that's just great, Mr. Patton," Donna cooed. "It must be a huge honor to be asked to assist in such a position."

Mark gave her a hazy stare and it was then that both Hayley and Donna realized that Mark was drunk. He wrapped his arms around Hayley and slurred, "This woman here is worth coming to Nashville for. She's gonna be great."

Shocked, Hayley said, "Thanks for being here, Mark." She slithered out of his arms and said, "Now, let me get the boys to do our version of 'Keep On The Sunny Side,' and show a little of what we do."

The band played and Hayley focused on her mandolin, singing the vocals with help from the band. Mark stumbled offstage, occasionally looking back at Hayley as though confused. When he got off-camera, a couple of stagehands grabbed his arms. They held him so he couldn't go back on camera. He started to protest, but they shushed him and pulled him further away.

When the song finished, Donna took over again.

"Thank you, Hayley Hopkins, for talking to us this afternoon and for bringing your band to give us a preview. We look forward to your performance this weekend."

Donna continued talking over the band's next song, reminding the audience again of the Sunday concert, suggesting that if they hadn't already gotten their tickets, they'd better do so quickly. The show was nearly sold out.

Someone offstage cued Donna to stop. The band finished playing and the lights went down. Hayley forced herself to smile and thanked Donna for her efforts.

Donna shook Hayley's hand stiffly and, although she didn't actively frown, her eyes told Hayley that she was not happy.

"I've already got my media passes for the concert Saturday," Donna said, "so I'm sure we'll see each other again soon." She stalked off, with a cameraman scuttling behind her.

Paige and Justine met Hayley backstage.

"How did we do?" Hayley asked.

"What the hell is wrong with Mark?" Paige snapped, ignoring her question.

"He's been drinking a little, that's all," Hayley said. "I didn't realize he'd had so much already."

"You didn't, did you? Well, just make sure that doesn't happen again anytime between now and Sunday. If this whole thing goes down in flames, it's on you!"

Hayley and Justine watched Paige go, and under her breath, Justine said, "You did great, honey."

"Thank you," Hayley whispered back.

"Best get Mark back on the wagon," Justine added.

Hayley nodded.

CHAPTER 21

Lower Broadway
Nashville, TN
Tuesday, April 27, 2010
11:45 A.M.

OLIVIA PARKED ON FOURTH AVENUE and unfolded her legs to get out of her blue Volvo, a 1985 four-door model that she lovingly called "The Tank." Despite a pleasant afternoon breeze, there was still enough heat to warm the interior of the car and make her perspire. She straightened her dress and picked up her tiny bag. All she needed for this trip was her phone and some cash.

She stood on the sidewalk by The Tank, looking down the street toward Broadway and scanning the surroundings. It was just a minute's walk to get to the corner occupied by Gruhn's guitar store. The street was almost empty. It was a beautiful day, but because it was Tuesday there weren't a lot of tourists around.

Not to say that there weren't any tourists at all. There were always people poking around Broadway, even on a Tuesday afternoon, looking for an open honky-tonk, a beer or three, and a fried bologna sandwich.

And sometimes there's a band playing for atmosphere, Olivia chuckled to herself.

She'd been secretly pleased that Dodd asked her to help track down the stolen Telecaster. This was the sort of thing she was good at. When she found out that the prize was taken from a bar on Broadway, she was more than a little interested. This latest rash of thefts was demoralizing to the city's musicians, so she was happy she had offered her services as part of the Task Force. She understood Watson Dodd's perspective. The stolen guitar wasn't a model that was of collectible value, but whatever its value, its owner wanted it back.

The theft took place the night before and the longer they waited to look for it, the harder the guitar would be to find. The bonus was that Olivia knew just where to start her search. She was looking for the sharpest set of eyes on Lower Broadway.

She was looking for Banjo Bob.

Olivia turned the corner at Fourth Avenue to walk up Broadway. She saw Bob just ahead of her, a few hundred feet from Tootsie's. Bob was dressed in his typical cowboy gear: jeans, dark shirt, light tan vest, scuffed brown boots, and his ever-present beat-to-hell-and-back Stetson. His upper body curved slightly over his banjo, and he was picking a tune that she knew well, "Blackberry Blossom." Bob's banjo case lay open next to him.

A few stray tourists stood by, listening, and Bob looked up long enough for his clear blue eyes to meet Olivia's. A quick nod tilted the Stetson. Olivia stood back from the group to indicate that she would wait. No need for Bob to lose any tips over this visit.

Olivia liked Banjo Bob. She stopped by to see him whenever she was downtown checking out the scene and Bob never failed to impress with his speed, dexterity, and endurance.

The thing Olivia really liked was that Bob was dependable. He was always there, rain or shine. It was, Bob once told her, what he did. All he did. All he wanted to do. Olivia had the idea that Bob had tried other things and that nothing fit as well, but she wasn't positive. Bob never talked a whole lot. He just played.

Bob finished the song and the group burst into applause. Bob thanked the group for their appreciation and wished them a good afternoon in beautiful downtown Nashville. Coins and bills hit the interior of the case and Bob smiled and thanked those who contributed.

Olivia waited until the tourists shuffled away. Bob's banjo was still strapped around him, but Olivia said, "Hey, Bob, can you take a break? I'll buy you a beer."

Bob looked unsure for a moment, then glanced around the street. "Yeah, okay," he said and slid the strap off his shoulder. He placed the banjo in the case, closed it, clicked the latch, and picked it up in what looked like one fluid movement.

"Henderson's okay?" she asked, and Bob nodded. It was just a few doors away and Bob would be able to step back onto the street when they were done.

They made their way into the smoke-filled atmosphere of the little bar and Olivia ordered two Pabst Blue Ribbons and pointed Bob in the direction of a tiny table to at least get him off his feet. She was looking for a certain amount of privacy, too. She didn't relish the bartender listening in on their conversation.

When they sat down, Bob removed his hat. Sitting next to him at the table, Olivia could see that Bob hadn't shaved for a couple days. His pale facial hair made it almost impossible to tell unless you were this close. It also made him look much younger than he was. *Blurring the lines of reality,* she thought.

"Business good today?" she asked.

"You saw my best crowd so far," Bob said, taking a deep drink of the beer. "I'm sure there will be more later. Thanks for this," he added, nodding to the bottle.

"I have a question for you."

"I figured. I think I even know what it might be about."

"The theft at Sweet's last night. Near Gruhn's."

"Yep."

"You saw it?"

"Yep." Bob took another drink. "Small guy, dark clothes, held the guitar up almost above his head so it didn't hit anybody." Bob raised his hands up in demonstration. "Moved pretty smoothly, considering the crowd."

"Must've had good upper body strength then."

Bob shrugged. "Guitar may not have been that heavy." He thought a bit. "Couldn't tell you make or model. It was in a gig bag."

"So, he wasn't a big guy?"

"No muscle if that's what you're thinking. Skinny guy. Moved like a slinky animal."

"A slinky animal? A snake?"

"Nah. Maybe a weasel."

Olivia almost choked on her beer, laughing.

Bob rolled his eyes. "Yeah, I know, but that's what he reminded me of."

"Okay. That's a pretty good visual. Did you see his face?"

"Nah, I was on the other side of the street." Bob took a moment to consider. "But I've seen him before."

"Yeah?"

"Yeah."

"Would you recognize him if you saw him again?"

Again, Bob considered. "Yeah," he nodded. "He's been around. But to be sure if it was him? Only if he was carrying a guitar over his head and running like someone was about to shoot him."

"Someone had a gun?"

Banjo Bob shrugged. "Sweet's bouncer."

Olivia nodded. Dodd had mentioned that there was some sort of security guy involved. Dodd wasn't sure if he was one of Sweet's or just someone that saw the guy taking off with the guitar. *Vigilante justice, maybe?* she'd thought at the time. *A friend of the guitar owner? But it made more sense if it was Sweet's guy.*

"Got it. Was he the only other guy?"

"Yeah, except for the guy that was yelling at him. I took him to be the owner of the guitar."

Olivia could picture the entire sequence of events in her head.

"All right, Bob, that's great. Thanks. I really appreciate your help." She slid one of her business cards across the table. "If you think of anything else, let me know."

Bob slid the card off the table with his fingertips. Olivia could see the calluses on those fingers and thought about the amount of playing it took to create those calluses. Bob looked at the card, then put it in his shirt pocket. They both continued to drink their beers.

"Are you planning to stay in Nashville for a while?" she asked.

"Been here twenty years. Wasn't planning on leaving anytime soon. Don't see many other options."

"Seems like a hard place to make a living."

"Maybe." Bob downed the last of his beer. "It ain't easier anywhere else."

Olivia nodded.

Bob replaced his hat and picked up his case. "Thanks again," Bob said. His mouth curved into a crooked, almost sly smile.

"Happy to do it. Thanks for the information," she said, slipping Bob a twenty-dollar bill. "If you see anything else, or if you see him again, keep me in the loop."

The Stetson tilted and Bob touched the brim. "Ma'am."

CHAPTER 22

KH Precision Machine
Nashville, TN
Tuesday, April 27, 2010
11:55 A.M.

HOSHI CAME OFF THE PRODUCTION FLOOR of KH Precision Machine and headed to his office. The men on the line had complained that the quality of some of the parts they'd received was poor. They were impossible to fit together. Hoshi had gone onto the floor to check for himself. The parts looked fine to him, but it was so long since he'd done any of the hand fitting himself that he wasn't sure. He attempted slipping pieces together but couldn't do it. Had he forgotten how they fit? Or were the parts themselves the problem? Unable to decide which and too embarrassed to ask for help, he came away frustrated and angry.

When he got to his office, he was surprised to find Bana there holding an open laptop. The screen paused on a video from a local television station.

"What's this?" Hoshi growled. "I don't have time to watch TV right now."

"It's the woman," Bana said. "The Hopkins woman. At The Station Inn."

Hoshi grabbed the laptop and put it down on his desk with a thump. He pulled up his chair and sat there, enthralled, as Hayley talked to the interviewer.

When the interview was over, while the band played, Hoshi looked at Bana and said, "Who was that guy?"

"One of the band members, maybe?"

"He didn't play anything." Hoshi's eyebrows were drawn together while he thought about this. "What kind of band member doesn't play in the band?"

"Sounded like he was a technical guy."

"So, he works on the mandolin."

Hoshi's brain churned, trying to figure out how to use this information.

"I want to talk to him," Hoshi said. "Bring him here."

Bana's eyes went wide.

"You know what to do!" Hoshi snapped.

Bana moved to take the laptop from Hoshi. Hoshi pulled it away from him and said, "I'll keep this."

Bana's eyes flickered, but he bowed slightly before he left the room.

Rocky has lost her mind.

Valerie was certain of this, now. Their room at the Hilton looked like a Western store exploded. There were bags and boxes spread out all over the sitting room of their suite, all of it loot that Rocky had acquired yesterday afternoon and this morning. Boots, several pairs in various styles, along with shirts, jeans, tank tops, and some cute sundresses.

"I thought you were going to ship this stuff."

"I was. I did ship some things, but these were too much fun to do that."

Rocky hummed to herself as she opened yet another box and pulled out a denim shirt with "Nashville" emblazoned on the back in gold rhinestones. She slipped it on over her t-shirt and paraded around the room, careful of her gait because she wore one of her new pairs of boots, this pair also covered in gold rhinestones.

"You do remember that we live in Philadelphia, don't you?" Valerie asked her.

"Of course, I do. What's your point?"

"How many sundresses did you buy? I don't think we have that many sunny days in Philadelphia."

"Yes, we do," Rocky insisted. "I'll just wear a sweater if it's too chilly. Besides, I'm always looking for sundresses. They have prettier ones here than they ever do at our malls at home. Might as well get them when I see them."

"And the boots?"

"What's wrong with them?" Rocky asked, pouting. She held out first one boot, then the other, for Valerie's inspection.

"Rhinestones? Really? You're not going to get much wear out of those once we get home."

"Of course, I will."

"Six pairs?"

"Different styles." Rocky tilted her head, thinking. "Maybe I'll buy another suitcase."

"I think you'll need it."

Valerie sighed and sank into one of the cushy chairs. The TV remote was on a small table next to her. Idly she picked up the remote and turned on the television.

Going through the channels, she scrolled past the news. Barack Obama was speaking about something; she wasn't sure what because she had the sound muted. It looked like something related to his birth certificate. Valerie was annoyed by the questioning of Obama's origins. As a mixed-race person herself, she thought it was great that he had become President of the United States. She didn't like that anyone thought he was less American for being mixed.

She clicked past the news and stopped on a local channel when she recognized Hayley Hopkins' face. She turned up the volume to hear what was being said. When Mark stepped into view next to her, Valerie's mouth dropped open.

Rocky stopped what she was doing. "Is that Mark?"

They watched as Mark draped himself over Hayley and then watched as he was pulled away by technicians. The band went into their song.

Valerie's mouth was still hanging open. She closed it sharply and said, "Well, that was not the Mark I know."

Sailor Lang and Paul Pratt sat at the bar in Hands Down, nursing their beers and discussing Paul's new job as part of the wait staff for the Athenian Towers.

"I've got the vest and shirt right here," Paul told Sailor, patting the black plastic bag he'd carried into the bar with him. "They sized me right there in the office, immediately after they hired me."

"Wow, I thought hiring would take longer."

"Yeah, me, too, but they said they're short-staffed."

"That's great," Sailor said. "How close did they look at your ID?"

"How close do you think?" Paul grinned. "They were more interested in how soon I could start. They want me back there tonight to learn the ropes from one of the other guys. The guy that you asked to vouch for me."

"Good." Sailor took another sip of beer. He was feeling happy about this job. Things were going very smoothly. Doing this little task for Suzume was going to be simple.

Paul tapped Sailor's shoulder and jerked his thumb up at the television above the bar. It was tuned to one of the local stations with the volume down to a barely listenable level. They had been showing the national news, but now the local news kicked in.

"Hey, isn't that the chick that owns the, you know, the instrument?"

Sailor looked up and saw Hayley Hopkins talking to some other woman. He recognized The Station Inn in the background. The chyron running at the bottom of the screen said, "Charley Hopkins' daughter to donate mandolin to Country Music Hall of Fame after concert Sunday," although it abbreviated the Hall of Fame to CMHOF.

Sailor glared at the words. *I don't think she'll be donating it to anyone but us,* he thought. When he turned to Paul to comment on the interview, he saw that Paul was watching the screen intently. Sailor glanced up in time to see some folks helping one of the band members off the stage and the rest of the band start to play. They both watched as Hayley Hopkins and The Storm played, their song faded out by the TV station long before they were done. *Just giving the audience a tiny taste,* Sailor thought.

When the segment ended, Paul turned to Sailor and said, "I think I see a weak link."

Part IV

THE CONFERENCE

CHAPTER 23

Hilton Hotel Downtown
Nashville, TN
Wednesday, April 28, 2010
2:30 P.M.

JUST OUTSIDE ONE OF THE MEETING ROOMS in the Hilton Hotel, Valerie glanced at herself in the mirror as she entered the ladies' restroom. She could see herself smiling. That alone was unusual.

The presentation couldn't have gone much better, Valerie thought.

She chose a stall and stepped inside. Alone with her thoughts, she let herself be proud that she and Rocky sounded and appeared so professional. They spoke well, their jokes got laughs, and people asked questions at the end.

She heard another woman enter and listened to the click of her heels as she passed Valerie's stall door. Then two more women entered, talking as they stood in front of the mirrors. They were laughing, but it sounded sarcastic.

"Well, that was an experience," one of the women said. "They must think we're completely stupid."

Valerie sat stock-still, not even daring to breathe. *Were they talking about our presentation?*

"I could have done what they did without even thinking twice. They made it sound like it was so hard," the other woman said.

Valerie didn't think they conveyed that in any way. *We tried to explain that the case was complex.*

"So, what did you think of Tokyo Rose?" the first woman said, and the sarcasm was absolute.

"Could she be any taller?" the second voice added with another haughty laugh. "She should have stayed with that basketball career."

The two of them finished whatever it was they were doing -- *checking their makeup, perhaps?* Whatever it was, they washed their hands and left.

Valerie stayed in the stall a few moments more, then came out slowly. She stood in front of the mirror, staring at her no-longer-smiling face, watching the tears slide down her cheeks. She heard her mother's voice. "Every time it happens, you feel worse."

It always hurts, she thought, *but this time it really cut. Why now? Why today?*

As Valerie washed her hands and blotted the tears from her face, the other woman, the one with the clicking heels who had walked by her stall earlier, came out of her own stall. She was a Black woman who looked a bit older than Valerie. She wore a high-quality navy suit that fit her perfectly. Her jewelry looked expensive, and her hair was in a natural cut appropriate for her age and style.

The woman washed her hands and dried them. She tossed the used paper towel in the trash, then looked at Valerie in the mirror.

"Don't take it to heart, honey," the woman said in a soft drawl. "You did a great job. I enjoyed your presentation." She pulled a small gold tube out of her handbag and applied some bright lipstick that complemented her look. "You know, it's not just because you're in the South. It's everywhere. People tell you one thing to your face, but when your back is turned, it's a different story."

She pivoted away from the mirror and looked at Valerie directly. "Who knows which person they really are?" She put on a broad, forced smile and said, "We do, don't we?" She patted Valerie's shoulder lightly and added, "You just gotta keep smiling, honey." Her heels clicked as she left the restroom.

Valerie watched her go. She had the feeling that this woman probably put on that smile multiple times a day. Just as Valerie always had. Just as her mother had.

At the midpoint of the conference, the conference planners left some Wednesday afternoon hours open so attendees could visit "The Emporium." This was the huge room where sales representatives hawked products and services for insurance investigators: surveillance cameras, audio equipment, the latest software to integrate services or provide quick record keeping. The company reps would be there throughout the conference, but Wednesday afternoon was the big sales push, with fully staffed booths and live presentations.

Normally, these things fascinated Valerie. Her visit to the ladies' room after the presentation, however, had left her deflated. All she wanted to do was go back to the suite and hide. She had to force herself to slow down by a booth to watch a demo or ask a question.

Rocky, on the other hand, kept darting ahead, picking up tchotchkes that caught her eye. She grabbed a tablet or eraser here, a hopping toy there, each with a company's logo and catchphrase on it.

"Stop that," Valerie said, lightly rapping Rocky's hand as she was about to take yet another tension-reducing squeeze ball from a display. "You already have at least two of those."

"Those are for me and after our program, I need them. You look like you should have some, too," Rocky said, and grabbed one from a booth. "Look how cute! It's got a teddy bear face." She dropped the ball into the plastic bag the organizers offered to all the members at the entrance to The Emporium. "Maybe I should grab one for Harry, too."

It's like going to the grocery store with a toddler, Valerie thought, fighting the impulse to pull Rocky out of the room by one arm.

Still, Valerie understood that even this part of the conference was important. She talked to salespeople who were able to answer questions and point her in the direction of new resources to use in investigations. As she got deeper and deeper into the room, she found a rhythm. She liked to be among other investigators who were asking some of the questions she had thought of but hadn't worked up the courage to ask – or the ones that reps ignored from her. *Because I look Japanese?* she wondered. *Or simply because I'm a woman?*

Rocky zipped along, eyes scanning the booths as they walked by, and Valerie thought she might even be listening to the conversations, at least some of the time. The tchotchkes served to keep Rocky entertained.

After roaming The Emporium, they took their stack of information, promotional items, and oddball toys back to their room. Once they returned to the lobby, they found the entrance to the hotel's Palm restaurant and ran into a few other investigators who recognized them and invited the women to join them for dinner. Once fully inside the restaurant they bumped into Olivia Farrell.

Olivia looked pleased to see them. "You and Rocky might want to sign up for one of the outings tomorrow night. There are several, but the one I'm hosting goes to Lower Broadway, a few blocks away. I'll take you to Tootsie's Orchid Lounge for a quick look around and a beer. We'll eat dinner at a great place called Leah's, then go for drinks afterword at one of the honky-tonks. I was thinking DaisyMae's. There's always a hot band playing there."

"We've been to a few honky-tonks already, but I like the idea of seeing more music. What do you think, Rocky?" Valerie asked.

"I'm always up for going out," Rocky said. "Sounds better than sitting in the hotel watching TV."

CHAPTER 24

Zimmer Investigations
Upper Darby, PA
Wednesday, April 28, 2010
8:00 P.M.

WHEN HARRY SENT VALERIE AND ROCKY TO NASHVILLE, he expected to miss them, but not to this extent. When he was busy with work, he was absorbed and didn't think about the empty office around him. But occasionally he'd look up and start to say something, little asides that he would normally share with them during the day or instructions he would call out to them. He had to remind himself that it was no different than when they were working on a case, just one that was out of town.

Still, their absence depressed him. *Just a little,* he thought. But he knew it was more than "just a little."

Harry kicked himself for not giving them any suggestions about keeping him informed of their progress. So, he was delighted when his phone rang, and he heard their voices when he picked up.

"Boss!" Rocky bellowed and he held the phone away from his ear a little. "We're having a great time! We have a phone with conference calling. Can you hear Valerie?"

"Hi, Harry," Valerie said.

"Hi, Valerie. How did the presentation go?"

"Good," she said. "It was good."

"No, it wasn't," Rocky interjected. "It was great! People loved us!"

Rocky proceeded to report everything they had done, from the flight to the Emporium, listing all the little gizmos and gadgets she was bringing back for him.

"I hope you learned something, too," he said.

"Don't worry," Valerie told him. "I got a lot of information from some of the salespeople. I'm bringing back literature for you to look at and a few contacts to pursue."

"That sounds good," he said. "But you might want to spend some time outside the sessions networking with other investigators, too. You know, go out to dinner, or have drinks with them at the hotel bar. You're going to learn as much from hanging out with them as you do in the sessions."

"We have plans to do that tomorrow night," Valerie said.

"We'll make you proud!" Rocky told him. "We're going to the honky-tonks!"

The honky-tonks! thought Harry. *Oh, how I wish I was there with you. I'd love to see that.*

"I hope Nashville is ready for that," Harry laughed. They said their goodbyes and Harry hung up, chuckling. The room, so full of life just a moment ago during the phone call, was suddenly barren.

Yeah, I miss those two, he thought. Abruptly he stood up to put on his jacket. He needed some air.

After their chat with Harry, Valerie called Mark to check in but got his voicemail. She figured he was busy with Hayley, although what that might mean made her shudder. She sighed, but knew it was part of the deal. He'd warned her about that when he told her about the job. But still.

Drunk at noon? Was that also part of the deal? Well, maybe he'll call later, she thought, but she was pretty sure that wasn't going to happen.

Instead, she thought about other calls she might make. Bic crossed her mind because he may have talked to Mark at some point. Ultimately that seemed like a bad idea. A call to Bic would signal trouble, she decided, so she tried to think of other people she might talk to, someone with whom she could share her experiences at the conference. Like they always did, her thoughts turned to her father. *Maybe I should check in with Dad,* she thought.

"How'd it go, honey?" Valerie's dad, Liam, asked. He sounded unusually buoyant. "The presentation was today, wasn't it?"

"Yeah," she said. "It went great. We told them about the case and got lots of questions afterward. Rocky did a terrific job."

"I'm impressed. I wasn't sure what kind of speaker Rocky might be."

"Turns out she's funny and personable. People really seemed to like her."

"That's good, but I'm sure they liked you, too."

The incident in the ladies' room stung Valerie's memory, and the phrase, "Not so much," crossed her mind, but she was determined not to share that part with her dad. He was sensitive enough about how people perceived Valerie. They often told Liam that she didn't look like his daughter, and he tried to laugh it off, but she knew he was touchy about it. She couldn't see the point in making him feel bad for her now.

"I suppose I did okay." It didn't sound persuasive to her ears. Grasping for something positive to say, she added, "You know how it is, Dad. We are our own toughest critics."

"That's so true," he said. "You learned that from your mom and me. I hope you're having a good time in spite of that."

"Yes. Better than I expected. We had dinner with some of the other investigators tonight. That was fun. Tomorrow night we're going downtown with another group. I'm looking forward to that, too."

"That's great." He paused and Valerie had the feeling that something was up. "I'm glad you called," he said. "I wanted to talk to you about something."

"Okay."

"You know I've been seeing Barbara for a while now."

He was referring to Barbara Wallingford Minnick. She was a chef and, with her four adult children, owner and operator of The Wallingford Inn near Kennett Square in Pennsylvania, a well-reviewed lodge that included a highly respected restaurant. Liam met her when he attended some of her cooking classes.

"I was thinking I might want to make things more permanent. But I wanted to make sure you knew about it first."

Valerie's throat suddenly had a huge rock in it that she hadn't noticed before. She croaked, "More permanent?"

"I'd like to ask her to marry me."

Valerie's mouth dropped open but this time nothing came out. The pause was long enough for him to say, "Are you still there?"

"Yes. I'm just a little surprised is all. I mean, I like Barbara and you two get along well. I just didn't realize…" she groped for the words, "you were thinking about getting married."

"This probably wasn't a great time to tell you, but her birthday is this weekend and I thought it was a good time to ask her," her dad said. "I guess I should've waited until you came home."

"No, no, that's fine," Valerie said. She realized that her reaction disappointed him. "I think it's really great!" she said, forcing herself to sound excited. "How soon are you thinking?"

Her dad laughed, his high spirits recovered. "Soon, I think. I won't know until I ask. If she says yes, we'll talk about a date."

"I suspect you don't need an 'if' in that sentence."

"I hope not."

Valerie could hear the happiness in his voice.

"Call me when she says yes, Dad," Valerie said.

"That's a promise."

CHAPTER 25

Tootsie's
Nashville, TN
Thursday, April 29, 2010
6:15 P.M.

THURSDAY NIGHT, AFTER ANOTHER DAY of conference sessions, Valerie and Rocky hung out with other investigators at the coffee bar in the atrium of the hotel. They were waiting to join Olivia and three other attendees from the conference to go downtown.

Valerie glanced up at the television screen above the coffee bar. Coverage of Governor Bobby Jindal declaring a state of emergency in Louisiana as the oil spill from the Deepwater Horizon explosion moved toward the Louisiana coast segued into a weather map, showing rain on the way. It was coming from both the west and the south. It looked like Nashville might get rain over the weekend.

"Well, don't you two look ready for some nightlife!" Olivia said, obviously approving of Rocky's choice of skintight jeans and "Party On, Nashville!" sequined t-shirt with one of her pairs of sparkly boots. Valerie had chosen a pair of black pants with a plain white tee and a thin fuchsia sweater to throw over her shoulders. The color was a bit strong for Valerie's taste, but Rocky encouraged her to wear it. Olivia certainly seemed to like it, so Valerie conceded some style points to Rocky, something she rarely did.

Olivia gathered their group together and directed them to board a shuttle headed for Tootsie's Orchid Lounge.

"We're going there to do the tourist thing," she told them. "If you don't stop at Tootsie's, no one will believe you actually visited Nashville."

There were only six of them, including Olivia. Valerie looked over the group. She already knew Rocky and Olivia, of course. The other three were guys she'd seen at some of the sessions she attended.

Olivia alerted them in advance that they would know they were at Tootsie's when they saw the purple building. Valerie saw the walls approaching and was surprised that the purple was not gaudier than it was. The orchid hue set the building apart, yet felt oddly welcoming, like it was beckoning you in.

The shuttle dropped them near the bar on a side street and they followed Olivia through a surprisingly well-lit back alley to get to an entrance. Inside, Valerie was immediately struck by the thick cloud of cigarette smoke and the scent of stale beer that Olivia referred to as "eau de honky-tonk."

They ordered beers and watched a pair of musicians play, but after about twenty minutes Olivia gestured for them to move along. Valerie gulped the last of her beer and followed the group as they left by the front entrance, exiting onto Lower Broadway. Night seemed to be setting in and lights that she didn't notice earlier were bright against the pale sky.

As they walked down Broadway, Valerie heard a banjo player picking as fast as she'd ever heard. She was pretty sure it was the same guy that she'd noticed the day she and Rocky were boot shopping. She craned her head to see who it was. Her view was blocked by a group of people watching him.

Valerie grabbed Olivia's arm to slow her down. "Who is that?" she asked, motioning to the cluster of people across the street.

As another knot of tourists brushed by the little crowd, the people around the player shuffled to either side so they didn't block the sidewalk.

Olivia corralled their dinner group to point out the banjo player to them. As they all gathered around Olivia to listen, she answered Valerie's question. "That's Banjo Bob," she said.

As his audience shifted position, Valerie got a better look at the musician. Banjo Bob was a lanky guy in a light-colored vest over a dark shirt and dark pants. His vest and hat were made garish by the wash of varying colors of lights on the street, the reflections of neon from the restaurants, and the intermittent flashes of headlights from passing cars. The dark colors of his shirt and pants were muddled by the oncoming evening light. They could have been dark red, green, blue, or black. He wore a light-colored cowboy hat pulled low over his face so there was no way to see his hair or eyes. From this distance he looked clean-shaven, so his mouth was slightly visible as a moving shadow in the eerily lit darkness, forming words that probably went along with his song, although Valerie couldn't hear him singing. All she could hear was the frantic melody line he played, the speed increasing as the song went on.

Valerie could see the outline of Bob's banjo case on the sidewalk next to him. The interior was one of those outrageous fluorescent colors that case-makers use to line instrument cases. Bob's was electric green and looked to be the color and texture of artificial turf.

The small audience around him called out their approval as the song whipped up to its big finish and when he picked the last note, they cheered and tossed tips into the case.

"Bob's a legend," Olivia told them. "He's here every day, rain or shine, tourists or no tourists. Plays all day and into the night."

"Wow," Rocky said. "Impressive. But why? Why doesn't he play in one of the bars? Seems like that would be more lucrative."

"It might be, but those slots are taken by other bands. Those bands rotate in and out of the honky-tonks. It's not a lasting gig, but really, no gigs are. I think I heard that at one time Bob may have played with some of those bands, but I've seen him playing solo on the street for a number of years now." Olivia, face turned toward Bob across the street, waited for a few minutes to see what he would play next. When he started the next tune, she said, "Nice. 'Banjo in the Hollow,'" and herded them along.

CHAPTER 26

Leah's
Nashville, TN
Thursday, April 29, 2010
6:45 P.M.

THEY FOUND THEIR DINNER STOP, Leah's, at the next corner. Shiny hardwood floors and a long, polished oak bar bordered a spacious dining room. A hostess greeted them.

As they were shown to their table, Valerie heard a trio playing at the far end of the room. She craned her head around their group to see a guitarist and an upright bass player on either side of a woman who played fiddle well enough to make Valerie want to cry. She wished she could play one-quarter as well. In an odd way, it reminded her of her mother, a consummate violinist, and Valerie felt tears welling in her eyes. *Mom would have appreciated this*, she thought.

Rocky, not seeing the look on Valerie's face, nudged her gently and teased. "Not quite your type of music, huh?"

"Maybe not," Valerie said, fighting the lump in her throat. "But she plays so well it doesn't matter."

In between the warm phrases of the fiddle, the vocalist sang a sad song about a bird caught in a cage. Valerie thought how unhappy the songwriter must have been when she wrote it. Tears clouded Valerie's vision. She tried to wipe them away so that no one would see, but Olivia caught her.

"Are you okay?" she asked, frowning.

"I'm fine," Valerie replied, shrugging off the question, but her voice catching a little. "It's a moving song."

"Yes," Olivia agreed, looking relieved. "The musicians in this town are among the best in the world, I think. Almost every bar or restaurant downtown offers music. Some nights when I go from venue to venue, I think each one is better than the last."

"It reminds me of my mother," Valerie said softly.

Olivia was about to respond when the waitress came to the table.

They ordered drinks and dinner. Rocky ordered another beer, but Valerie went for sweet tea. Even after the drinks arrived, Valerie couldn't seem to pull her eyes away from the fiddle player and her side men playing across the room, leaving Rocky to handle conversation.

"You'll have to excuse her," Rocky said to the table. "My friend knows about violins and probably wishes she could be up there with them."

"No, no, not at all," Valerie explained, pulling herself away from the music. "I just admire good players. I know enough about violins to know how hard it is to make it look that easy."

"You play?" Olivia asked, sipping her beer.

"No. Both my parents did, though."

"They were in the Philadelphia Orchestra," Rocky interjected.

"I'm surprised you don't, then," Olivia said. "I'm guessing there's a story there."

"Tell her," Rocky pressed.

"There's not much to tell. I tried to play when I was a kid, but the best I could do was make shrieking sounds that hurt everyone's ears." Valerie smiled at the memory of her grandmother's squinting face, trying to figure out where this child had come from. "Lessons were a useless cost for me, but one good thing that came out of it is that I learned how to work on violins."

"That's her side business," Rocky added. "Just in case this insurance thing doesn't work out."

When the food came, it was classic Nashville fare that Valerie had read about. Pork ribs in the house barbecue sauce, spicy chicken fried golden brown, biscuits with sweet cream butter and honey, collard greens, baked beans, and corncakes. The table went silent as they dug in.

"Wow, great food!" one of the agents said around a mouthful of chicken. He was Floridian Chris Jenkins, a pale blond with very fair skin. His cheeks were turning pink from the peppery heat of the chicken and beads of perspiration were sliding down his temples. He mopped his face with his napkin.

"I warned you that the heat would be a bit much," Olivia told Chris. "I've eaten in restaurants all over this town all of my life. I know what that chicken is like. Really tasty so you wolf it down, then it sets you on fire from the inside," she laughed. "We're proud of our food heritage here," she went on as she took a forkful of collard greens and held it up as an example. "If any of you get a chance before you leave, go to the Nashville Farmer's Market. It's a bit out of your way, but well worth visiting."

"Speaking of things to see," Rocky said, swallowing her mac and cheese and spearing a chunk of country ham off her plate, "I was hoping to maybe run into Bret Michaels while I'm here. Do you think he hangs around the honky-tonks?"

"Oh, honey," Olivia said, "Bret left Nashville a while back. I think I saw his house is up for sale."

"No!" Rocky said. "I came all this way..."

"To attend a conference," Valerie reminded her.

"Where did he go, do you think?" Rocky's tone was plaintive.

Olivia took a deep swallow of her beer. "I think he moved back to L.A. At least, that's what I heard."

"I'm so bummed," Rocky said, popping the ham into her mouth.

"There's plenty of other men around this town," Olivia said. "You just hang out with me. There's better men than Bret Michaels out there."

— • —

Conversation continued, loose and easy, around the table. While waiting for her banana pudding dessert, Valerie realized she was enjoying the group of agents that had gotten together. She didn't expect that to happen. Each agent had a quirk, but they all found things to discuss other than work, much of it music oriented. Valerie finally mentioned Hayley Hopkins, asking if anyone was familiar with her work.

"Ah, she used to be pretty good, but I think she gave it up," the investigator from South Carolina, Dan Messersmith, said from across the table. He'd ordered a second portion of ribs instead of dessert and was working his way through them, licking his fingers after every rib.

Robert Wheeler, a Mississippi investigator, suggested that Hayley "drank her way into rehab and never could get it back together." He opted for beer rather than pastry to finish his meal.

"You know, I just saw her play at Springwater a few weeks ago," Olivia said, picking her way through a slice of coconut cream pie. "I think she's trying to change her act somewhat. Less bluegrass, more, well, not rock exactly but headed that way. The crowd wasn't terribly kind to her, but I thought she was pretty good. Her voice is better than it was when she was young. More resonance. She never was much of an instrumentalist though, except for the mandolin. She played guitar that night at Springwater. I have to say that her guitar playing was not memorable."

"Did she have Daddy's mandolin with her?" Dan asked, wiping his chin.

"Why, yes, yes, she did," Olivia replied, looking like she was sorting through her mental file. "I'd forgotten. She played 'Will The Circle Be Unbroken' with it near the end of her show. Definitely the best song she played that night."

"And she told the story, right?" Robert said.

"Story?" asked Rocky, scooping up a forkful of chess pie. "What story?" She slipped the pie into her mouth.

"Her father was Charley Hopkins, a mandolin wizard," Olivia said. "Hugely influential. That mandolin she brings with her? He played that mandolin for every show he played."

"Well, almost every show," Robert interjected. "When he didn't have it with him, the shows never went as well. At least, that's the story. They say he only played a handful of shows without it."

"Yes, but the last time was crucial. It was the day he died." Olivia sipped a cup of coffee almost white with cream. "The story goes that he couldn't find his mandolin before he went on, so he borrowed one. Funny thing was, he found his right after the show. Later they discovered Charley laying on the road, dead. They guess he was headed for the parking lot, to go home with his band. The mandolin case was in his hands, the mandolin inside."

"That's horrible!" Rocky said. "What happened?"

"Don't know for sure, but popular opinion was that he had a heart attack," Olivia said.

"I read comments about that last show that said it was a little uneven that night," Robert added. "I suppose if your heart was acting up, you might not play as well as usual."

"Or if you didn't use your favorite instrument," Rocky said.

Robert drained his beer and was about to order another when Olivia stopped him.

"Let's go on to DaisyMae's. You can get another beer there." When the waitress stopped by their table, Olivia asked for their checks.

"So, this mandolin, the one that belonged to Charley Hopkins, that's the one that Hayley uses?" Valerie asked.

"That's what she claims," Robert said, his tone a tad snide.

"I believe it to be Charley's," Olivia said. "It certainly looks like the one I've seen in pictures with him. An F-style."

"F-style?" asked Rocky.

"Florentine," Robert said. "Has an ornamental scroll in the head-stock. Charley's was all scratched up and written on." Robert wrinkled his nose.

"How would you be sure, though?" Rocky asked. "I mean, just because it looks like one in an old photo, that doesn't verify anything."

"If you know the instrument, if you know where it came from, of course you can figure out if it was his," Olivia said. "You did that with the Gibson Les Paul you retrieved."

"Right," Valerie said. "So, the mandolin is coded with some sort of number?"

"Yes," Olivia replied. "Of course, in this case, it helps that Charley Hopkins played a Lloyd Loar mandolin."

"A Lloyd Loar?" Rocky asked, glancing at Valerie.

"Yes," Valerie nodded. "He worked for the Gibson Company and their instruments, even at that time, were well documented."

"He was hired to endorse Gibson's instruments," Olivia added, "but he wasn't a designer, like some people will tell you. He had input into the design of the F5 mandolin, but to actually sign it as the designer, well, let's just say someone at the company must have liked him."

"Like Lewis Williams," Robert said.

"Who's Lewis Williams?" Valerie asked.

"Gibson's General Manager at the time Lloyd Loar worked there," Olivia explained.

"Whether or not he was the actual designer is an old argument," Robert said, "and we probably won't settle it here."

Olivia shrugged. "I don't know for sure. I just know that people are willing to pay a lot of money to get one. And there are people who would love to have Charley's."

"Does that mean Hayley's family has a lot of money?" asked Valerie.

Olivia smiled. "I don't think so. Charley's dad got that mandolin from his own father, Vernon. Vernon would have been a young man when those mandolins were made. They weren't famous, they weren't collectible, not back then. They probably were available at a price Vernon could afford. Maybe he worked to save up the money. Or, as these things often go, it may have been a gift from his own parents. At any rate, Vernon handed it on to his son Charley. After Charley died, his wife gave it to Hayley."

They settled their bills with the restaurant and Rocky, restless after all the talk about mandolins, stood up from the table. "I want to dance!" she proclaimed. "Let's go!"

CHAPTER 27

DaisyMae's
Nashville, TN
Thursday, April 29, 2010
9:15 P.M.

OLIVIA LED THE WAY TO DAISYMAE'S, less than a block from Leah's, but more brightly lit. The crowd was thick and the music loud. The band was set up just inside the door on a stage about two feet above the floor of the bar.

Olivia shuffled the group into the honky-tonk and elbowed her way to the bar so they could get drinks. They had to split up to watch the band.

Valerie was uncertain how she felt about DaisyMae's. The energy of the band combined with the loud voices of the people around them was fascinating and frightening all at once. The bars she frequented in Philadelphia with Rocky, Harry, or Mark were much quieter than this one. She thought of the bands and shows she'd seen with Mark and couldn't think of anything quite like this. This bar was thick with noise, smells, wild abandon, and slightly seedy atmosphere. She thought she could reach out and touch it. It was all pressing in on her, but in an exciting way.

Some of the audience members were dancing in front of the stage and you could hear the clicking of their boots, depending on the song and the dance they chose. Olivia grabbed a guy near her and had him dance her right up to the stage so she could converse with the band. Valerie was horrified by her impetuousness, but she could see Rocky laughing and looking a little jealous, like she wished she had thought of it first.

"I want to dance," Rocky leaned over and called out to Valerie, competing with the music.

"You should've gone with Olivia," Valerie called back.

"She's got a guy with her."

"You could pick a guy."

Rocky scrunched up her face. "I don't know any of these guys."

"That never stopped you before."

Rocky scanned the room, then looked at Valerie again.

"Well, I'm not going to dance with you," Valerie said.

"I didn't expect you to," Rocky huffed. "Besides, you're a lousy dancer." She scanned the room again. "Maybe Dan would dance with me."

Rocky went off to ask Dan, who had moved across the room to watch the band from a different angle. Robert and Chris stood next to him. Robert was talking, but Dan seemed far more interested in the band than Robert. Chris stood behind Robert and appeared to struggle to hear what he was saying, as though Robert was intentionally cutting him out of the conversation.

When Rocky interrupted them, Dan quickly took her arm and led her to the dance floor, leaving Robert looking annoyed and Chris surprised. Robert turned in Valerie's direction.

Valerie quickly averted her head, not wanting to make any eye contact with Robert that he might perceive as inviting. When she looked back in Robert's direction, she was startled to find Chris standing right beside her, watching her with considerable amusement as he sipped his beer.

"Your friend reminds me of Olivia," Chris said, fighting to be heard above the music and the crowd.

"I can see where you would get that," Valerie responded in kind, her voice loud, also trying to make herself heard.

"Loud but lovable. Raises your blood pressure and scares you to death. Am I right?"

"Pretty much," Valerie nodded.

"But also a good friend who, when it comes right down to it, has your back," Chris said, watching Rocky thoughtfully. "A good partner for those of us with a more tentative approach."

"Tentative approach," Valerie echoed. "I like that. Rocky says I think too much."

Chris laughed. "Maybe she's right. Do you want to dance?"

Valerie shook her head. "I love music, but these feet don't have any dance in them."

"Oh, thank God," he said, visibly relieved. "I'm a terrible dancer."

Now it was Valerie's turn to laugh. "Then why did you ask?"

"I wanted to talk to you. Also, I think it's part of the conference agenda. You know, mixing and getting to know investigators from other areas."

"Was that in the program? I don't remember seeing that."

"That was the idea, according to the committee that put the conference together," Chris said. "Even if that means making a fool of yourself on the dance floor. Thanks for saving me from that embarrassment."

"You're welcome."

The song ended, but the band swung right into another. Chris motioned to the bartender to get two more beers. He slid one to Valerie and they clinked bottles.

"To not having to dance," Valerie said.

"Cheers to that," Chris responded. After the first sip, he said, "I can see that you have a lot of interest in the music here. And you mentioned knowing about violins. And there's the missing guitar you and Rocky talked about in your session. How can you NOT be a musician?"

Valerie shook her head. "It's easy, really. I just don't have the touch."

"Too bad," he said. "Have you been to the Schermerhorn? I understand Nashville has a wonderful symphony."

"I walked around it with Rocky, but we didn't have a chance to go inside or hear any music there. We won't be here long enough this trip to get there. Did you go? Are you a musician?"

"I played trumpet in high school and college but gave it up when I started working. And no, I didn't get there, either. Maybe next time." He slipped a business card out of his pocket. "Professional hazard," he said by way of apology as he handed it to her. "Let me know when you come back to Nashville, and I'll meet you for a date at the Schermerhorn."

She took the card, laughing, and gave him one of hers.

"You never know," she said. "I might just take you up on that."

The band's set ended. Rocky, Dan, and Olivia rejoined Valerie and Chris. They were joking with each other about the band.

"Shouldn't we be getting back?" Valerie said.

"Party pooper!" Rocky teased her.

"You won't say that at 6:00 tomorrow morning when we have to get up," Valerie reminded her.

"Oh, honey, I didn't think Philly girls went to bed so early," needled Olivia.

"We don't, generally. Just one of us." Rocky sounded peeved.

"The Asian element?" Olivia asked with feigned innocence.

"Oh, please, not you, too," Valerie said.

"All right, all right," Olivia laughed and waved a hand at Robert, still standing across the room looking annoyed. He made his way through the crowd to join them. "We're heading outside now," Olivia said. "It'll be a few minutes until the shuttle picks us up, but we should be out there waiting for them."

CHAPTER 28

THE INTERNATIONAL INSURANCE INVESTIGATORS Conference ended with a final, very brief, meeting and luncheon on Friday morning. Valerie and Rocky arrived fifteen minutes before the meeting so they could find a seat. Looking around the huge banquet room, Valerie was surprised by how many of the faces were now familiar to her when just a few days ago everyone but Rocky was a stranger. Attendees chatted in random groups around tables. Some hovered near the buffet.

Eyes sweeping the room, she wondered which two women were the ones she overheard in the ladies' room. She shook off the thought but realized that her mother was right: *Once you are targeted, you never forget. And every time it happens, you feel worse. It gets harder and harder to just let it go.*

Valerie was a kid when her mother told her that, maybe ten or eleven, and she remembered thinking at the time that her mother was simply overly emotional. But after it happened to Valerie, more than once, she knew her mother was right. *It's a weight that never leaves you, not completely,* Valerie thought. *The weight of being different.* And now the weight was a little heavier.

Across the room she caught Olivia Farrell's eye and waved. Olivia waved back and gestured to a table close to her. Valerie tapped Rocky's shoulder and said, "Let's sit over there," steering her to the table Olivia pointed out.

"This was a great conference," Valerie said as they sat down. "We learned a lot, didn't we, Rocky?"

"Yeah," Rocky agreed. "I especially liked our tour of Lower Broadway."

"I bet you did," Valerie laughed. Out of the corner of her eye, she saw Rocky's eyebrows arch and turned away from her to see why. Chris Jenkins slid into the chair next to her.

"Hi, Valerie. I'm glad I caught you."

"Hey, Chris," she said genially. "Ready for the big finale?"

"Oh, yeah. I'm ready to head back to Pensacola," he grinned. "But not really. I'd like to hit Lower Broadway again and spend a little more time there."

"Sounds like more fun than going back to work, right?"

"No kidding. I don't have to drive home until Sunday. Maybe you could take another day or two..."

Valerie could feel the expression on her face freeze.

"Uh, no, I don't think so. I'm meeting a friend tonight for dinner and my weekend is spoken for."

Chris's face fell. Clearly, he'd been expecting her to be available. *Why would he think that?* she wondered, but then their conversation last night about the Schermerhorn came back to her in a rush. She thought she'd been making small talk. Chris thought she was seriously considering going out with him.

The roar of conversation around her swelled. She thought about Mark and about how guilty this chat made her feel. She really wanted this conversation to end.

"Do you think you'll come back?" Chris asked, his eyes fixed on Valerie.

"To the conference? Or Nashville?"

"Either. Both."

"I would," Rocky interjected. When Chris didn't respond to her but kept staring at Valerie, Rocky said, "Hey, I see Dan Messersmith over there. I'm just gonna go say goodbye to him."

"Tell him I'll come over in a moment," Valerie said over her shoulder, then turned back to Chris.

"I'd definitely come to another conference," she told Chris. "If the company can afford it, I mean. We were lucky this year. Olivia was kind enough to invite us and Harry - that's my boss - really wanted us to come."

"I'm not talking about a conference." Chris said. "I'm talking about you. Would you come back just to visit the town? On your own?"

Taken aback, Valerie paused to consider a diplomatic response.

"Maybe. I might come back with my friend Mark. He has friends here."

"Your friend? As in, your boyfriend?"

"My friend," she said, emphasizing the word "friend."

"Oh. Okay." He stood abruptly. "Well, I should let you make your farewells, then," Chris said. "You have my card."

"I do. And you have mine." Their eyes were still locked. She felt like she should add something, but words stuck in her throat. Anything she might have added sounded false in her head. She should have just told him that Mark was her boyfriend. What was wrong with her? Why couldn't she say it?

Chris blinked and then said, "Maybe I'll call you. Would that be okay? Maybe I can talk you into coming to Florida."

Still staring at him, Valerie said, "Maybe." She regretted the word as soon as it left her mouth.

Rocky passed Chris as he walked away from the table.

"What was all that about?" Rocky asked Valerie, sitting down at the table again. She grinned as though she knew the answer.

"Darned if I know," Valerie said. She wasn't looking for Rocky's advice. To distract her, Valerie pointed a finger at the stage in the front of the room. "Look, Rocky. Guitars!"

Sure enough, there were electric guitars on stands, along with a drum kit, on a low temporary stage. To one side was a keyboard-looking thing with strings instead of keys that Valerie recognized as a pedal steel guitar, something Mark had introduced her to some months earlier. She'd come to love the instrument and the sound it made. It reminded her of wistful singing, of wind blowing through trees and the ocean rolling towards the shore. Beautiful and heartbreaking.

Olivia stood at a lectern on the other side of the stage from the pedal steel guitar. She was trying to get the crowd's attention but the volume level in the room made it difficult. The band shuffled to the stage and the front man, the tallest member of the band and the only one wearing a cowboy hat, grabbed his guitar and struck a single chord that got everyone's attention. Except for the sound of the chord reverberating, the room fell silent. All eyes were on the front man. Olivia would still have to compete for the crowd's attention.

"Who is this?" Valerie asked Rocky.

Rocky looked at a sheet of paper that was lying on the table. In addition to information about their lunch, the entertainment was listed as "Randall Barlow and Custom Made." Rocky read off the name and shook her head. "I've been listening to a lot of country music since we got here, and I honestly have no idea who this is." She looked up at the stage and added, "But he's going to be a lot of fun to watch."

Valerie could see why. He was just Rocky's type. Male. That alone would interest her, but he was also lean and muscular. Mid-30s. Long, wavy dark-blond hair. Angular face with a scruff of beard. *Yeah, just Rocky's type.*

Olivia leaned into the microphone on the lectern and began her thank-yous and in-appreciations. Among them she mentioned Valerie and Rocky, who stood briefly along with the other people who had presented programs. Together they accepted the group's applause.

Valerie couldn't help but think about the women in the ladies' room. The memory was like a jab to the gut. But she tried to emulate Rocky and smiled as brightly as she could. When they sat down again, Rocky looked over at her and whispered, "What's wrong with you? You look like you ate a lemon."

Valerie shook her head and said, "Later." Rocky shrugged and went back to examining the program.

Then Olivia introduced the band.

"We are beyond thrilled to welcome to our very own stage the hottest new band to arrive in Nashville. Folks, put your hands together for Kentucky's finest son, Randall Barlow, with Custom Made."

The band started out with a slow bluesy intro to the song "Cuts Like A Knife." Rocky's head snapped up and she grabbed Valerie's arm. Then she went a little crazy.

"Oh, my God, oh, my God, they're playing Bryan Adams' song!"

she swooned to Valerie, never mind that Valerie had no idea who Bryan Adams was. But the fact that Rocky mentioned him told Valerie he was some musician from the eighties.

Barlow's gravelly voice intoned, "Drivin' home this evenin', coulda sworn we had it all worked out." Valerie looked over at her partner, only to realize that Rocky had been transported to some other world. She removed Rocky's clenched hand from her arm.

Valerie listened while the lead guitarist did his solo in the bridge, thinking about Mark and wishing he could be here with her to see this. He would critique the band's performance and tell her whether the musicians were any good. Instead, she had to make that judgement for herself.

She thought about the music, the way the pedal steel guitar wound its moaning notes into and out of the work of the other musicians. She wasn't sure how the band stacked up against other country bands, but she decided that she liked them. It felt good to make that decision for herself, rather than waiting for Mark to suggest what she should think. Was she getting more certain of herself in this country music world? Maybe.

Sometimes she and Mark misunderstood each other, but she always thought they could talk things through. Even so, some of his actions here in Nashville baffled her. The weirdness surrounding his relationship with Hayley. The drinking, more than usual. Skirting direct questions. Long pauses when there should have been explanations.

For the past few months, she and Mark talked about living together but hadn't come to a definite decision before he left for Nashville. While it saved Valerie from telling her dad she was moving out of the house at the time, her dad's probable marriage meant she had to find another place to live, sooner than she had anticipated. The idea of changing so much at once left a cold knot of fear in her stomach.

She needed to discuss this with Mark. But Mark's trip to Nashville raised some other, more troubling, questions, specifically about their ability to be honest and clear with each other.

Then there was Chris Jenkins. She felt the flutter of attraction there, but was it enough to bring her back to Nashville? Or take her to Florida, Chris's home state? Why was she feeling his pull when she thought she was happy with Mark?

Custom Made moved on through their set, a combination of blues and country, including some slow tunes that surprised Valerie with their listenability. Country music was not her thing. Her background was rooted in classical music. But being around Mark over the past year exposed her to more than just the music that had surrounded her life before meeting him. He helped her to appreciate all kinds of music, including country, and increased her understanding of the connections between different types. She respected his knowledge. After all, it was his expertise that originally brought them together. But was that all she based their relationship on?

Late in the set, Barlow performed a catchy new song, "Women Like Wine," a raucous, feel-good song. By its end, the entire crowd was singing along to the chorus.

"Chardonnay, Cabernet,

Any kind is okay,

Any time of the day,

Women like wine."

Even Valerie could hear that Barlow had a hit on his hands. The band took their bows.

Olivia came back to the podium to dismiss what was left of the crowd. Some folks had left the room during the band's set, so it was a fraction of the attendees. She reminded everyone of next year's conference to be held in Seattle as the crowd shuffled out.

CHAPTER 29

Hilton Hotel Downtown
Nashville, TN
Friday, April 30, 2010
1:30 p.m.

AFTER AVIDLY WATCHING RANDALL BARLOW and Custom Made, Rocky collapsed across the table like a limp rag. Valerie laughed at her. *So dramatic. But that's Rocky.*

Rocky suddenly jumped to her feet and darted past Olivia to talk to Randall Barlow as the band packed up their instruments.

"Mr. Barlow?" Valerie heard Rocky say as she stepped up onto the stage. It looked like she was trying not to trip over cables or knock over guitars.

"Hello there," he said with that gravelly voice. He smiled tentatively at Rocky but kept unplugging equipment and wrapping cords to toss into one of the equipment boxes. Somehow, he managed to maintain eye contact with her.

"I thought your set was great," Rocky said breathlessly. "Fantastic. I loved your first song. What made you choose it? Do you like eighties rock, too?"

Valerie tried to decide whether she should interrupt Rocky and direct her away from the band so they could "tear down and load out," a phrase she'd heard Mark use more than a few times over the past year. Olivia caught up to Valerie first.

"That's some brass your partner's got," Olivia said. Her tone sounded gruff, but she didn't look angry. Her expression was almost admiring.

Valerie nodded. "She's quick, that Rocky."

"Let's hope it doesn't ever get her into trouble," Olivia said, still watching Rocky and Barlow on the stage.

"Wouldn't be the first time."

"I bet," Olivia said. "Valerie, I just wanted to thank you again for participating. Did you enjoy the conference? We loved having you here."

"We both had a terrific time. We appreciated your invitation."

Valerie offered her hand. Olivia took it and they briefly shook hands, something Olivia had not done when they first met. Olivia's grip was warm and firm, not at all what Valerie expected.

"When you get back, tell Harry I said hey and I'll call him soon," Olivia said. "Safe travels."

"I will. Thanks."

Olivia waved to an agent across the room and headed toward him, in the opposite direction from the stage. When she caught up to him, she chatted with him animatedly.

Valerie turned back toward the stage and saw Rocky now in serious conversation with Barlow. He had stopped packing and was talking intently to Rocky, who nodded frequently and looked mesmerized.

Valerie climbed the two short steps to the slightly raised stage to fetch Rocky. When she got to the stage, Rocky introduced her to Mr. Barlow as "my friend Randall."

Brass, indeed, Valerie thought as she shook Barlow's hand.

On their way back to their hotel room, Rocky told Valerie all about her conversation with Randall Barlow.

"He's so cool," she enthused. "That voice! Even when he talks, he makes me shiver. But guess what? His real name is Jake Yablonski. And remember when Olivia said he was from Kentucky? He's not. He's from Plainfield, New Jersey!"

"I didn't know Plainfield folks had that much of a drawl," Valerie observed.

"They don't," Rocky said. "I used to date a guy from Sayreville, near Plainfield. He didn't sound anything like that." She wrinkled her nose, thinking. Then she said, "Randall told me he picked up the drawl while working in Kentucky. His record company tells people that's where he's from. He said it works for his image and his music. They made up his name, too, can you believe that? He said it has to do with knives, both the Randall and the Barlow. That's why he sings 'Cuts Like a Knife' in his set."

"Hmm." Valerie watched as the band members toted their equipment toward the exit doors. "Makes me wonder where the rest of the band is from."

"I was so shocked about the New Jersey thing I didn't ask about them," Rocky said. "Randall said that country stars don't come from New Jersey, so when he moved to Kentucky, he just called that his home. The record company promoted the heck out of that." A frown developed on her face. "I don't know, Valerie. What kind of person does that? It just seems dishonest, you know, telling people your history is something other than what it really is. Why do you think he lies about it?"

Valerie was surprised that Rocky didn't accept this more easily. *That hard-as-nails Philadelphia girl has a naive streak,* she thought. *I think I like her for that.*

"Come on, Rocky," Valerie said. "Think of all the people we meet who try to swindle an insurance company. People are dishonest about who they are all the time. Sounds like his business isn't so different from ours."

"I guess." Rocky looked over at Barlow, still packing up on stage.

"Besides, as you pointed out, you don't know why he thought it was a good idea. Maybe there's something in his past that he wants to cover up. An ex-wife who tossed him out, kids he doesn't want to acknowledge." Valerie hushed her voice to add, "Maybe he was in jail."

Rocky's eyes sparkled when she said, "I bet that's it."

"You always did go for the bad boys."

"I'm not sure Mr. Barlow is actually a bad guy."

"Just trying to break into the business, right?" Valerie said. "You know, almost everyone I've ever known hides who they really are, at least until you get to know them well. And even then, they sometimes make things up."

"So that's why you're so suspicious of Mark."

Valerie's eyebrows flew up. "I am?" She didn't realize she'd been making it so obvious.

"Yeah. Look at you. You don't believe anything he tells you about Hayley. Do you think he's lying to you? I thought you knew him pretty well."

Yeah, so did I, Valerie thought.

CHAPTER 30

Bluebird Cafe
Nashville, TN
Friday, April 30, 2010
4:45 p.m.

MARK WAS RUNNING LATE TO PICK HER UP for the show at the
Bluebird Cafe. Valerie had hoped that they would have a chance to
talk about all the things that swirled in her head earlier in the day.
She wouldn't have a lot of time because the cafe was only a short ride
from the hotel, but she thought she'd give it a shot.

She immediately smelled alcohol on his breath when he kissed her
hello. The scent evoked the memory of his appearance on television,
and she felt herself instinctively pull away from him.

"Sorry I'm late," he said. "Hayley wanted to rehearse extra for the
Nissan workers' show tomorrow."

"Another show? When did that happen?"

"A few days ago, I think. I'm not quite sure. I just know that she's
angry about doing it. She was focused on the Hall of Fame show
Sunday. She blew up at Paige for agreeing to this other one. Paige

took her aside and talked to her and got her to calm down and agree. I guess she's over it because we rehearsed for it."

"Weird."

"Yeah, you'd think their schedule was well set by now, with the tour and all. And guess what?"

"What?"

"She's asked me to play guitar with the band."

"But I thought you were just doing the tech stuff for her."

"I am, but I think she's been trying to work this out all along. She wants Des to play fiddle more and leave the guitar to me. She says she really needs more fiddle than we've got."

Mark pulled into a parking lot of a strip mall. Valerie spotted the awning sign for the Bluebird Cafe and pursed her lips. She'd run out of time. The conversation she wanted to have with Mark was not going to happen until later, possibly much later. And when it did, she wasn't sure it was going to go well.

She expected The Bluebird Cafe would be in a freestanding building, not in a cramped strip mall next to a dry cleaner. The line to get into it was long.

"Wow. I thought there would just be a few people waiting for the doors to open. This looks more like seventy."

"Yeah," Mark said. "The place only holds about a hundred and twenty people. It's popular, so it fills up quickly."

Valerie could see that. People lined up on the sidewalk and across the parking lot, weaving around the cars parked there. She and Mark got into line.

"So, this is the Bluebird."

"It's a legend," he told her. "And a fine listening room. That's why I wanted you to see it. They feature singer-songwriters, many of whom have yet to be discovered. Garth Brooks, Kathy Mattea, and Taylor Swift all played here and made connections that helped jumpstart their careers. Many others, too. Tonight, my friend Max Lightfoot is playing here."

"Max Lightfoot?" she asked. She had some vague knowledge of Brooks, Mattea, and Swift, probably from Mark talking about them. But Max Lightfoot? She'd never heard Mark talk about him before.

"Yeah," he said. "Remember that I told you the band was rehearsing at Lightfoot Storage before they moved to the condo? The storage company is owned by Max's brothers, Tayloe and Brock. Maxwell's the youngest of the three."

Once inside the cool, dark cafe, they were seated at a table near the low stage that held three tall stools that would be used by the players. She thought they had an excellent view. *Although,* she admitted to herself, *the place is small enough that almost everyone has a good seat.* Valerie looked around the room, noting the posters and candid photos on the walls.

To the left of the stage, she saw a little area that jutted out, away from the tables, lined with old wooden pews polished to a high sheen. Because the tables were already full, newcomers were shown spots there. All around the room, people chatted and ordered drinks and meals.

Mark's beer and her seltzer arrived, followed shortly by their food. Mark encouraged her to eat right away, explaining that, as a listening room, The Bluebird asked the audience to be as quiet as possible during the time the players were on.

"They don't want to hear the rustling of paper plates and plastic utensils," he told her.

She tucked into her chicken fingers and sweet potato fries, even though her stomach was less than thrilled. It had been tied in knots all the way here and now, probably, for the rest of the evening. She glanced at Mark and realized he had no idea how tense she was or even that she was uncomfortable in any way. *I should have talked to him on the way here,* she thought, mentally kicking herself.

She finished most of her food by the time the players came out and servers removed their plates. Maxwell acknowledged Mark from the stage with a wave and a big smile. "We'll talk after," he called to Mark. Then he settled himself on one of the stools.

Across the room, a few stragglers came into the Bluebird. Most were shown to the pews. But the back of one head caught Valerie's eye. Shiny dark hair woven into a long braid, swinging between the shoulder blades of a tiny woman. At first Valerie took her for a child but didn't think that children were allowed here so she looked again. The braided-hair woman was with an Asian man who wore a colorfully decorated silk bomber jacket. When the staff showed them to a table not far from the stage and the woman turned around, panic rose in Valerie's chest.

It was Suzume Kojima. Valerie was certain.

The program began. The three singer-songwriters took turns chatting among themselves, playing new songs, almost as if the audience wasn't there. They told stories from their lives and their time on the road, as well as the background of the songs they played.

Later, Valerie would remember none of what happened on stage. She could hardly sit still. She felt a desperate need to get up from her chair and leave. She saw Mark glance at her several times. Even he was starting to realize there was a problem.

"I have to go," she finally said to Mark.

Mark shook his head and frowned at her. "Why?"

"Suzume Kojima is over there," she whispered.

Mark turned his head enough to see the Asian woman staring daggers at Valerie. And him.

"I just have to go," she said again. "I need some air."

"All right," he said. "Come with me."

As quietly as they could, the two of them stood and slipped out, trying not to disturb the other listeners.

Once outside, Mark pulled Valerie over to the windows in front of the dry cleaners.

"What's going on? Why is Suzume here?"

"I don't know. I had no idea she was in Nashville."

"Is she after you?"

"I didn't think so," Valerie said, "but I know she blames me for taking Reuben and that other guy away from her gang at the warehouse in Philadelphia last year."

Mark crossed his arms and leaned back again a row of bricks between windows.

"I know she used to crank call you. Does she still do that?"

"No. I think she gave that up. But this is the first time I've seen her in person since then. I don't trust her, Mark. I think she'd like to kill me."

"But you have no way of knowing if she's after you or just coming to see the performers."

"You don't believe me."

"I don't think she's going to hurt you." Mark scuffed the toe of his boot against the sidewalk. "You can't live your life afraid of her."

"I know that."

"Can we go back inside?" he asked.

"I don't think I can. You go ahead, go back in. I'll get a cab."

Mark shook his head but pulled out his phone. "I'll call the cab company and wait until they get here."

Part V

DURING THE FLOOD

CHAPTER 31

Athenian Towers
Nashville, TN
Saturday, May 1, 2010
8:45 A.M.

PAUL ADJUSTED HIS PURPLE VEST and looked in the staff bathroom mirror again. He had gotten a little wet in the rain this morning and had to neaten his look. He slicked back his hair and tied it at the nape of his neck, then flipped it up and wound a matching purple kerchief around it. He had practiced this maneuver several times at home until he got efficient at it and the speed paid off.

"Be proud of the uniform, young man," his new boss had intoned during his brief training. "Purple is the color of royalty. It is also the color of the highest chakra."

Whatever, Paul thought, tucking a loose hair under the kerchief. *He might be my boss, but what a flake.*

The important part was that he needed to look like every other worker on the kitchen staff except the chefs. The chefs wore all white. There were plenty of wait staff employees at the Athenian who dressed just like Paul, or a female version of him. White jacket, shit-brown pants, brown shoes with gum soles, and the little purple vest and head wrap that looked so ridiculous to him. *Still, I won't be easy to pick out of a lineup*, he decided, although he also guessed there wouldn't be one. Side by side by side, no one would pick him out.

Sailor's friend handled the Athenian's background check for Paul, even giving Paul a fake name. When Paul arrived in person, there were no questions asked. He signed a contract using his new identity. They took a photo for his ID, laminated it, and clipped it to his vest. Then they sent him to the kitchen.

In the kitchen, Sailor's friend, the one that apparently got Paul the job, explained what the Athenian expected from him: be prompt, be courteous, don't get friendly with the women, do what the chefs ask you to do.

I can do that, Paul thought.

He joined the rest of the waitstaff and did the tasks they told him to do. Most of the time that meant mopping, wiping down, and cleaning up around the kitchen. Occasionally one of the other staff members ran food orders to condos. The choice of server seemed to be random, but it looked as though, sooner or later, everyone was asked to do it.

That's why Paul was there. All he needed was a sixth-floor assignment. That's where the mandolin was supposed to be, according to Sailor.

Paul spent Saturday morning running from one end of the kitchen to the other, wiping up spills; loading dishes in one side of the massive dishwasher then unloading them when they came out the other side and burning his hands; capping hot meals; helping to load carts; transferring carts to the elevators. It was hot and he was sweating. He wished he didn't have all the layers of clothes on, the jacket, vest, shirt, and tie, but to remove any of it was forbidden.

Besides, his random opportunity to make a delivery could come at any moment.

Unfortunately, when the call for the sixth floor came, the assigned waiter, Larry Cable, got it and Paul felt his heart sink. Then he heard his name whispered. It was the waiter who'd gotten the call, beckoning to him. Startled, Paul responded, "What?"

"Take this order up to sixth. I've got to go to the john."

Paul's doppelgänger brushed past him with barely a look.

Paul tried not to look as surprised as he felt. He realized that this guy must've been told by someone, probably Sailor's buddy, that Paul needed the sixth-floor call. Paul grabbed the cart and pushed it into the elevator. It was heavy. He wondered how many people it was going to feed.

Well, this trip is just to look around. I'll plan the actual theft after I see the layout of the room and how many people I have to sidestep.

In the elevator, Paul swiped at the sweat on his face and felt his heart beating in his ears. He hoped he wouldn't get lightheaded from the adrenalin rush of the job, his surprise at being called, or the sudden upward movement of the elevator, however slow.

When will these damn doors open?

As the elevator bumped to a full stop at the sixth floor and the door opened, Paul felt the cool air of the hallway slap his face. He breathed in deeply and pushed the cloth-covered cart into the hallway, the elevator door closing behind him.

CHAPTER 32

Hilton Hotel Downtown
Nashville, TN
Saturday, May 1, 2010
9:30 a.m.

ROCKY LISTENED AS VALERIE went over the story for the third time.

"I couldn't stay there, not once I saw her," Valerie groaned. "Ugh. Suzume and that guy she was with. I bet he was her bodyguard. They certainly weren't a couple." She paused and tears leaked out of her eyes again. "I had to get away from her. I had no idea she was here."

"You knew her father was," Rocky reminded her.

"Yes, but that's not the same thing. He doesn't know me." Valerie dabbed at her face with a tissue. "Suzume does. I thought she might come after me. Physically. Or send that thug."

"I had no idea you were so spooked by Suzume," Rocky said.

"You know she's been harassing me."

"Yes, but we've always sort of laughed about it."

Valerie put her hands over her face. "She scares me. That's why I try to avoid talking to her."

"The police..."

"The police have done what they can. I filed a restraining order, but you and I both know that has limitations."

Rocky nodded. "I'm sorry that Mark wasn't more sympathetic."

"He was focused on his buddy playing onstage. He was angry with me for walking out." Valerie said, then added, "He'd had a couple beers."

"But he knows your history with Suzume. He could have been more understanding." Rocky looked puzzled. "It just doesn't sound like him. A couple beers shouldn't change that."

"He smelled of booze when I first got in the car, before we got to the Bluebird. He's so different here than he was in Philly," Valerie said. "The drinking, the attitude. His behavior in general. I just want things to go back to the way they were before this whole Nashville trip came up." Valerie felt tears well in her eyes again but was determined not to let them fall.

"All right," Rocky said, her voice softer now. She patted Valerie's shoulder "I understand that, for sure." Rocky sighed and looked at her watch. "Go wash your face, Valerie. Mark's going to pick us up in a few minutes."

The ride in the elevator was silent but Rocky squeezed Valerie's arm for support. When they got to the lobby, they shuffled to the hotel's front entrance doors where Mark was talking to one of the valets. Valerie's stomach churned. She wasn't sure what kind of greeting she'd get from Mark.

"Rocky," Mark nodded to her, then turned to Valerie. "How are you doing this morning?"

"Better."

Mark tentatively reached out to give her a stiff hug and a quick peck on the cheek.

"Did you get any sleep?" he asked.

"A little." Valerie fought the urge to ask him to take her home. To Philadelphia.

Rocky gave them a few minutes to reconnect. She stood by the floor to ceiling front windows of the hotel, watching the clouds roll up and blow through the sky. The sky looked strangely dark with a yellowish cast, and Rocky saw occasional streaks of lightning.

Behind her, Mark said, "Are you looking forward to the concert tomorrow, Rocky? I think it's going to be great!"

"You don't know the half of it," Rocky said, turning away from the window. "I read that Randall Barlow is on the bill, too. Did Valerie tell you he played for the conference? Since we have VIP tickets for the induction concert, I'm looking forward to going backstage. I want to talk to him again. We have a lot in common."

"I'm sure you do," Mark chuckled. He kept one arm around Valerie as he grabbed her bag.

"Oh! It's raining," Valerie said, noticing for the first time.

"Yeah, it's been going on since early this morning. They're calling for a lot of rain. Possible flooding around the Cumberland and the small streams near it."

A throng swirled around them. The automatic doors whooshed open and closed incessantly as people dashed for parked vehicles or asked about their shuttles. Some people were looking out of the huge plate glass windows at the pounding rain and chattering about the weather forecast. The valets were calling cabs for some of them. It seemed like everyone had somewhere they had to go despite the storm.

"We don't have umbrellas," Rocky told Mark.

"That's okay," Mark said. "The car is under the roof. I got the last spot in the covered area, but the rain is blowing, so be prepared. It's rough out there."

CHAPTER 33

Athenian Towers
Nashville, TN
Saturday, May 1, 2010
11:45 A.M.

PAUL'S EYES SEARCHED THE HALLWAY. He wished he had scoped it out in advance, but Sailor usually covered that angle. Besides, earlier access would have been difficult to arrange, even for Sailor. He didn't look like the type of guy that might be looking to rent one of these condos. They were too upscale.

There were four doors in the hallway. The one closest to him opened, spilling people into the hallway around Paul. There were maybe eight people skirting him. Paul recognized most of them as band members from the TV show. Paul tried to talk to one of them, but the guy dodged him, either not hearing him or choosing to ignore him.

Then Paul heard a woman's voice say, "Is that for us? Just bring it in here." He moved the cart forward, toward the open door, and was met there by a good-looking redhead.

"Just take it inside," the redhead said, waving one hand. She didn't bother to introduce herself. She held several sheets of paper close to her face, as though the print was hard to read. She seemed unconcerned about Paul's arrival or what he might need to do.

Paul took stock of the condo. Contemporary design, a large living space with plate glass windows overlooking the city. Draperies pooled on the floor by the windows at either end of the room, looking like parentheses around the glass. He looked out of the windows expecting to see skyscrapers, but the clouds were still hanging low. Rain drenched the city; mist covered building details. Occasionally, lightning cut across the sky. But inside the condo, the thunder was muted, and the room felt cozy despite its size.

Part of the room's coziness came from its clutter. Part of the clutter was a selection of instruments: two guitars, a violin on a stand, a banjo, bags, cases, cables, amps, and a small drum set filled the space. But no mandolin.

"Uh, ma'am?" Paul said tentatively.

"Yes?" She looked up from her papers, frowning.

"Where would you like this set up?"

"Over there on the table," she said, pointing to what he supposed was the dining area of the huge space. Twelve upholstered high-back chairs surrounded an oak table in front of the windows. A long countertop with five stools was to the left of the table, with a full kitchen beyond that. The kitchen looked largely unused but the bar next to the refrigerator was stocked and bottles of liquor with various levels of liquid inside littered the countertop.

The redhead shook her head as if to clear it, then said, "We'll only need five place settings. Everyone else decided to go out."

"Thank you, ma'am," he said and wheeled the cart into the space next to the table. The redhead stepped into an interior hallway that took her out of the room.

Paul moved the fresh flowers from the center of the long table to a side table near one of the couches and started his prep work. He put out the tablecloth, dishes, silverware, and glassware, just as he had been told. As he worked, he glanced around the room, keeping his eyes alert, moving quickly, assessing the situation. He made a mental note of where furniture was, where there were open spaces, how to best get around everything that cluttered his path to the door, and where other doors in the condo might open.

When he finally caught sight of a small case on the couch, his heart leapt. He was so focused on the meal setup that he almost missed it. It was two steps away from him, partially open, half-obscured by a throw pillow. The instrument itself was exposed, not really seated in the case. All Paul could see was the headstock, the neck, and the upper shoulders of the thing but he recognized it. He'd seen the picture often enough.

Oh, oh. So close.

Paul reached over and flipped the pillow away from the case with the back of his hand. He opened the case the rest of the way, uncovering the body of the mandolin, and almost choked. He'd seen the pictures, but to see it in person was shocking.

What a piece of trash!

Not only did the surface wood look nearly destroyed, chipped, and scratched, there was scribbling all over the body. Paul's eyes kept sliding over it again and again. It looked worse than the pictures Sailor showed him.

Who on earth would pay money for that junk?

Paul knew full well that there was far more to an instrument's value than how shiny and new it might be. Paul understood about collectors, obsessions, and provenance. Plus, Sailor had told him the story behind this one. But even so.

The redhead returned to the room, absorbed in her papers. Paul stepped back to his cart by the table. She didn't appear to notice him or the food he was pretending to arrange.

"Hayley?" she called out, her voice sharp and angry, and Paul jumped. "Can you explain this charge to me?"

She took the papers and left the room again, obviously looking for the person named Hayley. *Hopkins,* he thought. *That's Hayley's last name. The owner of the mandolin. The blond woman I saw on TV.*

He listened to the redhead talk to Hayley. Their voices faded in and out of clarity, but he heard most of the conversation.

"Mark can explain that," Hayley's voice was like the redhead's but less abrasive. "He's on the way now with his friends."

"Well, it's sure taking him long enough. He left here, when, eleven o'clock? Geez."

"He's probably having trouble with traffic. It's really raining," the Hayley voice said. "I'm sure that's the problem."

Paul looked out of the windows. The rain was so heavy now it was hard to see the buildings across the street. *Yeah, it's a problem, all right,* he thought. His return visit concerned him. *I might have to take the weather into consideration. It all depends on my exit strategy.*

"He'll be here. Just give him some time."

"I have no time to give for him anymore, Hayley."

Their arguing faded from Paul's consciousness as he looked at the mandolin. His fingers itched. The mandolin was tempting him.

Just pick me up and take me, the mandolin called out.

No need to be in such a rush, Paul told the mandolin silently. *I'll be back for you later.*

Paul carefully placed the flowers back on the table, set away from the platters so that the diners could get to the trays of food unobstructed. He checked the cart to make sure he laid out every-thing, then stood away from the table to survey his handiwork.

The redhead returned. Paul cleared his throat and said, "Uh, ma'am? Would you like to sign for the food?"

The redhead came over to the table and took the work order from him. She looked at it, apparently checking it for discrepancies as she compared the list to the table. Finally, she said, "Lovely," and flat-tened the sheet of paper on the table atop the other sheets she had, now anchored securely onto a clipboard. She held up the condo's electronic key. "Do you need this?" she asked.

"Uh, no, not if you sign."

"Fine." She put the key down and signed for the food.

Paul watched as she signed in heavy blue marker.

"Thank you," she glanced up at him, but her blank eyes indicated that she didn't see him, not really.

She is thinking about something else, something not-me. Paul looked down at the receipt. Her name was Paige. Paige Hopkins. *A sis-ter? Perhaps.*

"Of course," he said.

Outside the room, Hayley's voice echoed in the hallway.

"Paige! I found it! I think this is what you're looking for."

Paige grumbled, "Good," and scurried out of the room, leaving the signed work order on the table. Her condo keycard, forgotten, lay next to the order. Paul stared at the keycard.

It's a sign, he thought. *She's making it easy for me. These people are so stupid. I was going to jimmy the room lock later, but the keycard is right here.*

He turned to the couch.

But so is the mandolin. Why make a second trip when no one is paying any attention to a huge order of food or the key to the condo? Paul stepped closer to the couch. *Or a valuable instrument?*

He nudged the mandolin into its case and deftly closed and clicked the latches. He slid the case onto the lower shelf of the cart, completely hidden by the cloth covering it. He wheeled the cart out of the room, gently closing the condo door behind him.

At the end of the hall, he parked the cart inside the elevator and punched the button that would take it to the kitchen level. As the elevator doors closed, he grabbed the case and stepped out of the elevator. Taking the stairs down to the exit in the basement, the one that workers rather than guests used, he arrived on the parking level.

He stripped off the purple vest with the ID tag and the purple head wrap and stuffed them into a covered trash bin. Then he shook out his hair, combed his fingers through it, and headed to the gate that would take him to street level, the mandolin case's handle clenched in his hand.

CHAPTER 34

Fourth Street
Nashville, TN
Saturday, May 1, 2010
11:55 A.M.

THE RIDE TO THE ATHENIAN TOWERS was tense. Driving the city streets in the heavy downpour was horrendous and frightening. Although Valerie was glad Mark drove, she could tell it was difficult for him, no matter how familiar he was with the downtown area. His eyes were glued to the street, with snarled traffic and constant road blockages where the sewer lines and water runoffs were starting to back up.

"Wow, what a mess," Valerie said.

"Yeah."

As they made their way around town, cars hidden by gray sheets of precipitation appeared at the last minute and sent large waves splashing against their windows. Flashing lights and sawhorses blocking access to streets seemed to appear on every road they tried to travel. What should have taken about ten minutes took nearly thirty with a lot of low-grade cursing by Mark and nervous perspiring by the women. Even Rocky, sitting in the back seat, was silent.

The sound of the rain stopped instantly when Mark pulled the car into the ground level parking garage of the Athenian. When she got out of the car, Valerie fought the urge to kiss the concrete. The sound of dripping water and the smell of oil and gasoline hung in the air like a cloak.

Mark got their luggage out of the trunk, and they took an elevator to the lobby level two floors up. Mark signed them in at the reception desk and again with a uniformed guard near the secure elevators to the residential floors. Rocky managed to strike up a conversation with the security guard and got him to laugh at something she said.

She makes friends wherever she goes, Valerie thought. *Unbelievable. She's probably already got his life story.*

After the hotel and the garage, Valerie noticed the hushed environment and the oddly neutral smell of the interior. She felt as though she'd been wrapped in some thick cotton batting. Decor was limited to a vase in a glass case; human-sized statuary, also encased; and two framed oils hung high on one wall. Everything looked expensive.

But it was the lack of scent that really struck Valerie.

Now that was a real trick. Surely someone has walked through here wearing perfume.

No trace of any smell. At least, not that she could discern.

As the three of them rode the elevator, Rocky told them that the security guard was from Alabama. Valerie's shoulders shook with laughter. Mark looked down at the floor, suppressing a smile. They both knew how good Rocky was at getting people to talk to her.

When the elevator doors opened on the sixth floor, the volume of voices that assailed them felt like all hell had broken loose. Male voices argued in the hallway, female voices screamed from the room behind them, at least one person was crying, and none of it sounded intelligible after the peace of the lower floor.

"What the fuck?" Mark said.

Valerie and Rocky followed Mark as he ran toward the outer door of the condo. Three guys in blue jeans and cowboy boots stood there, yelling at each other. Mark shooed them into the condo. They went in, all of them talking to Mark at the same time. Valerie and Rocky followed. Rocky pulled the door closed behind her.

Inside the condo, everyone continued to talk at high volume and speed.

I sure hope the walls are soundproofed enough to contain all this noise, Valerie thought. Then she remembered the silence of the building as they stepped into the elevator. *Yeah, I'm pretty sure they are.*

The voices stopped when Mark crossed the room. There were two other guys further inside the room, standing with two women that Valerie guessed were the Hopkins sisters.

The tiny blonde wore a sequined shirt and sparkly boots in pink and gold. *Almost like the boots Rocky bought,* Valerie thought. The taller woman, a redhead, was dressed in well-fitted designer clothes all in a pale cream color with matching strappy heels. *Very classy. But you know, the redhead really doesn't need the extra height,* Valerie caught herself thinking and, with a jolt, immediately realized that's exactly what the two women in the ladies' room at the Hilton had mocked about her. *Well, maybe we could start a basketball team,* she thought.

Everyone else was looking at Mark.

Mark turned to the two women first. "What happened?" he asked.

Everyone started talking at once again and Mark raised his hand and tried to shout louder. He wasn't having an effect, so Rocky did what she did best, gave one sharp whistle and shouted at the top of her nasal voice, "Shut up! Let Mark talk!"

The entire room went silent, and heads swiveled from Rocky back to Mark. Mark nodded his thanks to Rocky, then said to the blonde, "Hayley, tell me what happened."

Hayley's face crumpled and although she tried to talk, she started crying so hard he couldn't make out what she was saying.

Mark sighed and turned to the redhead. "Paige?"

She glared at Mark, then looked back at her sister. "The mandolin is gone."

"Gone?" Mark was so surprised, his face looked blank.

Paige gestured to the table where the remnants of lunch remained. "We didn't notice anything until after we started eating. And I don't know what made Hayley look for it, but she's the one that saw that it was gone."

"I was just playing it earlier!" Hayley sniffed. "It should be here! I've looked everywhere, but it's not here!" She burst into tears again.

"She tried to blame it on me," Des moaned, running his hand across his bald head. "But I didn't take it. Why would I?"

"It's okay, Des," Mark said.

"No, it's not," Hayley stopped crying long enough to shoot back. "Why wouldn't you take it? It's the most valuable instrument you've ever touched."

Mark put a hand on her arm and said, "Whoa, slow down, Hayley. Let him talk."

"But he took it!" She started crying again. "I can't believe it's gone!" Her mascara and eye liner smudged, giving her a sad clown face, but a beautiful one.

"Where was everyone when it happened?" Valerie asked.

Everyone fell silent again, looking at Valerie like she'd grown an extra head. It was obvious that some of them didn't know who she was.

"I'm Valerie Sloan," she said. "I'm a friend of Mark's. And I'm an insurance investigator."

"So, you are Valerie," Paige said, looking her up and down. "That means your friend must be Rocky."

"Right," Rocky said.

"Well, you took longer to get here than we expected," Paige's voice was brittle as she addressed Mark instead of Valerie or Rocky. "We decided to go ahead and eat lunch. While Hayley and I were eating, she mentioned that she wanted to change one of the outfits she was going to wear tonight. So, we went back to her room to look at what she suggested. We heard the band come in. They were talking. Loud. Laughing. They were here for a few minutes before we decided to get back to our lunch."

"Did the entire band come in at the same time?" Rocky asked.

Paige swung around to look at Rocky with a why-are-you-talking? face, but she answered, "I don't think so. I heard Des and Boomer first. The other guys showed up a minute or so after."

"See, she thinks I did it," Des whined.

Valerie and Rocky exchanged glances.

"I'm calling Security," Paige said and made a show of whipping out her cell phone and leaving the room in a huff.

"Will they call the cops?" Des asked. "I don't want to go to jail."

"Des, you're not going to jail," Mark said. "Why don't you guys sit down for a while? Security is going to want to talk to all of us."

"I think maybe we should make a phone call, too," Valerie murmured to Rocky. They sidled out of the room and into the hallway. "Do you have Olivia's phone number?"

"Yes," Rocky said and at Valerie's request, made the call. She clicked off just as the elevator doors opened. The security guard from the desk in the lobby stepped out of the elevator. He looked less than happy to be there but brightened when he saw Rocky. He asked her what happened. Rocky gave him a quick summary and accompanied him into the condo, Valerie trailing them.

After listening to Hayley and Paige recite their version of the story, and before the band could jump into the conversation, the guard told them that he was going to call the police.

"I knew it," Des complained.

While they all waited, Valerie took Rocky aside. "What did Olivia say?"

"She's on her way. She thanked us for calling."

"To be honest, I can't imagine there's much she can do about it at this point."

"I don't know about that," Rocky looked at her phone as though she expected it to buzz at any moment. "She said she is Hayley's insurance agent."

"Oh, wow."

"She also said she was going to send the cops over."

"I heard the security guy say he was going to call them, too."

"Yeah, but Olivia knows exactly who to send."

"Because of the Task Force, right?" Valerie nodded, understanding Rocky's reasoning.

Across the room, the security guard looked trapped by the band, still squabbling with Hayley about who took the mandolin.

"Okay," Valerie said quietly to Rocky, "let's go through what happened."

"All right," Rocky nodded.

"Hayley and Paige sit down to eat. Hayley talks about a new outfit, and they leave the room. The band comes in, Des and Boomer first. Then the rest come in, making a lot of noise." Valerie paused. "There doesn't seem to be a lot of time between Des and Boomer coming in and then the rest of the band. That doesn't give Des a lot of time to grab the mandolin and hide it somewhere, does it?"

"Plus, there was an audience, " Rocky said. "Boomer. But he hasn't said anything so far, making me think he's either an accomplice or saw nothing because there was nothing to see."

"Right," Valerie said. "Do you think that Des had anything to do with this? I sure don't."

"Me either," Rocky concurred. "How could he? Boomer was with him. They weren't here all that long."

"Okay, we'll set them aside for now. If they didn't do it and the rest of the band wasn't here yet, who does that leave? Just Hayley and Paige."

"Do you think Paige hid it somewhere?"

Valerie thought about that for a moment. "What would she have to gain? That would just piss off Hayley and hold things up. Paige doesn't seem like a hold-things-up kind of person."

"Maybe she's taking revenge on a sister she's jealous of?" Rocky's eyebrows arched.

"That's a possibility." Valerie watched the sisters. "Is there anyone else we should consider?"

"If it happened before they sat down to lunch," Rocky said. "Only one other person isn't accounted for."

Their eyes met.

"The waiter who brought lunch," Valerie said as Rocky's phone buzzed.

Rocky answered and said, "Okay," tersely. She slid the phone in the back pocket of her jeans and murmured, "The Task Force is on the way," to Valerie.

CHAPTER 35

Athenian Towers
Nashville, TN
Saturday, May 1, 2010
11:45 A.M.

OLIVIA AND A DETECTIVE ARRIVED, with the local police on her heels, causing fresh chaos. There were two factions now: a couple beat cops, who had responded to the security guard's call, and a Task Force detective who accompanied Olivia. They were all trying to get information from the band, Hayley, and Paige with limited success.

Valerie listened to the cacophony of voices, all trying to talk, to explain, to blame. There were duplicate interviews, angry outbursts from Paige and the band, and frustrated tears from Hayley. Everyone's nerves were wearing thin. There was little progress, if any. Valerie wasn't positive that the mandolin would ever be found at this rate.

Olivia finally called out, "For those of us who are coming to the situation late, could one of you tell us, step by step, what happened?"

The room quieted.

Hayley's shoulders were still heaving, so Paige repeated the story to Olivia, in the end, blaming Des.

Valerie cleared her throat, loudly enough for Olivia to hear. "You have something to add?" Olivia asked.

"I think Rocky and I may have come up with someone else who might have been involved."

"The waiter," Rocky jumped in before Olivia could respond. "Didn't a waiter bring the food in?"

Paige nodded slowly, her expression thoughtful. "I let him in. He set up, I signed for the food, and he left."

"Were you in the room with him the whole time?" Olivia asked.

"No," Paige admitted. "I was talking to Hayley about some bills that I didn't understand. I went back the hall to her room to talk to her." Paige thought a little more. "Twice." She looked stricken.

Hayley stared at her, horrified. "You let this guy in unsupervised?"

"He was a waiter. I didn't..." Paige's voice faded.

"You let him take Daddy's mandolin?" Hayley grabbed Paige's shoulders and shook her, then pummeled her with her fists. Paige held up her arms to protect herself. Mark stepped in to pull Hayley back, but Hayley was focused on Paige and pushed him away.

"How could you do this?" Hayley screamed. "How could you be so stupid!"

Mark got between the two women again.

"Hayley, stop," he said. "This isn't helping."

"It's her fault," Hayley whined and then, falling into Mark's arms, started crying again.

Olivia, who had been watching the sisters, now turned to Valerie and Rocky. "You were saying?"

"We should find out about the waiter. He had the opportunity," Rocky said, "and enough unsupervised time."

"That can't be." The security guard had been listening and now sounded offended. "The management here has tight control over who they hire. Of course, they only choose responsible, reliable people, even in food services."

Olivia clucked her tongue. "Oh, honey, you're so sweet to think that, but you know, even a careful organization can make mistakes. Let's go have a chat with the fine folks in the kitchen and find out who brought this lovely lunch to our ladies. Maybe they saw something."

Olivia nudged the young Task Force detective with her elbow. "Come with me," she said, and he followed her without saying a word.

Valerie looked at Rocky, who shook her head. "You should go," Rocky said. "I'll keep an eye here."

Valerie nodded and followed Olivia and the officer into the hallway. Olivia smiled at Valerie and the three of them entered the elevator.

The detective was tall, a few inches taller than Valerie. He had a solid build and a head of curly brown hair. Most of the cops Valerie knew in Philadelphia sported buzz cuts and they had perfected a glare that usually meant she was infringing on their turf. But when this detective turned around to face the front of the elevator, his eyes connected with Valerie's, and she had a completely different feeling. His eyes were warm and friendly. His smile seemed genuine.

"What's your name again, dear?" Olivia asked the officer.

"Dodd. Watson Dodd."

"Oh, yes, I talked to you on the phone. Lovely to see you in person, Watson. Can I call you Watson?" she asked without waiting for his answer. "This is Valerie. She's also an investigator. Insurance. Like me."

Olivia left out the fact that Valerie was from Pennsylvania and probably had no real jurisdiction here, even in the insurance industry. Valerie thought that was probably intentional.

"Ma'am." Dodd nodded to Valerie politely his curls bouncing ever so slightly.

"Nice to meet you," Valerie said, then felt her stomach lurch as the elevator jerked into gear.

The kitchen had its own floor between the lobby level and the garage level. They got off into a bright white workspace with steam rolling around the room and fogging the glass partitions. Heat exploded into their faces.

"Lordy!" Olivia said and started fanning herself. "They keep it warm in here, don't they?" She looked around and targeted the white-coated cook with the highest toque to accost with her questions. "Excuse me, are you the person in charge here?"

"I am the Chef de Cuisine," he responded with gritted teeth, "and I am very busy. Who are you?"

"Olivia Farrell, Davis Insurance." She tugged Watson's arm so that he stood in front of her. "And this is Detective Dodd and Valerie Sloan." Dodd showed his ID to the chef. "And you are Nathan DeFries?" Olivia added, pointing to the name sewn into his white chef's coat.

"Why are you here?" DeFries demanded without answering her question.

"We are looking for one of your waiters," Olivia said sweetly. "The server who took food to the sixth floor at one o'clock."

The head chef stared at her, then glanced at a large white wall clock with black numbers hung where everyone working in the kitchen could easily see it. "One o'clock? That was ages ago." He started to turn away, but then whipped back to face Olivia. "And why are you asking me this? I would have no idea!" He threw his hands up in the air.

"Well, maybe you could send us to the person who would know," Valerie suggested.

DeFries shot her an angry look. "You need Cheryl, in the restaurant. She's the Head Server. She assigns the wait staff." He turned away and barked, "What are you all looking at?" at the other chefs and cooks and wait staff, who had paused in their actions when the investigators arrived. He walked behind the cooks and bellowed, "Step it up!" and "Watch what you're doing!"

Olivia fluttered her lashes and said to his back, "Thank you so much for your cooperation," and led Valerie and Watson back to the elevator. They could hear the chef harrumph behind them.

"The restaurant is on the level above the lobby, I imagine," Olivia said, reaching past Dodd to press that button in the elevator. She gazed at him and said, "You are so talkative, my dear."

Dodd chuckled and said, "You were doing just fine back there. I didn't think you needed me to say anything."

She rubbed his shoulder and said, "Oh, honey, I love a man who doesn't talk much."

Valerie could feel her eyes roll and she looked away, but not before she saw the officer blush.

CHAPTER 36

KH Precision Machine
Nashville, TN
Saturday, May 1, 2010
1:15 P.M.

"HEY, SUZUME," SAILOR LANG SAID. "How are you?"

Suzume shifted in her office chair and stretched. She'd lost track of time while she worked on her desktop and now her body was achy and stiff from being in one position so long. Taking advantage of the empty offices on a Saturday, she'd been poring over local auction and sale listings for pieces she might want to acquire, possibly legally but probably not. It was the kind of research she resorted to when her other contacts and feelers returned nothing to her. She had even pressed Ryu into service—after all, if he was going to be with her at all times, he might as well be useful —letting him use one of the company laptops to do some general searching for her.

Suzume's eyes burned from the intense scrutiny of looking at the screen. She was happy for the break the phone call offered.

"I'm fine," she said, rubbing her eyes with one hand. "But I'd be better if you had some good news for me."

Across the desk, Ryu looked up, curious.

"I do," Sailor said. "I have the item you were looking for."

Suzume's heart beat a little faster. Her first thought was, *oh, Daddy, you'll be so surprised.* Her second thought was, *I'm in! You can't hold me back anymore, Daddy!*

"That's excellent," she said to Sailor. "When can we meet? And where?"

"I don't exactly have it in my hands," Sailor said.

Suzume's heart stopped.

"Then why are you calling?" Each word sounded like it was chipped from ice. *If you don't have it now, you'd better get it soon, buddy.*

Ryu turned to squint at the phone, eyebrows drawn together.

"My operative has it," Sailor told her. "I'm going to meet him to pick it up. I thought if you could meet the two of us, you'd be able to pay us right away. Five thousand each, right?"

Suzume's brain went on red alert. *Is he setting me up? Why is he in such a hurry? Why does he think I want to meet his operative? That's just one more loophole to close if the deal goes sideways.*

"That's an interesting idea," she said aloud. "I'm not sure I want to handle it that way."

"We'd be meeting in a public place," Sailor wheedled. "I was thinking maybe Hands Down, you know, that bar on Church."

"I know where it is," she said. "How about if you guys split five thousand?"

"But you said..."

"I didn't know you'd be calling me today, so I don't have that much cash on me. It would take a few days to get the rest. If you want your money now, today, you'll split the five thousand," Suzume said. She could almost hear his frown as he expelled an angry breath.

"All right," he said. "Meet us at three."

CHAPTER 37

Athenian Towers
Nashville, TN
Saturday, May 1, 2010
1:30 P.M.

ON THE RESTAURANT LEVEL OF THE TOWERS, Valerie, Olivia, and Watson encountered loosely organized bedlam. It took a few minutes of watching to figure out who was in charge. It helped when one of the reception staff peered into the room and called out, "Cheryl?" and a head bobbed up to reply, "Over here, Jane!"

As Jane made her way to Cheryl from one end of the restaurant to the other, Olivia, Valerie, and Watson wound around the tables and chairs to approach her from a different angle. Cheryl was already talking to Jane when they got within speaking distance.

"I know it looks rough right now, but we'll be ready by five," Cheryl said with all the brightness of a woman who is trying to convince someone that she has complete control of a situation when she does not. "The entire wait staff is here and working on getting things ready."

"But that's what I came to tell you. The club is thinking about cancelling the dinner tonight." Jane said.

"Oh, no!" Cheryl's face fell.

"Yes, members have been calling to cancel their reservations and now the organizers called to say they are going to postpone. They've asked us to find another date that will work for them."

For a moment, Valerie thought Cheryl might cry. Then she broke out a smile that was like the sun breaking through the storm clouds outside. She looked as though her brain was whirring.

"As long as they didn't simply cancel. We can store most of the decor they asked for that we didn't already have. It's the food…"

"I know," Jane said. "I haven't talked to Nathan yet."

"Nathan? DeFries?" Olivia asked.

Both women's heads turned. "Who are you?" Jane asked.

Watson was faster with his ID this time and Cheryl and Jane were suitably taken aback.

"We're here to ask a few questions about your wait staff," Olivia said as gently as Valerie had ever heard her speak. "You're in charge of them, is that correct?"

"I'm the scheduler," Cheryl said. "Jane is the restaurant manager. We work as a team."

Olivia glanced at Jane, who nodded. "That's correct."

"We'd like to know about one of your wait staff in particular." Olivia's voice was still quiet enough that the rest of the staff didn't hear.

Cheryl glanced at the waiters scampering around the tables. "I think you'd better stop for now," she called out to them, her voice calm. They paused in mid-motion and blinked at her. "The meeting has been cancelled. Just put the place settings back in their boxes and put all the decorations on one of the tables so we can pack them up later. I'll be back in a few minutes." Turning to Olivia she said, "Let's discuss this in the office." She was back to looking like she might cry.

The entire group followed Cheryl to a cramped office just off the restaurant floor. A petite desk and chair were squeezed into a corner there. A laptop computer rested on the top of the desk, its lid open. As Cheryl slid into the tiny chair, the laptop screen popped on. The rest of them gathered in a small arc around her. It felt claustrophobic.

"So, you want to know about my waiters?" Cheryl asked.

"Just one of them," Olivia responded. "Who was assigned to take the lunch to the sixth-floor condo at 1:00 today?"

"Does this have to do with Security being called there this afternoon?" Jane asked. "I heard about it but didn't know what it was about."

"Yes," Olivia said. She took a beat before she added, "A valuable item was stolen from there and we want to question the waiter. We think he may have some information about it."

"I understand," Cheryl said, visibly relieved. "He could have seen something or noticed someone that others might not. Our waiters are trained to be observant."

Olivia skirted the desk to look over Cheryl's shoulder while she searched. Valerie took a similar position on the other side. She saw the service schedule on the screen and followed Cheryl's fingertip when she located the information.

"Yes, here it is," Cheryl said. "A recent hire. He was assigned to take the food to Six. Laurence Cable."

"Oh, yes," Jane said. "I saw his paperwork come through."

Olivia glanced at Valerie, who was shaking her head. "No one I've ever heard of," she said. "Do you have a picture of him?"

"Yes, we take one for their ID." Cheryl tapped some keys and a head shot clicked into view. It was a photo of the young man before his hair was slicked back and tied up for service.

Valerie and Olivia craned around the screen to look at the photo. Olivia waved her fingers at Watson for him to look, too.

"No one I know," Watson said.

"Me, either," Olivia said. "Can we talk to this waiter?"

"Of course," Cheryl said, and picked up her cell phone.

Larry Cable met them in the tiny office outside the restaurant. He surveyed the group, then turned to focus on Cheryl. "You wanted to see me?"

"Yes, these folks want to talk to the waiter who served lunch on the sixth floor at one. Your name is assigned to the duty."

"I did it, then," he said. "Was there a problem with the service?"

"No, not that. A valuable item is missing from the suite. These folks were wondering if you saw anything happen while you were there." The waiter's face blanched. Cheryl looked up at him from her chair, smiling brightly, trying to put him at ease. "Do you remember anything?"

"No, I didn't see anything," he said.

"How long have you been a waiter here?" Olivia asked.

"A couple months."

"You like your job?"

"Yeah, sure. Everyone is pretty nice. The work isn't hard."

"But I'm sure the chef keeps you on your toes."

Larry chuckled. "Yeah, you could say that."

"Where did you work before?" Watson asked.

"Other restaurants," he said, no longer chuckling. "Downtown, mostly." He looked uneasy.

"I have a list," Cheryl said, gesturing to her laptop.

"How did you get the job here?" Olivia asked.

"A friend suggested I might like working here. He knew one of the other waiters."

"And who was this friend?"

"I don't remember the guy's name."

"You don't remember your friend's name?" Valerie asked.

Larry was starting to visibly sweat. "I have lots of friends," he said.

"Do they all work here?" asked Olivia. "Or just the one who suggested you apply here?"

Larry looked confused. "Say, what's this really about? Is my friend in trouble?"

"Only if he delivered food to the sixth floor at one o'clock," Olivia said. "But you did that, didn't you?"

Larry didn't answer her.

"Didn't you?" she repeated.

Larry's Adam's apple rode up and down. He pulled a handkerchief from his pocket and wiped his face. "I didn't see anything," he said.

"Because you weren't there," Valerie said for him. "So, who was? Who delivered the food for you?"

Larry looked at Valerie, then at Cheryl. "I didn't want to do it, but they threatened me."

"Who?" Cheryl asked.

"I don't know," Larry said, his voice suddenly thin and high. They called me on the phone and threatened to hurt me if I didn't let this other guy do my delivery. I thought it was a joke but then the guy showed up at work today."

"You're saying that someone else delivered the food to the

sixth floor," Watson said, making notes. "And you don't know him or his name."

"I never saw him before. Am I going to lose my job?"

<hr>

Cheryl asked them to help her escort Larry to Security's office, to have them go over all the information they possibly could about the situation. "It's a major breach," Cheryl explained to them, "and Security will want to investigate the people who threatened our staff member."

"I'll take a statement and take care of the paperwork on our end," Watson said.

"I'm sure Security will have a few choice things to say to Larry. It's never pretty when someone gets dressed down," Olivia sighed to Watson and Valerie as they followed her.

"Will he be fired?" Valerie asked.

"He was afraid someone would hurt him if he didn't comply with their request. My guess is he won't be fired. At least, not for that."

CHAPTER 38

KH Precision Machine
Nashville, TN
Saturday, May 1, 2010
2:00 P.M.

THUNDER CRACKED and Hoshi stared out the windows of his office at the rain. It was raining hard again, like it had been this morning. *Still just a passing storm,* he thought.

Hoshi knew he should be looking at spreadsheets, to make sure the shipments he had promised to his bosses in Japan were on their way. But he couldn't get his mind off the mandolin or the concert tonight at the hotel where Naoki was arranging the Workers Day event.

Hoshi had been careful to form his plan. Funded the band. Sweet-talked the Hopkins sisters, particularly the redhead, Paige, the sister who handled the business end, into playing at the hotel where Naoki was putting together the entertainment. Let them think he was prepared to pay all their expenses just for an opportunity to talk to the man's daughter and see the instrument played one last time before it went to the Country Music Hall of Fame for display. And then, just maybe...

He glanced out his windows again. The sound of the rain followed a pattern. It was as though barrels of rain poured over the city, paused to be refilled, then began again.

The phone on his desk buzzed. Hoshi looked at the blinking light. The receptionist wasn't there. The answering service should pick up unless the caller knew his private bypass code. The phone continued to buzz. Exasperated, he answered.

The panicked voice on the other end of the line spoke quickly. "Hoshi! Have you seen the forecast? Should we cancel tonight's concert?" Naoki said. "They say the Cumberland is flooding!"

"That's ridiculous!" Hoshi barked back. "For this rain? It's not that bad. It will be over this afternoon. The concert will go forward tonight as planned."

"But they say the rain could last into tomorrow," Naoki pressed. "We can reschedule the concert for later."

"No! Everything is arranged!" Hoshi insisted, his anger at the man's weakness rising. "The concert will go on!" He clicked off the phone.

Bana rapped on the door and Hoshi told him to enter. Bana stopped short when he saw his boss's face split with an angry scowl.

"Sir? What happened?"

Kojima's face was hot pink, his eyes widened and bulged. "Naoki wants to call off tonight's concert!" Kojima yelled. "Because of a little rain!" And he shook his fist at the windows. Outside, grey sheets of water poured amid lightning flashes.

———————•◆•———————

Bana had seen Hoshi Kojima angry before, but not like this.

"He can't do this to me," Hoshi was ranting to the room. "Just because of a little water." With a sweep of his arm, Hoshi knocked a stapler and small calculator to the floor.

Bana jumped back from the desk to avoid being hit by the stapler. "Sir?"

"Naoki. He can't just call and cancel the concert."

Bana had seen what Hoshi did to men when he was this angry and Bana was not happy to be sitting within a few arms' length of all that heat. He didn't understand what set Hoshi off to this extent. A concert at a local hotel? Baffling.

Bana sat very still, waiting for calm to overtake Hoshi. He tried to make himself smaller, not an easy task for a man with a well-developed chest and thickly muscled arms. If Hoshi went on the attack, he would grab Bana as a Naoki substitute. Bana could try to stop him, but it would be a dangerous, well-matched duel. They could easily kill one another. Bana thought there must be a different way. Brute force would not be helpful here.

"The weather was not your doing," Bana said carefully. "Surely Naoki would reschedule."

"I just told you! I don't want to reschedule!"

A wooden box holding note paper sailed by Bana's head, showering leaves of white around the room. Bana followed his instinct to duck. He was relieved to see the desk was almost cleared, leaving little there for Hoshi to throw. Just Ichi's photo in its frame and Bana was pretty sure Hoshi wasn't going to throw that.

Then Hoshi turned to the bookshelves behind him, apparently ready to toss their contents, as well. He pulled a leather-bound financial journal from the bookshelf. Bana knew that if he didn't stop Hoshi soon, the rest of the office would be a shambles on the floor.

"Sir, please don't throw that." Bana's tone was calm. To his surprise, instead of tossing it, Hoshi opened the journal on his desk and reviewed some pages.

"No, no, I won't. I just want to check our position."

Hoshi leaned over and unlocked a hidden drawer under the desk. Bana had only seen him open this drawer twice before, both times when he needed cash unexpectedly.

Hoshi glanced up at Bana, eyes sharp and angry. "I need to make a payment to the office in a couple days. I was counting on receiving some items that our customers were waiting for, but they haven't arrived yet."

"The items from Suzume."

"Correct, although I expected she would not be successful. As always, I will have to take matters into my own hands. I'll have to come up with something else to offer them."

"You don't have much time."

"No. But I have some reserves that may hold them off." Hoshi gestured to the drawer with cash, hanging open. He pushed it closed and locked it.

"What if you could get the Hopkins woman's instrument, the mandolin," Bana asked. "Would that be worth something?"

Hoshi laid a hand on the ledger, thinking. His eyes took on a misty look.

"With the instrument, you would have a bargaining chip," Bana went on. "Appease the bosses with it. At least one of them must be interested. Or perhaps tell them you'll sell it to recoup the money."

Bana could almost smell the smoke of Hoshi's brain at work.

"It could be done." Hoshi's eyes clicked onto Bana's, and he suddenly seemed clear and in the present. He glanced at the mess on the floor and with his hands made two little brooms. "See that this is cleaned up," he told Bana. "I have some phone calls to make."

CHAPTER 39

Athenian Towers
Nashville, TN
Saturday, May 1, 2010
2:15 P.M.

LEAVING WATSON DODD WITH CHERYL, Valerie and Olivia returned to the sixth floor, where things seemed quiet. A little too quiet. Everyone was sitting down, no one was talking, just sitting and staring.

"Hello?" Olivia said. Faces turned her way, but no one answered. Everyone looked glum.

Rocky headed across the room to Valerie. When she got within whispering distance, Rocky murmured, "The induction and the concert have been cancelled."

She nodded at Hayley, who was sitting on one of the couches, holding a spare mandolin tight to her chest. Justine talked to her softly. Paige sat in a side chair near them, staring into space.

Rocky sighed. "Someone at the museum called to tell her that the weather made conditions too dangerous."

"Are they rescheduling?" Olivia asked.

Paige pulled herself out of her chair to join them. "They haven't told me that, at least, not yet."

"First the mandolin, now this. This is the last thing I wanted to happen," Hayley said.

"There's nothing you can do about the weather," Olivia said, gesturing to the huge windows, where rain continued to pour. It would soon be dusk, and the view would be even more dismal.

"I'm not surprised they cancelled," Valerie said. "They have to be concerned about people's safety, the audience and the people working for them. I'm sure they will reschedule."

"We've worked so hard to prepare," Hayley squeezed her eyes shut, but at least she wasn't crying anymore. "The tour," she added miserably. "This was supposed to be my big comeback, my chance to crossover into country and not just play bluegrass like Daddy did. I wanted to play his mandolin, to show everyone it didn't have to be used just one way."

"The induction concert is a big deal," Paige added. "They'll do it later. You'll still have your chance." She tried to smile at Hayley, but it was a sour effort at best.

"Look on the bright side," Olivia said. "This delay gives us time to find your father's mandolin so you can use it for the tour. And for the concert, when they reschedule."

Hayley brightened a little. "Well, maybe you're right. I wasn't looking forward to telling the Museum it was missing. Do you think you can find it?"

"We're working on it. We're just getting started."

Valerie wondered if one of Olivia's strengths was her Southern charm, helping clients ignore bad news. She seemed so positive they would be able to track down the thief. Valerie knew that wasn't likely to happen, since investigators often took years to find most missing instruments. Still, they weren't far behind the thief for this one.

When the phone rang again, Paige picked it up, spoke to the person on the phone, then called out, "It's for you, Hayley."

Hayley took a deep breath and then palmed the phone from her sister. "Yes?" she said and listened to the voice on the other end of the line. "Yes, I heard. No, no other date was mentioned to me, either."

The voice on the other end, from what Valerie could hear, carried a wheedling tone that told her someone was trying to convince Hayley of something. She squinted her eyes as though that would help her to hear better.

Hayley listened for a few moments, then said, "So the concert at the hotel is still on? I thought you might cancel because of the weather. Isn't the hotel next to the river?"

The voice responded, sounding much less accommodating.

"I know. But..." She turned her head away from the phone. She looked shocked. "Paige, can you talk to this guy?"

"Of course," Paige nodded.

The voice was still talking. Hayley interrupted him, saying, "Let me put you on speaker. My business manager needs to hear what you are asking."

The man's voice boomed into the room. "Your business manager? Your sister, I believe. And I'm sure she will agree."

There was a haughtiness to his voice that set Valerie's teeth on edge. It reminded her of something that she couldn't place. She tried to assess the voice. *Was he trying to convince Hayley to play? In the middle of what looked like a full-fledged flood? Was he bullying her because the induction concert was called off? Why did he care so much?*

"We have a contract," the voice said. "You signed it and agreed to play 'rain or shine' according to my copy."

"But this is a flood! It's too dangerous to play near the river tonight."

"Dangerous? This is just a little rain shower. The river won't crest until tomorrow at the earliest."

Hayley hesitated, looking at Paige. She mouthed the words, "Is that right?" Paige made an I-don't-know shrug and held her palms up.

"I take it that losing the money you would be paid doesn't concern you. As the person who has been paying for your expenses, it does concern me. I expected you to be able to repay at least part of my investment."

"So, that's why you set us up to play this gig? So, we pay the money to you?" Hayley was talking to the disembodied voice, but she was staring daggers at her sister.

"I'm a businessman. Of course, that's part of the contract. Your sister should have told you that."

Hayley shot another quick look at Paige and saw her nod. Hayley turned her back to her sister.

"Then you must know that profits are not the reason I'm performing this show or any show. This is about my father's legacy," Hayley said. "Money is of far lesser importance."

"But what about YOUR reputation and legacy," the voice continued. "What will your fans think of you for not honoring their desire to see you perform? What will your critics say? They've already driven you from the business once. Are you prepared to let them destroy you again?"

Hayley blinked. She looked like she'd been shot.

"What, exactly, do you propose?" Paige asked, standing closer to Hayley now.

"This is not a negotiation." The voice became insistent. "Let me remind you of your obligation to me. Contractually, you are bound to play a concert. Tonight. With your father's mandolin. Or you pay me to cancel."

"It's too dangerous," Hayley repeated.

"The contract is specific."

"No," Paige said.

"You will do this!" the voice shouted.

"And how will you force us to do this? Send your henchmen for payment?" Paige laughed drily. "I'd like to see that."

"You don't know who you are dealing with. Never laugh at me. Ever."

"Then what is it that you want us to do?"

"I'll send my men to pick you up and take you to the hotel." The click of the phone was so loud it echoed in the room.

Valerie suddenly realized who the voice reminded her of. She grabbed Paige's arm and shook her head violently. "Don't do this!" she hissed into Paige's face.

"I have to," Paige hissed back. "We owe him. He's paid for everything!"

Paige and Hayley stared at each other, then at Valerie.

"Who was that?" Olivia asked.

Valerie suspected that she already knew.

"One of our benefactors," Paige said. "A very generous one. Hoshi Kojima, the man who owns Oriental Exchange, the big exporter. Hayley and the band are supposed to play a couple sets tonight for workers at one of the car plants in town. A friend of his runs the plant."

"We're going to have to do this, aren't we?" Hayley asked.

"Yes," Paige replied. "I'm sorry."

Valerie's heart sank. She and Rocky exchanged glances. Olivia, behind them, said, "Someone you know?"

"Oh, yes," Valerie said. "I think he might have been responsible for my mother's death."

CHAPTER 40

Athenian Towers
Nashville, TN
Saturday, May 1, 2010
2:25 P.M.

OLIVIA INHALED SHARPLY. "Really? He killed your mother?"

"Not directly, but I think he was behind it. You already know our story about the guitar in Philadelphia," Valerie said. "We had quite a time tailing the thieves."

"Yes, you mentioned that in your session at the conference," Olivia said.

"Ultimately, we tracked them to a warehouse in downtown Philadelphia where they were trying to retrieve the guitar themselves."

"From someone who acquired it from them at the guitar show," Olivia interrupted. "Yes, you told the group that. I thought it was a legal transaction. Go on."

"It was. The problem was that when the client caught up with the thief, he heard that the thief was trying to get it back. On his own. The client insisted on going with him to meet with the man who had the guitar."

Rocky jumped in at that point. "They went to a warehouse where they would supposedly find this guy, Mr. Itoh. But when they got there, the only person they saw was a young woman who they took to be a high school student waiting for her father to pick her up. The story gets murky here, but if you believe the guys, they were just trying to ask the girl some questions."

"The girl, on the other hand," Valerie said, "thought they were trying to kidnap her."

Olivia looked from Valerie to Rocky and back again. "And which was it?"

"Knowing the client, I'm guessing he bumbled from the asking of questions into possible kidnapping, but it didn't get that far."

"And who was the girl?"

"Hoshi Kojima's daughter," Valerie said. "Suzume Kojima."

Olivia looked confused. "I don't understand. I know Kojima owns the shipping facility here in Nashville, but you seem to know something about him that I don't. I don't understand why everyone seems to be in awe of him."

Valerie winced. "I'm not sure 'awe' is the right word. 'Afraid' might be better."

"Afraid of what?"

"Hoshi Kojima leads a gang in the United States that has clear ties to a Yakuza family in Japan."

Olivia took a moment to process this. Then she said, "And how, exactly, do you know that?"

"Through our investigation. Through an uncle of a family friend who works for the FBI. Through them contacting me and discussing how I might be of service to them."

Olivia's mouth hung open.

"My mother died in a car accident in 1984. Someone arranged that accident and it may have been Hoshi Kojima. I was fifteen at the time. I just found out the details last year."

Valerie's voice broke. It was still hard to talk about her mother's death all these years later. It didn't help that the new knowledge was still so fresh.

"I can't prove it, not officially, but that's what I was told. And I believe it."

"Oh, honey," Olivia grasped Valerie's arm. "I am so sorry."

Valerie tried to smile, but it didn't reach her eyes.

"When Rocky and I searched for the men who sold our client's guitar, we stumbled into the alleged kidnapping of Kojima's daughter," Valerie explained. "Suzume saw Rocky and I drive off with the two perpetrators. She thought we helped them get away. She didn't know we were hauling them back to face the police."

"Suzume has been harassing Valerie ever since," Rocky added. "She won't listen to Valerie's explanation. Apparently, she had a falling out with her father about the whole thing and she blames Valerie."

"All along I thought Suzume was in Philadelphia," Valerie added, "but I saw her at the Bluebird Cafe last night. So now I know she's here and now I know her father is, too. He's the one I really want to talk to."

"That doesn't mean he's not trying to help us," Paige said.

"You can't believe that," Valerie said. "He's a dangerous man. You can't go along with this."

"We don't have a choice," Paige said flatly. "We have a contract."

Hayley reached out and touched Valerie's arm. "She's right. We've got to go. I'll play the show with this instead." She held up the mandolin she'd been holding.

As Valerie silently stewed, Olivia said, "And all I was worried about was finding a mandolin thief. It sounds like we have bigger fish to fry."

CHAPTER 41

HandsDown
Nashville, TN
Saturday, May 1, 2010
2:30 P.M.

PAUL PRATT AGREED TO MEET Sailor Lang at one of their favorite bars, HandsDown, near a high-rise under construction on Church Street. It was a small place, just a ten-seat bar with three tables for the hard core, stay all day, drinkers. Dark inside, no one asking questions, no one talking, just the heavy silence of locals who like to avoid the tourist hubbub. Every time the door opened, everyone in the bar looked at the door furtively, then looked away. If you dared to enter, you had to expect to be scrutinized but not greeted.

The wood of the bar was burnished with age but battered by use. The mirror behind the bar was mostly covered by liquor bottles, the original name of the bar hidden somewhere behind them. Parts of golden letters showed around the shoulders of spirits lined up over five heavily laden shelves.

The bartender was craggy-faced and crabby. He was always there when Paul visited. Paul thought of him as the owner, but he never asked, just as the bartender never acknowledged him even though Paul drank there several times a week.

Paul swung the mandolin case under the bar and propped it between his legs. He ordered a beer to drink until Sailor joined him. His hoodie was matted to his back and his hair clung to his head in wet strings, but Paul wasn't thinking about that. He was thinking about the mandolin. He was thinking about the money.

Sailor was soaked when he came into the bar. His umbrella had collapsed in a gust of wind outside and the storm hit him full force. He hung his umbrella on a hook on the wall and took a few minutes to wipe himself off and get comfortable on the seat next to Paul. Two other drinkers moved away from him as he inserted himself there. They headed for a suddenly deserted table, away from the wet newcomer.

Sailor eyed them as they moved, then remembered what he was doing there.

"So, you got it?" Sailor asked Paul

"Yep."

"That was quick. Any trouble?"

"Nope. It went great, better than I hoped."

Paul proceeded to tell Sailor the whole story: how he not only made himself an integral part of the wait staff at the Athenian Towers in record time but also how he was able to get into the condo on the sixth floor and lift the mandolin earlier, faster, and easier than he ever anticipated.

"No one cared," Paul said, still a little stunned by the experience. "No one noticed. No one came after me. No one yelled at me. I passed several cops on the street, but they were more interested in trying to direct traffic near the river. I guess it's flooding over there."

"Too busy to pay attention, huh?" Sailor said. "All the better for us, right?" He slapped Paul's shoulder and pulled his hand away when he felt the spray of water from Paul's hoodie.

"Yeah, but it just seemed like everything was too easy."

"Never too easy. Easy is good, buddy. Just means it was meant to be."

"Right."

"So where is it?"

"Right here," Paul said and pointed down between his knees.

Sailor grinned. "Great. Didn't see it." Sailor pretended to stretch, looking down at the case from his position at the bar without letting anyone around them notice. "Good, good. I called Suzume to meet us here with the money." Sailor's expression shifted into a frown. "There's a hitch, though."

"A hitch?" Paul said, louder than he intended, as he pulled himself out of the hunch he had developed to hover over his beer.

Sailor leaned over to Paul and said, "Keep your voice down."

"Okay. What hitch?" Paul whispered.

"Instead of five thousand each, now we're splitting five thousand."

Paul frowned. "Splitting?"

"Yeah. At first I was going to argue with her, but then I thought maybe we'd deal with this when she gets here."

"Deal with this?" Paul bristled. "What are we gonna do, slap her around? Here? Tell the cops she's cheating us?"

Sailor slid his empty bottle forward so the bartender would bring him another.

"No, no, of course not. But at least we can get paid right away. I thought maybe it was better to accept her deal on the chance to get more work from her."

Paul's eyes widened. "Did she say that?"

"Well, no, but that's how these things usually work." Sailor shrugged. "She's just testing us." Sailor left out the fact that he'd worked with Suzume before. He thought he had a track record with her. Tests be damned.

"Huh." Paul looked at his beer, seething.

"What's the matter?"

"Well, everyone's been talking about how important this mandolin is. How much people admire it. How much they were gonna get paid to play it and show it off."

"Yeah? So?"

"So, maybe twenty-five hundred each isn't enough. Maybe we should hold out."

Sailor shifted uncomfortably on the stool. "I don't like negotiating with this woman. Her reputation is..." he searched for the right word, "ugly."

"If she wants this thing, she should pay for it, right?"

"Yes, but I'm looking at the bigger picture, the future work."

"Yeah. Future work you don't know we'll get."

"C'mon, buddy, this is the way of the world," Sailor coaxed. "We'll make it up later."

"Hey, she should be grateful! We got the thing. I got the thing. And fast." Paul raised his voice. He couldn't help but let his pride shine. "She owes us. More than twenty-five hundred."

"Shh. Hold it down," Sailor said. "I don't know, Paul. She's been pretty good to me when I've worked for her before. Normally she's upfront with the deal."

"Have I been your partner before when you worked for her?"

"Probably. You just didn't know." Sailor took a long swallow of beer. He should have explained this to Paul earlier.

"Even better. She knows our work. Come on, man, you know I'm right. We should push a little." Paul leaned toward him, breathing beer fumes into Sailor's face. "We can get what she promised. I bet we could even get more." Paul's eyes drilled into Sailor's. "And if we don't, you know people, too. You don't have to sell it to her."

Sailor arched back, away from Paul, to dodge the fumes and think. "All right," Sailor finally agreed. "But let me do the talking." The decision didn't feel good.

Then the door opened behind them and Suzume and one of her henchmen stepped inside the bar.

CHAPTER 42

Athenian Towers
Nashville, TN
Saturday, May 1, 2010
2:50 P.M.

ATHENIAN TOWERS PRIDED ITSELF ON PRIVACY. When Mark, Hayley, and the band stepped out of the elevator, Mark wasn't surprised to see a clutch of white vans and shuttles with no markings on their sides. The van nearest the elevator was running. He guessed that was their ride.

"I bet that's our driver," Hayley said, adjusting the weight of her gig bag on her shoulder. She pointed to a tough-looking Asian gentleman standing next to a white cargo van. He wore a dark slicker over a white shirt. "Stay here," she told Mark and went toward the Asian man, who met her halfway.

Mark saw the scar on his cheek and wondered briefly how that happened. But the gentleman, after a few brief words to Hayley, led her to the van. Hayley waved the rest of the band over. The Asian man helped Hayley into the front cab. Hayley put her gig bag on the seat between her and the driver. The driver motioned for the guys to get in the back.

The door to the cargo area opened and a second Asian man, this one much younger, climbed out of the back and stood aside for them to enter. His face was so smooth and clean, Mark wondered just how young he was. The young man kept glancing at the driver, so Mark assumed he was following orders from the man with the scar.

The van was not going to offer a luxury ride for the band, that was certain. Seating was just two metal benches bolted longways to the back of the van. Hand straps hung from the ceiling above the benches.

Boomer leaned over to Mark and whispered, "Hey, are we being kidnapped?" and the two of them laughed.

After the band got into the back of the van, the young man followed them inside. He locked the door and sat down at the end of the bench opposite the entry door. His eyes roamed over them constantly, watching them jostling to get settled. Mark thought he seemed jumpy but the young man's hand was steady when he reached up to grab onto one of the hand straps. *Maybe I'm the one who's jumpy*, he thought.

Mark noticed that the only means of communication with the front cab was a small oblong door set at head level for the driver. There was no latch or knob on the cargo side that he could see, so he guessed that it only opened from the cab side. He also guessed that this van was usually used for hauling boxes, not people. He wondered why they chose this bare-bones van rather than borrowing one of the fully upholstered shuttles from the condo. They could have just sent them to the hotel that way.

The van lurched off. As it left the garage and turned into the street, the rain suddenly pounded on the van's roof, defeating any attempt at conversation. As the band sat there silently, Mark looked from face to face and realized they were all uncomfortable with their circumstances and with the young Asian man sitting with them.

Kenny, especially, seemed edgy, constantly looking at the man in their midst and then glancing at Mark quickly before turning his eyes to the floor. Kenny looked like he wanted to say something, but the noise of the weather prevented him. Kenny was usually so quiet and reserved that Mark was surprised at his response to the young man.

Mark suspected that they all just wanted to get to the hotel to check the setup and rehearse. But Kenny's eyes kept going to the young man. Mark was getting unnerved.

The van made several turns, and without windows, Mark lost all sense of direction. When the van finally came to a stop, he and the rest of the guys started to move around, preparing to get out. "Wait," the young man commanded, and the band sat down again.

After a few minutes there was a bang on the side of the van. The young man stood and quickly opened the door. It was pouring outside the van. Thunder rumbled in the distance. The young man got out and hurriedly closed the door behind him. Then Mark heard the click of the lock.

"Hey!" Mark yelled and pounded on the door. "Hey, what about us?"

When there was no response, the rest of the guys started pounding on the walls of the van and yelling, too, even Kenny.

Mark finally shouted, "Wait! Stop!" at them and they quieted down. He went to the little door in the wall between the cab and the body of the truck and listened. He tapped on the tiny metal door and waited. Then he heard Hayley's voice, muffled, on the other side of the wall.

"Hayley?" he called. "Hayley? Are you there?"

Her voice sounded far away, but he could make out her words. "Mark!" she screamed, "Help me!"

Boomer's head jerked toward the front cab. "What the hell?"

Mark turned to Boomer and said, "Holy shit, you were right! We have been kidnapped! Fuck!"

CHAPTER 43

KH Precision Machine
Nashville, TN
Saturday, May 1, 2010
2:50 P.M.

SUZUME WISHED THAT BANA was with her for the trip to HandsDown, but he had told her hours ago that her father needed him for a special project. Instead, she relied on Ryu, the swaggering young buck who Daddy assigned to her and who followed her like a puppy. Well, a puppy with an attitude. She asked Ryu if he would drive her downtown in her sporty little Nissan. He seemed inordinately pleased.

Asian men baffled her, but she enjoyed using them. She had to remind herself not to trust them.

Still, she found herself admiring Ryu's style. He constantly wore that silk bomber jacket embroidered with a snarling tiger on the back. The front panels of his jacket had additional embroidery, circlets of vine embellished with leaves. The jacket was a beautiful example of the hand-stitching that her countrymen were so good at -- and which she sneered at as too traditional. Under the colorful jacket he wore black, black, and more black: shirt, pants, shoes.

Still, Ryu was a nice piece of arm candy. Dark hair swept into a well-groomed pompadour, one curl swooping over his high forehead. Dark eyes looking almost liquid. Attractive in that way of young Asian men, seeming so subservient, so desirous to please. She understood how effective he could be, allowing an adversary to be less defensive.

Bana could never be that. Not with the face he had, the scar, the lines, the hard eyes. His very build was brutal.

But Ryu was no traditional man in the hierarchy of her father's business. He was, from what Suzume could tell, Bana's man, not Hoshi's. It made Suzume wonder about Bana's true loyalty.

Was Bana loyal to her father, or was he considering becoming an independent businessman with his own workforce? And if that was the case, where will I fit when a confrontation inevitably happens? Thoughts for another time, she told herself. *I have immediate business and Ryu is here to help me.*

She buttoned up her rain cape and flipped her single braid out over the neck. "We have something to take care of," she told Ryu. "I'll explain on the way."

• ● •

Suzume was fond of places like HandsDown. Low lighting, hard-core drinkers mixed with locals, a place where you could do business with no one asking questions. She liked that it wasn't far from her dad's office or from Lower Broadway.

With all the rain, parking was hard to find. It looked like everyone had parked downtown. When Ryu finally found a spot, it was almost a block away from the bar. He apologized for the distance.

"That's what rain gear is for," she needled him. His silk bomber jacket was no protection against the rain. She didn't know how he'd feel about walking in the rain dressed the way he was, but he didn't argue or complain. And he seemed completely comfortable following her into the bar. She was starting to like this guy.

Inside the bar, Suzume realized that it was so gray outside that her eyes automatically adjusted to the gloomy interior. She saw Sailor and another man at the bar, nursing beers. They turned as one to see who had just come into the bar. Sailor stood and waved her over but when he saw the man in the silk jacket coming along with her, his face froze.

Ryu moved a few steps away from Suzume, taking a seat at the end of the bar. She liked that he had a sense of her power, that she was in charge, that she needed to be front and center. She felt him nearby rather than saw him. She relaxed, feeling his protection.

"Who's your friend?" she asked Sailor, pointing at the man next him.

"Who's yours?" he growled back. He gestured loosely toward the man at the end of the bar. "The guy in the fancy jacket."

"You first," Suzume said.

Sailor eyed her suspiciously, but Paul reached over Sailor to hold out his hand to Suzume. "Paul Pratt. The gentleman who found the item you were looking for."

Sailor glared at Paul.

"Really? Where is it?" Suzume asked.

Paul was holding the case between his knees, effectively hiding it in the shadows under the bar, but made no move to indicate that to Suzume.

Sailor said, "We'll get to that. Who is that guy?" he asked, pointing again at the man who'd come in with Suzume.

"My bodyguard, Ryu," she said.

"Bodyguard." Paul snorted a laugh. Suzume shot him a dark look that caused the sound to die. His mouth had suddenly gone dry. He sipped his beer.

Suzume hopped up onto the stool next to Paul, with Sailor retaking his seat on the other side of him. The bartender brought Suzume a drink, even though she hadn't asked. She nodded her thanks to the bartender.

Paul watched, amazed. *How did he know what she wanted?* Followed by the realization, *she's been here before.* He swallowed hard. *Maybe this is a bad idea.*

Sailor cleared his throat. Then he said, very quietly, "Paul and I think maybe you could do a little better on your offer."

Paul, watching how this interchange was going and considering the man at the end of the bar, was suddenly not so sure. "Uh, Sailor?"

Sailor shook his head. "Not now," he growled.

"I don't think so," Suzume said, her voice kept low and even to avoid attention. "You've already gotten a down payment."

"Down payment?" Paul's head swiveled to Sailor.

Sailor waved him off. "Expenses. Before the fact. Nothing to do with you."

Suzume wondered if the contract between Sailor and Paul wasn't as clear as hers with Sailor. "Not completing a contract is a dangerous thing," she pointed out.

"Yes, it is," Sailor shot back. "What are you going to do if we just walk out of here? It's too public for a showdown, even if you've brought your..." he paused, "bodyguard." His voice sounded like thick, oozy oil.

Suzume snapped her fingers at Ryu, who pulled out a pack of cigarettes and extracted one for her. She took it delicately, waiting for him to light it. When Ryu pulled out his lighter, it jiggled out of his hands and dropped to the floor. Ryu had to bend deeply to pick it up.

As he came up to light her cigarette, he smiled at her and gave her a quick nod.

Sailor's heart sank. Ryu must have seen the case under the bar. He couldn't miss it. "I think our business has concluded," Sailor said and turned his face away from Suzume.

"I don't think so," she said, her voice taking on a deeper, ominous note. "Where is it?"

Ryu stood and moved closer to Suzume.

Paul shifted his weight a little to put himself more solidly between Suzume and the mandolin under the bar. He hadn't counted on the second set of eyes on him. And Silk Jacket's eyes were sharp. Paul, too, guessed that Ryu knew exactly where the mandolin was.

"We can just take it with us," Ryu said to Suzume, pointing down at Paul's legs.

Suzume tilted her head down to follow his gesture. Sure enough, there was something between the feet of the skinny man with the stringy hair. She turned to Ryu.

"Take it and let's go. They're too stupid to get any more than what I've already given them."

When Ryu reached forward, Paul instinctively did what he had trained himself to do all his life: he grabbed the mandolin and headed for the door.

The rain hit him like a brick wall when he opened the door, but Paul knew better than to let that stop him. Holding the mandolin close to his body, he started running, running harder than he'd ever run, conscious of footsteps behind him.

He heard Sailor yelling. "Go, go, go!"

Suzume screamed "Stop!"

He wasn't sure how close either of them was, or where Silk Jacket might be. The rain was loud, and the occasional crash of thunder deafened him momentarily.

All he could do was run.

CHAPTER 44

Athenian Towers
Nashville, TN
Saturday, May 1, 2010
3:00 P.M.

WATSON DODD BURST INTO THE CONDO and headed straight for Olivia.

"I think I found something," he said, showing her a several sheets of paper in his hand. He pulled one out to show her. "This is a photo from the security footage earlier today."

She took the fuzzy photo from him and looked at it. "Just looks like one of the waiters," she said. "All the waiters look like that."

"Yes, but this one entered the garage level and took off parts of his uniform." He offered her a second picture. "Same guy, but without the vest and headwrap. He headed for the exit ramp on foot."

Valerie looked over Olivia's shoulder. "He's got a small case with him. I imagine that's the mandolin."

"Too bad I can't see his face," Olivia murmured. "There's something about him."

The condo door opened again, and the security guy entered the room with another photo printed on paper. "Detective Dodd?"

"What do you have there?" Dodd asked and took the sheet.

Olivia, Valerie, and Rocky crowded around Watson to see the picture. It was still slightly fuzzy but a much clearer angle of the waiter's face.

Olivia's eyes went wide. "Paul Pratt!" she exclaimed. "I should have guessed!" She saw Valerie's puzzled expression and added, "Local guy, known thief. We've been looking for him for another theft downtown."

"The cameras caught him outside the building. We think he was headed south," the security guy pointed out.

"That would make sense," Olivia said. "He lives in an apartment on the other side of the pedestrian bridge, south of here."

"Here's the weird thing," the security guy said, "he didn't look like he was in much of a hurry, even though it's pouring outside. From the footage we were able to see, he stayed close to the building to keep as dry as possible. But his actions were normal, not calling any attention to himself."

"Huh," Dodd huffed. "Maybe we should see if he's at home," he suggested to Olivia.

"That sounds like a very good idea," she agreed.

CHAPTER 45

KH Precision Machine
Nashville, TN
Saturday, May 1, 2010
3:10 P.M.

BANA DROVE THE VAN into the partially paved parking lot of a low manufacturing building. A few cars filled the spots in front of the entrance to the building. Three small box trucks were parked on the pavement near the building, partially blocking a tractor trailer parked in one of the two bays at the building's loading dock. The trailer and the loading bays were both dark and silent. No one appeared to be working there.

"Hey! This isn't the hotel. Where are we?" Hayley said.

"We're not going to the hotel."

He guided the van to the far end of the parking lot just beyond the tractor trailer where there were more stones than pavement. The spot overlooked what Hayley assumed was the Cumberland River.

The river ran high and fast, the water choppy and brown. The parking lot sagged low in this area, tilting the van slightly in the driver's direction. Looking out the front window, Hayley felt like she was only a few feet above the river.

Bana turned to Hayley and said, "Give me your hands."

Startled, she pulled them back against her chest. He reached out and grabbed her wrists anyway.

"Ow!" she said, "what are you doing?" She wriggled a little to pull away from him, but he overpowered her movement easily.

Bana held her wrists together in one of his hands while he pulled a length of thin rope from the side pocket of the cab with the other. Despite her struggling, he expertly wrapped the rope around her wrists, then tied them to the steering wheel of the van. He picked up her gig bag and opened his door.

"That's my mandolin!" Hayley shrieked. "Where are you going?"

Bana got out of the van, leaning forward slightly to protect the gig bag. Rain poured over his slicker. Hayley kicked after him with one leg. Glaring at her, he locked the cab door behind him and moved out of her sight behind the van. She heard a thwack as he hit the side of the van once with his hand.

It hurt Hayley's wrists and shoulders to turn around to watch him, so she faced the driver's door and twisted and turned the rope at her wrists.

She was so stunned she had gone completely silent while he tied her to the steering wheel. But then he took her mandolin, too. She couldn't believe it. *Is he coming back?*

Hayley heard the door to the back of the van open and then close and lock. She turned her head to see who'd gotten out of the van. It was the young helper, whose back and shoulder appeared briefly as he scampered off. Then she heard shouting in the back.

The band. The band is back there. With Mark.

"Mark!" she screamed as loudly as she could. "Help me!"

———•———

Bana stepped inside the doors of KH Precision Machine and looked around the lobby. The place was empty, silent. But he knew that Hoshi was here, waiting for his report. He frowned at his young companion, who had followed him to the building like a lost puppy. Bana ordered, "Stay here." The young man's eyes told Bana he would do anything he was asked.

Bana walked down the hallway to Hoshi's office and knocked gently. "Enter."

The lights were bright in Hoshi's office. Bana squinted to see him. Hoshi was looking at a catalog of some sort. *Equipment for the machine shop, maybe?* Bana thought, but when he approached Hoshi's desk, he could see the book's pages were full of musical instruments.

"I've got them," Bana said. "In the parking lot. Here's the instrument."

"Excellent." Hoshi's smile was gleeful, but his eyes were not. He grabbed the case from Bana and laid it on his desk. The droplets of water draining from the case onto his desk seemed not to matter to him. He opened the case and, for a moment, stood transfixed. Then he roared, "This is not the instrument I wanted!"

Bana cowered slightly, forgetting for that he could probably kill Kojima if he chose. "I didn't know," he said quietly. "What can I do?"

"Nothing, you imbecile! You're no better than my daughter! Get out of my sight!"

Bana turned to go when Kojima said, "Wait."

"Yes, sir?"

"You have the girl in the van?"

"Yes, sir."

"Bring her in here."

"Yes, sir." Bana turned again to go, then paused to ask, "But what about the rest of the people in the van?"

"Eliminate them."

A few minutes after Olivia and Dodd left, Paige's phone rang. She looked puzzled. "It's Kojima," she said.

"I have your sister," Kojima's gritty voice emanated from the phone. "And her little band. She thought she could fool me by bringing someone else's mandolin with her. If you want her back, you must bring your father's mandolin to me."

A shock ran through Valerie. *Has Suzume engineered this?*

"Ask him where," she whispered to Paige.

"Suzume?" Rocky mouthed to Valerie, who nodded curtly.

"I'd bet on it."

"But we don't have..." Paige started to say into the phone.

"Ask him!" Valerie hissed, grabbing Paige's arm and shaking it.

"Where should we meet you?" Paige's voice shook as she asked the question.

"Bring the mandolin to KH Precision Machine."

"KH... I don't know where that is."

"I'm sure you can figure it out. If you want your sister back."

"Is Hayley all right?" Paige asked, her voice frantic.

"Meet me there," he said, ignoring her question. "I'll be waiting."

The phone in Paige's hand clicked.

"But we don't have the mandolin!" Paige shouted, shaking the disconnected phone in her hand. She looked to Valerie and Rocky. "Now what do we do?"

"Do you have a car?" Valerie asked.

"Yes."

"Let's go."

CHAPTER 46

KH Precision Machine
Nashville, TN
Saturday, May 1, 2010
3:30 P.M.

MARK LOOKED AT HIS CELL PHONE for the hundredth time. No messages. No phone calls. No cell service.

Mark had been surprised that no one took their phones. But when he tried to use his, he understood why. Phone service was almost non-existent, probably because the cell towers and reception were affected by the storm. The connection indicator blinked at a very low level. He tried calling Valerie, but only got her voicemail. He left a frantic message. After a few minutes he tried again and left a second message, this time forcing himself to calm down and tell her more clearly what happened.

He also tried calling the police but couldn't get through. Then cell service went off entirely. His phone suddenly felt like a brick in his hand. He shoved it in his pocket.

It felt like years had gone by and no one had come to check on the van. The guys pushed and prodded the vehicle doors and pounded on the little window to the cab but couldn't force anything open. The air inside the van smelled rancid with sweat and fear. The hammering of rain on the van's roof made it hard to talk.

Mark pressed his ear against the cab wall again. He shushed the guys and then called out, "Hayley? Hayley, can you hear me?"

"Yes!" It sounded like she had to yell to make herself heard.

"Are you okay? We're locked in back here. Can you get to the door?"

"No!" she said. "I'm tied to the steering wheel."

Mark's anger blinded him for a moment, but he knew he had to tamp it down and get the band and Hayley out of the van.

"I can see where we are," Hayley called out. "We're next to the river, I think. The water is really moving fast and it's getting higher. I'm scared, Mark."

"I know," he said, ignoring the panic making his own heart pound. "Can you see anything else?"

"We're in a parking lot," she said. "We're at the edge of the lot, at the top of a bank. There is a one-story building across the parking lot, but I can't see what it is. There's a sign. I can see two big letters, a K and an H. Does that mean anything to you?"

"No," he said. "What else can you see? Cars? People?"

"Just trucks. No people. I think the driver went into the building. With the other guy."

"Okay, Hayley. Stay calm. Everything will be okay." He wasn't sure about that, but he wasn't going to tell her. Mark turned around to look at the guys, who had been hanging on every word of their exchange.

"We're at KH Precision Machine," Kenny said. "I used to work there. The guy who rode over here with us? I remember him from there. He's a flunky for the owners."

"KH Precision Machine?" Mark asked.

"I was a machinist. They do a lot of stuff for export."

"What do they want with us?" Luke asked.

"I don't know," Mark said. "Do you?" he asked Kenny.

Kenny looked as baffled as Mark felt. All the guys looked whipped. There was no point in trying to cheer them up, they'd been working hard to open the van. They had no tools and the van itself seemed somehow reinforced. Mark's brain whirled, trying to figure out what to do to get out of the van or at least help Hayley.

There was a sudden shift in the angle of the van. The guys all yelled, and Mark heard Hayley scream again. A second, stronger jolt followed, knocking all of them off their feet, leaving the guys scrambling for an upright position. Des cracked his head against one of the seats and was bleeding from a cut on his temple. Mark gave him the handkerchief from his pocket and Boomer and Clay helped Des up. Boomer positioned the cloth to cover the cut.

Mark pressed himself tight to the wall between the van and the cab, steadying himself with one of the handholds in the ceiling. "Hayley! What's going on?"

She was sobbing, he could tell. She stopped long enough to yell, "The bank is washing out from under us!"

Another shift and the van tilted again. Mark was overcome with vertigo, but the van settled onto what felt like a pillow and the sensation stopped. They guys grabbed onto anything they could to stay upright, mostly the bolted seating or the handholds above them. At first Mark thought they had just rolled down a hill and had come to a stop, but he had a strange sensation of movement. Then he heard Hayley yell, "We're in the water! Mark, do something!"

CHAPTER 47

Fourth Avenue South
Nashville, TN
Saturday, May 1, 2010
3:25 P.M.

THE RAIN LIGHTENED CONSIDERABLY while Paul ran. At first he'd wanted so badly to stop, to take a breath, but he'd hit that point in his run that his breathing was starting to smooth out despite the adrenalin and the physical effort he was making. He knew where he was going, and he knew how to get there, so he let his mind drift.

His thoughts wandered back to what an old girlfriend had told him in high school when she'd tried to get him to compete in track, that he was able to get to a "runner's high" more easily than anyone she'd ever seen. It would make him a great competitor, she said.

Running like this was a mental break for him, his breathing heavy but deep and full, regular in rhythm and replenishing to his system. The rain was merely showering him, sweeping across his face. He had a vague sense of going home.

Oh, right, he thought. *I am going home.*

The voices behind him had faded. Paul figured that none of them had been able to keep up with him. He was loping now, running the streets he knew so well. Church to Sixth to Commerce to Fourth. Few pedestrians were on the streets. He ran past the jammed traffic and the high water at the curbs, ignoring the sloshing of his sneakers, heading toward the Hilton Hotel, then the Schermerhorn, taking the walkway to the pedestrian bridge over the Cumberland. He could see the Cumberland's brown water rising over its banks, higher than he'd ever seen. But the bridge, the bridge was safe. He just needed to get over the river and onto the street on the other side. He'd be back at the Crystal before he knew it and into the hall, up the stairs and into his room, door locked, before any of them could catch up, even Sailor.

And only Sailor knew where Paul lived. Sailor would find him. Later. They'd deal with the mandolin. Later. For now, he was certain that Sailor was trying to lead the others away, to give Paul a chance to disappear with the mandolin.

Paul saw the Schermerhorn, then the bridge. The river was swollen out over its banks, covering everything near it, but he was safe on the bridge. And across the river was home.

He was hit from behind with what felt like a large, heavy bag of clothes. He lost his balance, tumbling forward, the mandolin case in front of him. He didn't want to land on it, he didn't want to break it, and he didn't want to get hurt by it. He jerked his arm away from his body so that the mandolin case whipped to one side.

Paul felt like a projectile, shooting over the walkway. In those few seconds of being airborne, he knew that coming down was going to hurt. He knew he would be brush-burned and possibly broken in places. Still, he flew. Then he hit the ground and slid forward flat on his chest and legs and arms, the case flung out to the right. His cramped fingers released the case, and he watched it skitter across the concrete. Paul screamed in pain as he felt his assailant's boot connect with his arm. Then he saw the man's other foot clip the mandolin case.

A few feet away from him on the bridge, the mandolin case's latches hit the concrete just so. They clicked open. The mandolin popped out of the case and slid close to the bridge's railing. If it went past the bottom lip, it would surely end up in the Cumberland. Paul screamed louder.

———•———

Olivia and Dodd came out of the Crystal Hotel disappointed. No Paul Pratt. Ethel, the manager of the building, was loath to let them into Pratt's apartment, even after Dodd showed his ID. If anything, it made Ethel even less inclined to cooperate. Olivia had the feeling Pratt wasn't the only questionable tenant in the building. Under Ethel's watchful gaze, they looked around, then thanked her and left.

As they came out of the front doors, Olivia marveled again that this eyesore of a hotel was still here.

In more favorable weather, this location would be beautiful. You can see the Cumberland in all its glory, backed by the bustling downtown of the city, with its distinctive towers and — Wait, what's that?

On the pedestrian bridge, Olivia could see a slender man in a black hoodie running at high speed toward them, holding a small, rounded case in his right hand. He was followed by another man, this one in a colorful silk bomber-style jacket, who appeared to be gaining ground on him. Behind the second man, further away and less clear to Olivia was a third man in a bedraggled suit and, following him, a woman in dark clothes who was shouting and waving her arms. Her long braid swung back and forth in the air as she ran.

It only took Olivia a moment to realize that the man with the case was Paul Pratt.

"There he is!" she shouted and pointed to Dodd and the two of them took off running toward the bridge.

As she ran, she saw Silk Jacket throw himself at Pratt's back to make him fall. Pratt flew through the air and landed face-down on the middle of the pavement. The man in the silk jacket had momentum. He flew forward toward Pratt. His legs tangled and his foot caught under Pratt's arm. His next step kicked the mandolin case further across the pavement.

The mandolin case skated away and popped open. The instrument inside slid even further away from Pratt and came to rest near the edge of the bridge.

"No!" Olivia yelled.

Silk Jacket's forward motion carried him over Pratt, into the air, and to Olivia's horror, over the railing of the bridge. His arms paddled as though he was trying to stop his fall, but to no avail. Her eyes followed him into the angry churn of the water. She could hear him screaming all the way down until he hit the surface.

His screams would haunt her dreams.

She and Dodd were still running. She watched as the man in the suit finally got close enough to throw himself over the mandolin as if protecting it with his body. The woman with the braid jumped on top of the man and tried to choke him.

The man protecting the mandolin jerked hard and turned over to free himself. The woman took advantage of his shift and threw a hard punch to his face. His head snapped to one side, and he flopped back onto the pavement. She jumped up, grabbed the mandolin, and shoved it back into its case. She maneuvered the case into her backpack and shouldered it in a quick movement, then turned around, and ran back the way she came.

Olivia and Dodd were on the bridge now. As they got closer to the group, Olivia called to Dodd, "Take the guys. One of them is Pratt. I'll go after the woman."

Dodd veered toward the men. Olivia gave chase as best she could but realized even before she crossed the bridge that she was no match for the lithe woman with the substantial lead. She had completely disappeared from Olivia's view.

Olivia returned to Dodd, who was talking with the two men. Still panting heavily, she stood next to Paul Pratt, whose face was bruised and bleeding. He seemed to be in shock, but not badly hurt otherwise. Mostly he was brush burned and the bleeding from his cheekbones and forehead was superficial, but she knew he should have some medical attention.

The man in the suit introduced himself as Sailor Lang, another name familiar to the Task Force. He didn't appear to be in shock or even seriously hurt by the punch to the jaw, but he was concerned for Pratt, who he said was a friend.

"What about the guy who went over the bridge?" Dodd asked.

"Don't know. Don't care," Lang said. "He was with Suzume. He threatened us. If she wasn't so greedy, we could have worked this out."

"The woman is Suzume?" asked Olivia.

"Yeah."

"Kojima?"

"Yeah."

"I'd better call this in," Dodd said.

The four of them walked toward the Crystal Hotel, where Dodd had left the car.

CHAPTER 48

Athenian Towers
Nashville, TN
Saturday, May 1, 2010
3:40 P.M.

FROM THE BACK SEAT OF PAIGE'S HONDA CIVIC, Paige fussed at Valerie about asking Rocky to drive her car. She had gotten over the initial shock of her sister's kidnapping and now was simply angry. "I don't know why you don't just let me drive," she said.

"Do you know where KH Precision Machine is?" Valerie asked.

"No." Paige wrinkled her nose. "Why would I?"

"Oh, I don't know, because you live here, and we don't?" Rocky said. Rocky had already taken her spot behind the wheel and was just waiting for Valerie's next instruction.

Valerie fiddled with the car's GPS, which recognized the company name. "Rocky's good at driving under pressure." Valerie couldn't believe she was defending Rocky's driving, but it was an asset now.

The car leapt forward at Rocky's touch. Valerie recognized Rocky's grin. *She likes the car. Good.*

Paige fumed in the back seat, muttering to herself. "This is nuts!" Valerie heard her say to the window. "We have nothing to trade for Hayley. How are we going to get her away from Kojima?"

"Not to mention the rest of the band," Valerie added.

"He won't care about them. Just Hayley and that damned mandolin."

Rocky was right where she wanted to be, on the bumper of the car in front of them. "Hey, he's going to have to give up all of them, not just Hayley," she said. She made a quick left turn where a street was blocked and immediately drove into water that lifted the car slightly, making all of them go silent. When Rocky got the car back onto solid ground safely, she said, "Well, that was interesting."

Paige immediately continued ranting. "I'm telling you, Kojima won't care. I'm not even sure that Hayley is safe."

"If you don't trust him, why did you decide to work with him?" Valerie asked.

"He paid our bills, bought us publicity, made sure we had plenty of cash to throw around and make people love Hayley again."

"And you didn't think he'd ask for his money back one day? That there was no loophole?"

Paige's face took on a distant look. "I was trying to negotiate like Mama always did."

"And how did that work out for you?" Rocky asked, glancing at her in the rearview mirror.

She pursed her lips. "It worked, at least for a while."

"And how did your mother handle people who wanted more than you could give?" Valerie asked.

"She'd just tell them no. To get lost. In her way."

"Meaning?"

"She was good with a shotgun."

"Oh, yeah, that's great," Rocky snorted. "I'm sure Kojima will be scared if you do that."

"Do you even know how to use a shotgun?" Valerie asked, genuinely curious.

"No. But I know how to give him a piece of my mind. What he's doing is illegal!"

"The man trades in illegal activity," Valerie reminded her. "It's crazy to think you can stop him."

"And you think you can?"

"I know who we're dealing with. I know some of his background. When we get there, let me do the talking," Valerie said. "I need to see what the situation is. Maybe we can string him along until we get the band back."

Rocky glanced at Valerie, then whispered, "You know he'll kill us all if we don't give him the mandolin."

"I know that." Valerie whispered back. She searched her phone and pulled up Olivia's contact information.

———— •●• ————

Olivia wasn't used to being in on the arrest and capture end of police work, so she wasn't thrilled to be riding with Lang and Pratt in the car. Something about having both men in the back seat scared her, even though they didn't strike her as violent. She also knew that there wasn't anything Dodd could do about it short of putting one of them in the trunk.

Sailor Lang sat at the window behind her. Paul Pratt, whose face was a bloody mess, sat by the window behind Dodd. They weren't cuffed and their proximity to each other made her nervous. At least

271

there was a dark metal grill separating the suspects from Dodd and herself.

Olivia's phone buzzed and she pulled it out. She had a text message, which she read twice to make sure she was reading it correctly.

"Skip the station, Dodd," Olivia said. "Head for KH Precision Machine, over in the manufacturing district."

"What? Why?"

"I just got a text from Valerie. She and Rocky and Paige are headed there. Hoshi Kojima kidnapped Hayley and the band."

"What?" Dodd gasped. Shaking his head, he accelerated and turned on the siren.

When Rocky pulled into the KH Precision Machine parking lot, Valerie saw trucks lined up in the lot, but she was more interested in the three people standing in the rain, looking at the river. The three turned at the sight of the car and two of them started running toward the women, waving their arms.

"Go away!" the younger man yelled. "Get out of here!"

Rocky stopped the car and got out. "You called us here. Now you want us to go?"

"Yes!" the man shouted, "You've got to go!" the man started pushing Rocky, trying to shove her back into the car. Rocky pushed right back until the older man, the one with a nasty scar on his cheek, pulled him away from her.

Valerie jumped out of the car. "Where's Hayley Hopkins?" she demanded, looking at the older man.

"Out of my hands," he said and turned his head to face the corner of the parking lot, where the third man stood watching the van bob in the water.

Paige was out of the car now, too. "Where's my sister?" she screamed, pounding the older man with her fists. "What have you done with her!"

"I believe they're still alive. In that van. For now."

They all turned to look at the van. The back end of the van sank lower than the cab, a large metal cookie being dunked in the river. Waves washed over its back wheels, but the cab floated high, its doors not touching the water. Yet.

Valerie thought she was about to faint, but she saw Rocky take off, running toward the van as fast as she could. Valerie snapped herself out of the dizziness she felt and set off after Rocky.

Rocky had run past all the trucks and was at the far end of the parking lot now. The man watching the van sink moved toward her, as if to stop her. She stopped running and sized up the situation. As Valerie caught up to her, Rocky said, "Look, they're stuck on that tree trunk."

Sure enough, the van was caught in the limbs of a downed tree, keeping it, at least for the moment, from floating along with the current.

The man came toward them, glowering. Rocky ignored him and kicked off her boots.

"What are you doing?" Valerie screamed at her.

"I'm going out there. The boots will just weigh me down."

"You're crazy!"

"As you've always known." Rocky grinned up at her for one millisecond, then hugged her hard.

"In case I don't make it back," she said.

Rocky turned and ran through the grass at the edge of the parking lot to get to the flooded riverbank. She waded into the water that had spilled over the bank and flowed into the grass.

"Stay away from us!" Valerie yelled at the man who was working his way toward them. Unsure of what he was doing, Valerie's eyes shifted from Rocky to the man and back again.

Rocky made her way to the tree trunk, root end sunk partially in the mud of the bank. She crawled up onto the trunk, steadying herself with the tree's water-slicked branches. Carefully, one step at a time, she moved closer to the van. She called out and immediately heard pounding and screaming, both male and female.

Rocky turned back to Valerie, waved, and gave her a thumbs-up.

"Well, you're going to need some help," Valerie yelled aloud, to herself as much as Rocky, who was too far away to hear. Valerie kicked off her own sneakers and headed across the grass, still glancing over at the menacing man on what was left of the parking lot.

At the riverbank she felt the weight of the water as it was fully absorbed into her jeans. It felt different from being rained on, like a vortex sucking at her legs. As Rocky had done, she made her way holding onto branches of the tree until she could pull herself up onto the trunk. The water was up to her thighs by then. She held on tight to one of the limbs and pulled herself up out of the water and the muck beneath it.

"Thought you'd never get here, Boss," Rocky called to her as Valerie got closer.

"Don't call me..." she started to say but stopped when she heard what she was sure was Mark's voice.

CHAPTER 49

A tree trunk near KH Precision Machine
Nashville, TN
Saturday, May 1, 2010
3:50 P.M.

"WE CAN'T OPEN THE DOORS," Mark called out slowly, word by word. "We need a crowbar!"

Valerie was on the tree trunk with Rocky now, edging her way closer to the van. At first, she was afraid the tree trunk would turn and flip them off its surface, but the force of the water combined with the van seemed to have pushed it deep into the mud. It felt solid under her feet, a feeling she was not prepared to trust since the water ran fast and choppy around them. The van wiggled in the water every few minutes, not as stable as the tree trunk. The guys were probably moving around inside the back of the van.

"We've got to get them out," Valerie called to Rocky. "The van could break loose at any time."

"I'm going to jump onto it," Rocky said.

No, no, don't do that, Valerie thought, but instead she yelled, "Be careful!"

Rocky stood up on the trunk and gauged the distance. Then she jumped, scrabbling her fingers against the van's roof for a handhold. The force of her landing caused everyone inside to yell when the van shifted.

Rocky latched onto the rain channel at the top of the windshield. She pulled herself onto the roof of the cab and looked into the cab upside down.

Hayley screamed in surprise, then burst out with nervous laughter. She stopped immediately.

Rocky looked at Hayley, then back at Valerie. "Hayley's in the cab. She's tied to the steering wheel." Rocky looked inside the cab again, cupping one hand around her face to see better. "Hayley, what shoes are you wearing?"

"Boots," Hayley said, her voice muted by the glass. She shifted in the seat, pulling up one leg so Rocky could see her foot. She was wearing pointy-toed, high heeled boots, one of her many pairs coated with rhinestones.

"Good," Rocky said. "Can you turn yourself around, so your feet are near the driver's side door?"

Hayley twisted herself around, fighting the rope that held her to the wheel. Although she was small, the van's weight shifted slightly in the water as she moved. Rocky scrambled to hold on. Again, the voices in the back of the van called out.

Valerie watched Rocky. She shivered, knowing that at any moment Rocky could lose her grip and slide into the brown water swirling around them. How deep was it here? Impossible to tell. How Rocky was holding on to the cab's roof was a mystery to her.

The rain was starting to pick up again. If the Cumberland rose much more, the van was liable to pull away from the trunk and float downstream. Or sink, Valerie wasn't sure which. She heard Rocky talk to Hayley again.

"Okay, now straighten out your legs," Rocky said.

"Like this?" Hayley responded, barely audible through the glass.

"Right. Now straighten your arms," Rocky told Hayley. "Good. Now, see if you can hit the door's latch with your boot."

Inside the cab, Hayley must have understood what Rocky meant, and kicked at the door. She missed several times. Valerie heard her boots hitting the window and saw the van bounce slightly. Rocky called out to her, "Don't kick, Hayley. Use the toe of your boot and pull."

The driver's side door opened a sliver.

"I did it! I did it!" Valerie heard Hayley scream in surprise, her voice suddenly clear through the open door.

"That's terrific, Hayley." Rocky responded calmly. "Now, straighten your legs and move as far away from the door as you can."

Rocky took a deep breath. Now it was her turn. She sized up the door and pushed it from the top, trying to open it further. When it opened, it only opened a few inches more. It was stuck against the upper limbs of the tree.

Rocky looked over at Valerie, who was very close to her but still on the tree trunk.

"You're doing great!" Valerie encouraged her. "Can you get in?"

"I don't think that I can fit in the door," Rocky admitted. "I'm too wide."

Valerie saw Rocky's cheeks flush and felt a wave of sympathy wash over her. Rocky was so close to getting into the cab.

They locked eyes. Valerie suddenly realized what Rocky wanted. She nodded silently and carefully stood up on the tree trunk.

I'll only have one shot at this. I'd better get it right.

As Dodd fit the two men into the back of his car, Olivia took a quick look at the river flowing under the pedestrian bridge, hoping to see someone paddling in the water, perhaps crawling up the bank. No luck.

"Did you tell the bureau about the guy in the water?" she asked Dodd as she got into the car.

"Yes. They'll look into it."

"Let's hope they find him," Olivia sighed. "Maybe even alive." From Dodd's silence, she guessed that wasn't going to happen. Her phone buzzed and she pulled it out of her pocket to see who was calling.

Banjo Bob?

"Bob?" she said.

"Hey, Olivia. I just saw something. You told me to call."

"What'd you see?"

"Some woman running down Broadway from Fourth Street. She was really moving. Had a backpack on her back with part of an instrument case poking out the top. She ran right past me and jumped into a car and took off."

Olivia brightened considerably. Dodd glanced at her but tried to stay focused on driving.

"Any idea who she is?"

"No, but it just didn't look right."

"Okay, thanks for letting me know." Olivia was frantically motioning to Dodd that she had information for him.

"One more thing," Bob added. "The edge of the case, at least the part that I could see, had some big letters on the side. "H-O-P-K, then I couldn't see the rest. But I've seen pictures of that case. I think it belongs to Hayley Hopkins. I know what Hayley looks like, and that wasn't her."

"Small woman, dark hair braided down her back?"

"That's the one."

"What kind of car?"

"Small. Sports car. Low to the ground. Bright red."

Ah, jeez, could she make herself any more conspicuous?

"Thank you, Bob. I'll talk to you soon."

She hung up and said, "Suzume was just spotted on Lower Broadway. She's driving a red sportscar."

"Are you kidding me?" Dodd asked.

"No," Olivia said.

Dodd turned toward Broadway, calling in the information as he drove.

CHAPTER 50

BRACING HERSELF TO PLUNGE INTO THE RIVER, Valerie stood up on the tree trunk and threw herself toward the van. She didn't make the leap as cleanly as Rocky had. Hayley screamed and male voices clamored as the van shifted. A wave of water washed into the van from Valerie's jump. The front of the van was starting to sink.

Valerie found the door handle of the cab and hung on, her heart racing. She looked up at the cab's roof and saw that at least she didn't knock Rocky off the van. The cab's door was open in front of her but wedged firmly against the tree. Valerie was going to have to use some body English to get in.

Hayley pulled herself as far away from the door as she could to give Valerie room. Valerie maneuvered herself through the door, feeling the weight of her clothes and the extra water she was dumping into the cab. The van bobbed and wobbled. In the back, the guys called out, but their voices sounded less upset and more surprised.

"You okay?" she asked Hayley.

Hayley nodded.

Valerie waited until the van's movement subsided, then looked up at Rocky, staring through the window upside down. "Now what?" Valerie asked.

Hayley spoke up first. "Open the little door and see how the guys are."

Valerie turned to the back wall of the cab and saw the button to press. The door popped open, and she said, "Everybody okay back there?" and a roar of happy male voices greeted her. She felt herself smile, even though she knew there was a lot more to do.

A set of fingers pushed through the open door. *I'd recognize them anywhere,* she thought. So many times, she'd watched him play instruments with those slender, tapered fingers. She reached out to touch them and peered through the slot. In the tiny space behind his hand, she saw tears in Mark's eyes. They looked haunted.

"Can you untie me?" Hayley asked, and Valerie laughed.

"I should have done that first," Valerie said.

"No, I wanted you to check on them. I don't think they have much fresh air back there," Hayley said.

Valerie untied the intricate knots Bana had used on her wrists. Hayley rubbed at the soreness.

"Are you okay?" Valerie asked her.

Hayley nodded. "I am. Let's get the guys out."

"Okay, ladies," Rocky said from the roof. "See if you can find the door release for the back."

Working together, Valerie and Hayley tried several buttons and levers in the cab. Finally Rocky suggested a switch that was on the lower ridge of the driver's door.

"I thought that was for another window," Valerie said, but when she pushed it, she heard the telltale whir of the door being released.

In the back, she heard the guys' excitement turn to fear.

"The door is sliding open," Mark called out.

"It's letting water in!" Valerie was pretty sure that was Des's voice.

"Move up further," suggested Boomer. "Stand on the seat if you have to."

"We're gonna sink!" Des whined.

"No, we're not," said Clay, surprisingly calm. "Take your time and we'll swim out before we sink."

"But I can't swim!" Des said.

Valerie thought she heard Clay mutter "For crying out loud."

"Anyone else in here that can't swim?" Clay asked. When no one else answered, he said, "Pull it together, dude. We'll get each other out of here. The rest of us can swim. We won't leave you behind."

In the distance Valerie heard sirens. She looked up at Rocky, still hanging onto the roof, looking down into the cab at Valerie and Hayley. "What's going on?" Valerie asked.

Rocky looked away from the van for a moment, then looked back inside the cab again. "I think the cavalry just got here. I see lights, lots of lights." She paused. "And when we get home, I'm going on a diet."

———————•◆•———————

Suzume's little red Nissan zoomed into the parking lot. She saw the car following her and guessed that it was an unmarked police car, but she knew her father would protect her from whoever was inside. She missed Ryu, but only a little. Still, it made her very angry that those two stupid thieves were responsible for his accident. She'd have her father see to them later.

She slowed the car when she saw her father standing in the corner of the lot with Bana and his henchman, along with some woman. They were all staring out at the river. As she drove closer to them, she saw the damage to the corner of the parking lot and the van floating on the water.

Finally hearing her engine get closer, her father looked over at her car. Her presence registered with him, and he looked displeased.

He'll feel better when he sees what I've brought him, she thought with satisfaction. She parked and got out, past caring if the rain drenched her.

"What are you doing here?" her father asked.

"I've brought you something," she said.

"Not now, Suzume."

"But it's important."

"I said, not now!"

The unmarked police car pulled up behind her. Her father's scowl grew deeper.

"What have you done?" he asked Suzume.

Dodd got out of the police car and directed his first comment to Kojima.

"What's going on here?"

"This van was parked at the edge of the lot and the river apparently damaged the bank there," Kojima said, waving one arm expansively toward the river. "I have no idea who would be stupid enough to park there."

Olivia was out of the car now. "That's Rocky!" she called to Dodd. "On the roof of the van!"

Dodd squinted through the rain at the van, then back at Kojima. He pulled out his phone and called the bureau.

CHAPTER 51

KH Precision Machine
Nashville, TN
Saturday, May 1, 2010
4:10 P.M.

VALERIE SAT IN THE PROTECTION of the open door of an ambulance, wrapped in a blanket, after being examined by emergency medical technicians. She was soaked through, and her teeth chattered. She wasn't sure how much the blanket helped but it was better than just sitting in the rain and wind in wet clothes.

Rocky had already been released by the medics and she stood next to the ambulance, also wrapped in a blanket, holding an umbrella. It was a laughable effort to protect an already-soaked person from a little more water, but Valerie was in no mood to laugh. She was looking anxiously at the other ambulance, where the band members were taking turns being checked over by another set of paramedics. Mark appeared to be overseeing the process.

So that means he's fine, right?

Olivia came over to check on Valerie and Rocky. She peered inside the ambulance where Paige hovered over Hayley. The paramedics had to twist around Paige to do their job. They were patient with her and didn't force her out into the rain, but they had very little space to work.

"Would it be okay if we take some of these folks into the building over there?" Olivia asked, waving a hand at the KH Precision Machine building.

"That would help us a lot," one of the medics said, adding quickly, "I'm sure it's warmer in there."

"Come on," Olivia said and pointed Rocky and Valerie to the building. "Paige?" she added. "Come on, honey. Hayley's in good hands. She'll be fine. Come with us."

Grudgingly Paige followed them to the lobby of the building. Hoshi, Bana, and the younger man were there, lined up in chairs normally meant for visiting businesspeople, under a police officer's watchful eye. As the women came in, he directed them across the room, away from the three men. Olivia stepped outside to check with Dodd.

Valerie and Rocky stood close together near the reception desk. Paige, glaring at everyone, stood a few feet away. Valerie unexpectedly made eye contact with Kojima. He looked at her sharply. Jutting out his chin, he said, "I know you."

Valerie swallowed. "I don't think so," she said. "But I know your daughter."

"It's your face," Kojima said. "I know your face." Then, very quietly, he added, "The face of a dead woman. Who are you?"

"I'm Valerie Sloan," she said.

Light dawned in his eyes. "Mai-Ling Yoshida's daughter."

"Yes."

"Your mother was lovely," he breathed. Then his eyes sharpened. "She should not have meddled."

Valerie's throat constricted, hearing the threat.

The police officer with Kojima was talking to Olivia. He didn't hear the conversation between Kojima and Valerie. Olivia caught some of it, however, and her expression darkened. The officer told Olivia that his partner was outside helping Dodd with the people in the back of the unmarked car, Sailor Lang and Paul Pratt. The problem, apparently, was Suzume.

He tried to keep his voice down, but everyone in the room had gone silent now, listening to him.

"I understand that the woman is giving Dodd a hard time," the officer said. "She won't answer his questions and keeps asking for 'her property.'"

Valerie saw Kojima wince. His daughter was a handful.

"She probably means the mandolin case," Olivia said.

"You have it?" Paige perked up.

"We do," Olivia replied. "Dodd saw it on Suzume's front seat and put it in his car. She's been screaming ever since."

"Thank goodness! I've got to tell Hayley," she said and headed for the entry door. The police officer stopped her. "Please have a seat, ma'am," he said. "We're trying to gather everyone in here."

"Why don't you sit down on the couch over there?" Olivia suggested. "Hayley will be finished soon, I'm sure. You can talk to her then. In fact, how about if all three of you ladies have a seat there?"

Valerie and Rocky sat down, clinging together as if they were appreciating each other's warmth. Paige joined them, as far to the other end of the couch as she could sit from them.

"Have we determined who fell into the river?" Olivia asked the officer.

"I don't have any information on that," the officer said. He held open the door as Hayley came in, also blanket-wrapped. She immediately went to Paige.

"Thank you for finding me," she wept into Paige's shoulder. "I thought I'd never see you again. Or Justine." Hayley pulled away from her, cheeks wet, and looked around. "Where is Justine?"

"She's at the condo."

"Why didn't she come along?"

"Did you really want her in danger, too?"

"No, I just... I need her."

"You know how that looks, Hayley. How smart is that, to tell everyone you two are a couple? You won't get anywhere in this town if people find out!"

The sisters glared at each other.

"It's always been about my career for you, hasn't it?" Hayley growled. "You don't care at all if I'm happy."

"I made a promise to Mama. I'm just keeping my promise."

"Yeah, to the other person who got all the cash from my career with none of the work," Hayley fumed. "I'm calling Justine." Hayley took out her phone and went into the hallway, away from the crowd in the lobby. Valerie heard Hayley say, "Hey, honey, I'm okay."

Valerie could guess what kind of emotions Justine was feeling. It was the way she felt when she heard Mark's voice in the van while it was still in the water. Tears welled in her eyes.

The rest of the band drifted in, person by person, until they were all there. Des had a bandage on his head, but it was smaller than Valerie expected. Clay and Boomer looked wet and exhausted. They hung close to Des and kept asking if he felt okay.

"Tell us if you feel dizzy or sick," Boomer said. "They said you should tell us right away."

"Don't badger him," Clay said, obviously annoyed. Boomer must have been overdoing it. "He'll let us know."

Luke looked a little shell-shocked and immediately sat down in a chair by the door. Kenny sat down next to him, saying, "I can't believe this happened. I'm just glad to be alive," over and over.

When Mark came in, Valerie stood to go hug him. To her surprise, Paige practically leapt across the room and got to him first.

"How could you let this happen?" Paige assailed him. "How could you let me down like that?" Then she burst into tears and threw her arms around him. "I thought you were dead! I couldn't go on if you were dead!"

Mark looked like he wanted to slide away from her but couldn't. Paige had him fully engulfed. His eyes found Valerie's.

CHAPTER 52

KH Precision Machine
Nashville, TN
Saturday, May 1, 2010
4:25 P.M.

VALERIE'S JAW SAGGED OPEN. She didn't get it until now. Paige's rigidness, her anger at Mark, even at times ignoring him, and her disdain for Valerie. Paige was in love with Mark. Maybe she always had been.

How could I be so clueless?

Rocky clutched at her arm. "Are you okay, Boss?" she asked.

"I think I need to sit down."

Dodd came in with the police officer's partner, as well as Sailor Lang and Suzume.

"Paul's still being examined by the paramedics," Dodd said to Olivia. "They want to take him to the hospital, but he's arguing with them. Most of his damage is surface, I think."

Hoshi exploded when he saw Suzume.

"What did you do this time? Why were the police following you? I knew you would get into trouble!" he shouted and stood up as if to go after her.

Dodd put out his arm, stopping Hoshi. "That may be true, but there is nothing you are going to do about it," he said, forcing Hoshi back into his chair.

Hoshi glared first at Dodd, then at his daughter. "You are going to pay for this!"

"But Daddy," Suzume whined in her unpleasant nasal voice, "I got you the mandolin! These assholes won't give it back to me."

Dodd's eyebrows shot up and Olivia laughed, counting heads, thinking of all the witnesses their lawyers could call.

"So, where is this mandolin?" Hoshi spat at her. "I see no mandolin."

"It's... It's..." Suzume looked helplessly at Sailor, who just shook his head.

"I don't know why you're looking at me," Sailor said. "I don't know anything about a mandolin."

Olivia laughed again. *This from the man who jumped all over it on the pedestrian bridge. This is one thief who is well-trained in evading charges.* But she had a feeling that she could still manage to build a case, especially since the evidence that had been in Paul Pratt's hands was now in the trunk of Dodd's unmarked car.

"So, there was a mandolin?" Kojima asked Dodd. "Could I at least see it? Assuming you actually have it, of course." He looked triumphant when he added, "I would not be surprised if what my daughter thinks she found is some sort of fake."

Dodd looked suspicious but Olivia agreed. "Sure. Why not? We've got the expert here to identify it."

Mark peeled Paige's arms away from him and nodded his assent. Paige looked hurt.

Dodd braved the rain again and went to the unmarked car. He returned, toting the case into the lobby. The Nashville sticker and the name "Hopkins" were clearly visible on the side. He handed the case to Mark, who placed it on the waiting room's coffee table. He knelt on the floor with the case in front of him.

Everyone leaned in together to peer at the case. When Mark clicked open the latches and lifted the top, the entire group seemed to sigh as they saw the instrument in person.

Yep, Olivia thought. *Just as ruined as the pictures looked.*

Mark pulled the instrument from the case and checked it over.

"This is it. Definitely." He looked at Olivia. "It needs to be dried out. And then it should be checked thoroughly. The case, too." He pulled his hand away from the damp interior.

Kojima held out his hands as if to touch the mandolin, but Dodd stopped him again. "Looking's okay. Touching is not," Dodd told him.

Kojima looked crushed, but only for a moment. His disappointment turned to anger directed at Suzume. "You will never be part of the family! I will see to that!"

Dodd looked back and forth between Hoshi and Suzume. "The family? Isn't she your daughter?"

"In name only," Kojima grumbled. "She will never be part of the business."

"The family business?" Dodd asked.

"Yes," Hoshi snapped.

"Oh, the shipping-stolen-goods-to-other-countries business?" Olivia asked.

Hoshi looked like he wanted to swallow his tongue. Suzume was silent and looked at the floor. Bana and his young assistant looked away from Hoshi, careful not to meet anyone's eyes.

The rain had gotten heavier again, pounding the pavement outside KH Precision Machine. Clouds roiled overhead. The van, cab roof still visible in the Cumberland River, had taken on enough water to be all but submerged. A few workmen had arrived with a tow truck to pull it back up onto the parking lot. Covered head to toe in wet-weather gear, they stood on the bank, pointing and discussing, heedless of the rain.

Satisfied that they had done all they could do, the paramedics drove away. Olivia, Dodd, and the two police officers assisting them herded everyone in custody out of the lobby and into vehicles to go to the police station.

As they were leaving, Hoshi called to Valerie, "I will see you again, daughter of Mai-Ling. You and I have unfinished business."

Valerie stared back at him. "Yes, we do," she said. Her mother's words echoed in her head. *Once you are targeted, you never forget. And every time it happens, you feel worse. It gets harder and harder to just let it go. It's the weight of being different.* Was that why her mother got involved with Hoshi Kojima? And now, was that Valerie's burden to bear as well?

Rocky offered to drive Paige's car to take Valerie, Paige, and Hayley to the condo. There, she said, she would change into dry clothes and drive back and forth to deliver all the guys to the condo, too.

Mark opted to return with the rest of the band. Valerie suspected he didn't want to be in the same car with Paige, who was still struggling to get over her feelings for him.

CHAPTER 53

BNA/Nashville International Airport
Nashville, TN
Wednesday, May 5, 2010
11:00 A.M.

BY WEDNESDAY THE AIRPORTS were scheduling flights again. Valerie, Rocky, and Mark got seats on the same flight, although not together. When they touched down in Philadelphia, they prepared to go their separate ways, Valerie and Rocky to Chestnut Hill, Mark to Phoenixville.

Valerie felt a tug of regret when Mark said he had to check in with Bic about the shop. She would have liked to talk with him, without Rocky, without working a case, and without worries about what anyone else might think.

"We need to talk," Valerie told him.

"I know," Mark nodded. "But Bic texted me. There's work waiting for me."

Valerie suspected there would always be work waiting for him.

Mark saw the expression on her face and lifted her chin so her eyes would meet his. "Let me check in with him and see where things stand. I'll call you tonight."

"Okay. How soon do you have to go back for the tour?"

"I told Hayley I was going home and not coming back. She's going to have to do the tour without me."

"Really?"

"Yes. It's time to get back to my real world, the one that means something to me. Nashville is Hayley's world. She can have it."

They hugged as Mark got into his cab. Just before he closed the door, he said, "Love you, Valerie."

"Love you, too," Valerie said. She waved as the cab negotiated the heavy traffic and watched Mark's face at the cab's window, his hand pressed flat on it, until the cab faded into the distance.

Behind her, Rocky asked, "You okay, Boss?"

At first Valerie couldn't answer her. But finally, she said, "Take me home, Rocky."

The car was still running, Rocky at the wheel. Valerie looked out the passenger side window at the house that had always been her home and thought about her history. Toddler, grade school, high school, her mother's death. The life, such as it was, that came after. Struggling with memories, with jobs, with other people. This home was always her sanctuary.

It was painful, thinking about having to leave this place.

"Do you want me to come in with you?" Rocky finally asked. "Maybe hang out for a while?"

Valerie put her hand on Rocky's shoulder.

"Do you know how good a friend you are?"

"Yes," Rocky bobbed her head up and down. "Of course, I do. And do you know how good a Boss you are?"

Valerie pursed her lips to keep from laughing. "Go home. You need some rest. I'll see you in the morning."

"I'll be here." Rocky said. "I'll pick you up at 8:00."

<hr>

Inside the door, Valerie sat her suitcase on the floor and looked around the room. She saw the furniture her parents had collected, the items that marked events in their lives, the things that still meant so much to her dad. And to her. The violin, the baby grand piano, the sheers at each window, the open and airy rooms.

She stuck her head inside her workroom, with its neat rows of bottles and cloths, horsehair and strings, and her beloved tools. The current crop of violins that she had in various stages of repair and refinishing were on stands or flat on her worktable. The instruments for sale hung on display hooks around the room.

Today she saw everything with new eyes.

Nothing had changed. Not yet. But Barbara was waiting in the wings, waiting to enter her father's life. And Valerie's. It would be awkward for a little while, until they both found a safe footing around each other. They'd get along, there was no doubt.

After all, Valerie liked Barbara, even admired her. Barbara had raised her kids alone after her husband died when she was in her thirties. She opened the Inn on her own. She made it a success. She was a tough woman but a loving one. And she loved Valerie's dad. The tone of her voice, the little touches of her hand on his arm, the sparkle in her eyes when she looked at him.

But Barbara's arrival here meant changes. Big ones.

After years of trying to keep everything the same, or close to the same as when her mother was alive, Valerie realized that everyone was right. Her dad, Rocky, even Mark had said that she had to live her own life, that she had to stop worrying about her dad and worry about herself instead.

She picked up her suitcase to take it to her childhood bedroom on the second floor.

CHAPTER 54

Maggie's Pub
Philadelphia, PA
Friday, May 7, 2010
5:00 P.M.

AS HARRY PROMISED, on Friday night, he, Valerie, and Rocky lined up at the bar of Maggie's Pub, drinking beers and waiting for cheesesteaks. Even though Harry had heard the Nashville story multiple times since they got back, Valerie and Rocky had talked to Olivia that afternoon and updated Harry.

"So, let me see if I have it all straight," Harry said and started counting on his fingers. "Theft, kidnapping..."

"Corruption for Hoshi Kojima, aggravated assault for Suzume..." Rocky added.

"And according to Olivia, they'll add receiving stolen goods charges for Suzume, too," Valerie said.

Harry sipped his beer and shook his head. "That Kojima is one foolish man."

"And his daughter is one foolish woman," Rocky said. "Obviously she learned that from her father."

"It's the family business, remember?" Valerie said. "You know, it sounded like he wasn't even thinking about stealing the mandolin at first. He made a deal with Paige to have Hayley play at the hotel so he could see the mandolin up close. But he was so smitten with the idea of having it in his grasp that when the flood came and Hayley refused to play, he imploded. He was so desperate to have it."

"It never ceases to amaze me that people with money and resources cross the line all the time. Can't they be happy with doing things legally?" Rocky mused.

Harry laughed. "Ever the optimist."

"Me?" Rocky said. "Hardly. My job is to expect the worst, right, Boss?" She grinned and craned around Harry to look at Valerie. "And right now, I expect my Boss to yell at me for calling her 'Boss.'"

"Good call," Valerie said as Mark slid onto the stool next to her. She felt herself blush. "Hi, honey," she said.

"Hi," he said, kissing her cheek gently. "I love Friday night happy hour at Maggie's. And Bic was thrilled to take over for the evening. The shop is only open till seven tonight." A beer slid over the bar to Mark from Harry's direction. "I'm not so sure he's happy I'm back. I think he liked running the store on his own."

"Just don't ask him to do paperwork, right?" laughed Rocky.

"Right."

"Cheesesteak okay for you?" Harry asked. He jerked his thumbs at Rocky and Valerie on either side of him. "I'm so happy to have these two back, I'll buy one for you, too."

"Sounds great," Mark said. "I'm hungry."

"Good." Harry flagged the waitress and told her. He turned back to Mark. "And welcome back to you, too," Harry said, his mustache twitching. "Enjoy Nashville?"

"Hmm. Interesting question," Mark said. "I would have enjoyed it more without the flood. And the kidnapping." He appeared to consider it a little more. "Let's just say I'm really glad to be back in Philly, too," he said and squeezed Valerie's arm.

As their happy hour broke up, Mark offered Valerie a ride so Rocky could go straight home. They were both quiet on the drive to Valerie's house, lost in their own thoughts. After Mark pulled into the gravel parking area next to the house, they sat in his truck, holding hands. They were there long enough for his windows to start fogging.

"We haven't talked much about moving in together since we came home," Mark said.

"We've talked," she said. "Maybe not as much as we'd like, but we both had jobs to get back to, things to do."

"I know, but we should start looking for a place again."

"I'd like that."

"Nashville really opened my eyes," Mark said. "I know I didn't act the way I do here. Something about the atmosphere, the memories. It brought out the worst in me." He gazed out of the window. "The way those guys grabbed us. In the van, I thought I was gonna die. Without even seeing you." He swallowed hard. "I realized how much you mean to me, how much I want to be with you. I know we've been talking about living together for a while, but when you put off telling your dad, I wasn't sure you really wanted to move in with me."

Valerie was silent. He was right. She hadn't been sure. But things were different now. And yet, living together seemed like such a huge idea to her.

"Look," Mark went on, "I know we have to figure things out. It means finding a place close to the shop, but close to your dad, too."

"Well, about that," she said. "Dad and Barbara are getting married."

Mark's eyebrows shot up and his mouth dropped open. "When did this happen?"

"While we were in Nashville."

"Why didn't you tell me?"

"There wasn't a good time. But I'm telling you now."

Mark's eyes searched her face. "How do you feel about it?"

"I think it's good for them." Valerie took a deep breath. "But I think that maybe this isn't a good time for us to be making such big changes."

Mark sat back, looking at her as though she'd struck him. "What are you saying?" he asked. "You don't want to live with me?"

"No, no, I just need a little more time. Let me talk to my dad, get a better idea of what he needs from me."

Mark blinked at her. "Valerie, your dad has to live his own life. You can't live it for him. And you can't let his need for you to be here keep you from living yours."

"I know," she said. "I'm not even sure he will need me here. But I have to work that out with him first."

RETURN TO NASHVILLE

CHAPTER 55

Grand Ole Opry House
Nashville, Tennessee
Tuesday, September 28, 2010
3:00 P.M.

THERE WAS AN AIR OF EXCITEMENT all around the Grand Old Opry House that Tuesday afternoon. Fans gathered outside on the walkways and patio areas, watching for familiar faces. The buzz of voices and flurry of activity lifted Valerie's heart. The Opry House was open again!

With the VIP passes that Hayley provided them, Valerie, Rocky, and Mark followed other country music fans into the building and headed toward the stage to see the early sound checks. They sat in the front pew of the audience area, watching the beaming faces of the performers and technicians as they worked. It was a glorious day for them, too, even more than for the fans, since they considered the Opry their mother church, their home.

Hayley and The Storm arrived. During the technical check, their start was tentative, but it didn't take them long to find their rhythm and become the band that people enjoyed hearing. They played enough to get their footing, and then moved out to let the next act prepare.

Just off stage left, Justine met Hayley and gave her a hug. Justine gestured toward them, and Hayley saw them and waved. When Hayley came over to talk to them, Valerie saw Paige look out from the curtains, frown, and disappear backstage.

"I am so glad y'all could make it," Hayley said, and the sentiment seemed genuine. She hugged Mark first, then Valerie, Rocky, and Olivia. "I know you had to make special arrangements."

"Not a problem, thanks to Olivia," Valerie told her. "We really wanted to see this happen, to see you play here."

"This isn't exactly the concert I pictured doing in May," Hayley said. "I don't know what my daddy would think about all this," she added, sweeping her arm across the entire room, "but something tells me he would enjoy it. Especially the part about him. Oh, and the Opry being open again, of course!"

"Are they going to induct him tonight?" Rocky asked. "That's what we heard."

"Well, the official announcement is tonight but the actual induction will happen in a few weeks. And even though the Museum has had the mandolin for a while, I got it back today for the concert. The official transfer of it to the Hall of Fame will happen tonight, too. Are you sure you don't want to join us, Mark?"

"No, Hayley, I'll be just fine, watching."

"Too bad."

A deep, familiar voice boomed out of the microphones, snatching Rocky's attention. "Ooh, Valerie, look! There's Randall Barlow! I've got to go talk to him." She snaked out of her seat in the pew and headed toward the stage to wait for him to finish his sound check.

Valerie laughed, "Oh, that Rocky!" she said, and Hayley smiled.

"Barlow's a nice boy. He's been opening for us some places we've played. He's gonna have a good career." Hayley's eyes went back to Rocky standing on the side of the stage. "Don't think he's looking to settle down anytime soon, though."

"Don't worry, neither is she," Valerie said. "Hey, isn't that Banjo Bob over there?" She saw his cowboy hat tilting up and down while he talked to one of the musicians who had stepped off the stage.

Olivia saw him, too, and said, "Yes, I got him a ticket. I wasn't sure he'd spend the money. I consider it a little perk for helping me out a few times. Looks like he took advantage of it. Think I'll go say hello."

"Always good to see the locals here," Hayley said as Olivia headed for Bob. "I tried to get Bob to play with us, but he turned me down."

They watched Olivia and Bob chat near the stage. Mark asked Hayley, "How's Paige?"

Valerie felt the air around her go cold.

"Angry, honey. She knows she lost." Hayley said. "But it sure has taken her a long time to realize it."

Mark shook his head. "There was nothing for her to win. Is that why she's not here?"

"Oh, she's here, but I don't think she'll be coming out to talk to you."

Valerie glanced at Mark. He had been forcing himself to be cheerful in case he had to face Paige, and now his face changed, collapsed subtly.

"It's probably for the best," he said and went back to watching Rocky and Randall. "Seeing Paige just opens old wounds." He put his arm around Valerie and hugged her.

"I'd better get going," Hayley excused herself. "I have a lot to do yet this afternoon, some press and whatnot. Will I see you tonight?"

"Of course," Mark and Valerie said in unison.

THE MYTH, THE WOMAN, THE MANDOLIN

Grand Ole Opry House
Nashville, Tennessee
Tuesday, September 28, 2010
9:00 P.M.

THE GRAND OLE OPRY HOUSE had been closed for repairs for five months since the flood. During those months, the Opry's radio show broadcast from various venues around the city, mindful that the show truly must go on, but tonight the House itself was finally open again.

After Brad Paisley and Little Jimmie Dickens opened the show, an all-star cast played and sang "Will the Circle Be Unbroken." The performers and their bands followed with their short sets, one by one. Later in the show, Randall Barlow and Custom Made performed their set, including his recent hit "Women Like Wine."

Then Hayley Hopkins stepped out onto the smooth wooden boards of the stage, boots clicking, and positioned herself. She stood on the white oak and maple circle of wood taken from the Ryman Auditorium in 1974 when the Opry was moved to this location. She rooted herself in front of the microphone, holding her daddy's mandolin in her hands. She'd borrowed it back from the Country Music Hall of Fame to play for this special night, celebrating The Grand Ole Opry House's reopening and her daddy's upcoming induction into the Country Music Hall of Fame.

At first, she heard just a few people clapping at the front of the house but when the house lights came down and the spotlight hit her, applause swelled as people recognized her on stage.

In a quiet drawl she said, "Good evening, y'all," drawing out the syllables as though she had all the time in the world. She felt her father's hand on her shoulder and took a deep breath. "I'm Hayley Hopkins, Charley Hopkins' daughter." The crowd exploded with more applause and shouts. "Here's a song I think you'll remember. It's one my daddy loved."

She positioned her hands on the strings of the mandolin and played the intro to "Ashes of Love."

The End

APPENDIX: THE ORIGINAL SONGS

Never Be As Good As You
WORDS AND MUSIC BY BILL NORK

You always taught me right from wrong
Taught me to sing a Country song
Gave me hope when I was in despair
All my life I knew you'd always be there

Now I'm standin' in your shoes
Tryin' to sing these lonesome blues
But no matter what I do
I'll never, never, never, never
Never be as good as you

So many roads I've travelled down
Searching for that high lonesome sound
But you kept calling me home
I knew I had to make it on my own

Now I'm standin' in your shoes
Tryin' to sing these lonesome blues
But no matter what I do
I'll never, never, never, never
Never be as good as you

Now that you're gone I can't forget
That I'll always be in your debt
A debt I can never repay
Except to love you more and more every day

Now I'm standin' in your shoes
Tryin' to lose these lonesome blues
But no matter what I do
I'll never, never, never, never
Never be as good as you

Women Like Wine
WORDS AND MUSIC BY BILL NORK

I like football, she likes shoes
I like country, she likes the blues
Every February she's my funny Valentine
Forget the candy and the flowers cause
Women like wine

Chardonnay, Cabernet
Any kind is ok
Any time of the day
Women like wine

When we go to the cabin
We always stop at the store
Buy a couple bottles
And a couple bottles more
I said we're just goin' for the weekend
She said that'll do just fine
Cause everybody knows
Women like wine

Chardonnay, Cabernet
Any kind is ok
Any time of the day
Women like wine

[Bridge]
She goes to karaoke and sings Purple Rain
But she never gets behind the wheel when she's feelin' no pain

Chardonnay, Cabernet
Any kind is ok
Any time of the day
Women like wine

AUTHOR BIO

SANDY NORK is the author of the Valerie Sloan crime novels set in the world. of insurance investigation of musical instruments. After a varied career in business, Sandy was a librarian in Pennsylvania for 23 years at both the local and state level. She retired from libraries to spend more time with her fictional characters. She lives in the Harrisburg area with her musician husband and his collection of guitars. You can find out more about her at sandynork.com.

ACKNOWLEDGMENTS

THANKS TO MY HUSBAND BILL, my inspiration, my favorite musician, and my biggest fan. Your love of bluegrass and country music, as well as Nashville, is infectious and your insights on music are invaluable. You have been gracious enough to put up with me no matter how the writing is going. Once again, this book is as much yours as it is mine.

Thanks to all the people who have encouraged me along the way: Don Helin, Dennis Royer, Dave Tamanini, Joel Burcat, Tory Gates, Gina Napoli, and Bill and Teresa Peschel; The 4th Wednesday Critique Group (especially Carrie Jacobs & Tina Crone, who always have a space for me at the table, whether online or in person); Ramona's Sprint Club (Wende Dikec and so many others there who unknowingly keep me afloat during the day); the Night Owl Writers (Fritz Roberts, Babs Mountjoy and all the crew who keep me on track at night); and all my friends and mentors at Pennwriters (including my heroes, Annette Dashofy, Nancy Martin, Susan Meier, Hilary Hauck, D.J. Stevenson among others).

Thanks to The Olde Orchard Hill Breakfast Club and The Soft Addiction Round Table (SART) who constantly remind me that readers are waiting. Your curiosity and enthusiasm keep me going.

Thanks also to all the people who helped with my research: Tom Cook, who provided fascinating historical and technical information about the mandolin; Mike Slusser, who inspired me with his life in Nashville; Bill DeMain and his Walkin' Nashville tour, who showed me a side of Nashville I never would have seen on my own; and of course the reference librarians at the Nashville Public Library, who assisted with my research on the 2010 Nashville flood. No book gets written without the help of librarians!

For the original music in this book, I'd like to thank not only the composer Bill Nork but also Teresa Gonzalez for her vocals on Never Be As Good As You and Ronnie Rhoads and Big Riff Studios for producing Women Like Wine. These songs really came to life just as I'd imagined them! The recorded versions can be found at sandynork.com.

Thanks to Beth Dorward, my editor at Reedsy, who helped me wrangle these words into a book. As always, your help was invaluable.

Thanks to Tara Mayberry at Teaberry Creative, for once again making the cover and interior look so beautiful. You are so talented!

And heartfelt thanks to all the readers of the first book in the series, *Special Risk*, especially those who sent me your reviews and comments. I look forward to your feedback on *Flood Risk*.

In memory of
Bill Noll
(1956-2003)